New Beginnings

at the

Harbour Inn

Also by Elise Darcy

The Living Apart Together series

Living Apart Together

It Takes 2 to Tango

Dear John

Love on the Rooftop

Standalone books

Lola & The Man

A Mallorcan Affair

The Villa in Sicily

We'll Meet Again

The Sunrise Coast Series

New Beginnings at the Harbour Inn

The Secret of the Summerhouse

The Cottage by the Sea

New Beginnings at the Harbour Inn

A Novel

ELISE DARCY

Penny Lane Press

ISBN 978-1-913147-07-5

"Every moment is a fresh beginning." – T.S. Eliot

1

Lili woke when her phone buzzed. She glanced over her shoulder, wondering if it had woken Alex too, and discovered he was no longer in bed. That wasn't unusual. It was Saturday, and he always went out for an early morning run at weekends. She reached over to the bedside table for her mobile. One of her friends who she'd been out with the night before had texted.

Lili and Alex were close friends with two other couples, and the six of them all loved the old Coach and Horses in Kew. They often met up there on Friday nights. The start of this weekend had been no different, except that Lili had overheard something in the bar, which she'd then confided to her girlfriends.

Lili had been making her way back from the loo, weaving through the crowded pub which was full of city-types blowing off steam after a long working week, when she'd spotted Alex at the bar getting another round of drinks. She was about to join him, but one of Alex's colleagues – a guy in his late twenties like Alex – got there first. She overheard him say to Alex, 'So, have you asked her yet?' Alex shook his head, no. 'I'm going to ask Lili when we are away.'

'Oh yes, that's right! You've booked a break in a hotel.' Alex's companion winked at him. 'Good plan.'

'She doesn't know about that either.'

Lili's eyes went wide. Was he intending to take her on a romantic break to propose to her?

Alex glanced around the crowded room.

When she caught Alex looking about him, making sure she wasn't in earshot, Lili ducked behind a group as though she had dropped something. When he turned back to his colleague, she retreated to their table outside in the beer garden, where their four friends were waiting. 'Do you think Alex needs a hand with the drinks?' she asked the two men in the group, Toby and Max. When they left their seats, she confided in her girlfriends, Abigail and Charlotte, what she'd just heard.

Lili had attended both their engagement parties, and their weddings, and Charlotte had recently become pregnant. Now, on Saturday morning, she was texting Lili to find out if Alex had told her yet about the romantic break away.

He had not.

After Lili replied to say there was no news, her friend suggested that, knowing Alex, the surprise holiday would be somewhere exotic. But Lili didn't mind where he proposed.

She got up, slipped on a pair of jogging bottoms and a sweatshirt, and walked over to the little dormer window in their bedroom. She thought she heard voices and glanced across the rooftops before her gaze dropped to the street below. Alex was standing outside the Victorian terraced house which housed their tiny two-bedroomed top-floor flat, taking some letters from the postman. She had been right: he'd been out for a morning run in Kew, their local neighbourhood. She knew he loved the small village feel of the London borough, as did she – the neighbours were friendly, and there were green open spaces. The only downside was the cost of the properties in the area. In the five years they'd been living here, as with other areas, house prices had shot up yet again. They continued to save, but Lili was doubtful they'd be able to buy a home there unless Alex landed a good promotion.

She watched him from the window. He was dressed in his running gear as expected, but this morning he was also holding a small brown paper bag. She knew he must have stopped at the local deli around the corner and brought home coffee and croissants – something that he didn't do unless it was a special occasion. It wasn't either of their birthdays or their anniversary, though.

She was getting excited. She saw him disappear up the small flight of stone steps into the house, so she undressed and crept back to bed. She plumped her cushions and had just picked up her gardening magazine when Alex walked into the bedroom. He smiled at her from across the room and held up a disposable cup of barista coffee in one hand and a buttered croissant sealed in a clear plastic bag in the other.

'Is that for me?' Lili said, feigning surprise. 'What's the special occasion?' she added breezily, remembering to sound innocent, given that the trip was a surprise – as was their impending engagement.

'I've already had breakfast. I thought I'd let you sleep in.'

Lili yawned and stretched. They'd had a mammoth weeding session at work the day before, and her back was a little sore. Not that she was complaining – she loved what she did. She wondered how many people in their twenties could say the same.

Alex walked over and placed her takeaway coffee and croissant on the table next to the bed. She smiled at her boyfriend, pulling him closer and giving him a kiss before he went for his shower. She felt that at twenty-seven, everything was coming together. She'd been living in a single room in a shared house, working in an admin job she hated, when he'd walked into her life. Now they rented a lovely little flat in Kew, and she had just completed her horticulture degree. Things were looking good; she'd quit her job and become a volunteer at Kew Gardens, the world's most famous botanical garden, a few minutes' walk from their flat.

Lili hoped she could step into a coveted permanent job as soon as one came up. She wouldn't earn a huge salary, but you couldn't put a price on a passion. She knew she was lucky. Alex, who earned good money working as a lawyer in a prestigious firm of solicitors in the city, had supported her so that she could complete her degree.

She'd been reticent about leaving work and being reliant on him for a time to concentrate on her volunteering role at Kew, but they'd been together for six years, and it was five years since they'd moved in together.

She was just finishing her coffee when Alex stepped out of the en suite, dressed in jeans and an old sweatshirt with the emblem of the university he'd attended emblazoned on the back. He was carrying his toiletry bag. She watched him get his suitcase out of the wardrobe and toss the bag inside. Breakfast in bed had already surprised her this morning, but she knew why he was packing. 'Are you going away on a business trip?' she asked, feigning disappointment. She was still waiting for him to tell her about the romantic holiday he'd booked.

'Nope.' He turned around and grinned his lop-sided grin at her.

Lili suppressed a smile. 'Are *we* going on a trip?'

'Yep.'

Lili put her empty coffee cup down on the bedside table and closed her magazine. She gave him her full attention. 'For the weekend?'

'Nope.'

Lili was getting a little irritated by the one-syllable answers. When was he going to tell her about the holiday?

'I've booked a week away.'

'A holiday!' Lili did her best to act surprised. 'A week – wow!' She hadn't believed it until that moment, but now she'd heard it from Alex himself. With his busy work schedule, he rarely took a long weekend break, let alone an entire week. 'That's just wonderful. Well, when are you going to tell me all the details? And why are you packing right now?' Lili looked at him askance.

He found another suitcase at the back of the wardrobe.

'That's my case,' said Lili, realising she was stating the obvious.

'Yep.' He turned around and placed it on the bed. 'You'd better pack. We're leaving today.'

'I beg your pardon?'

'Our train is this afternoon.'

'What?' Lili's mind was racing. 'But I haven't told the manager at Kew. I must give them notice.'

'Why? It's only a voluntary job.'

'But they depend on volunteers.'

'Well, they will have to depend on someone else.'

Lili frowned at his back as he returned to the wardrobe to

pack. 'Alex, this is genuinely nice of you, booking a surprise holiday, but it's such short notice …' She trailed off. She couldn't just drop everything. 'I can't just not turn up on Monday.' All that hard work, that dedication to her course and to her volunteering role at Kew Gardens would be for nothing if she didn't continue to show her commitment. She had filled out a job application for a full-time position, and there was the replanting project she was planning. However, if it was true, and he was intending to propose …

'Can't we postpone the trip for a little while?' she asked.

Alex, not the tongue-tied type, clammed up. *This is a rare event*, thought Lili. Alex had arranged time off work to go away for an entire week. She saw no sign of his laptop or his work phone. A proper holiday. Lili guessed it was true then: Alex *was* intending to propose. She turned her head and eyed her phone; she couldn't wait to tell her friends she was going to be getting married.

Despite her reservations about phoning Kew and letting them know she wouldn't be there on Monday, Lili wasn't going to pass up this opportunity. However, the question of why they were going right now was still troubling her. She understood that Alex must be keen to propose, but this last-minute approach just wasn't like him.

She wondered if there was something else he wasn't telling her. 'You haven't lost your job – have you?'

He laughed at that. 'Of course not.'

'Another bonus?'

She knew he was getting irritated. 'Look, I have got something to ask you, but I want to do it when we are away, okay?' He returned to packing, but not before she saw him check his jacket pocket for the umpteenth time. Was there a ring inside? Lili was dying to see it. It took all her willpower not to ask.

'Okay, no more questions – I promise. But can you at least tell me where we are going? If it's somewhere hot, I need to pack sun cream.' She noticed there was no sign of their passports and assumed that they weren't holidaying abroad. Even better. She was not fond of flying.

'It's in Suffolk – Aldeburgh.'

Lili looked at him, stunned. 'Why there – of all places?'

He turned around and looked at her. 'I thought you liked the Suffolk coast. It's only two hours from London. Not too far to travel. No planes.' He smiled at her. 'I was trying to think of somewhere you might like to visit.'

Then why didn't you ask me, thought Lili. She had already spoiled his surprise by moaning, though, so she kept quiet.

'I thought you'd enjoy a trip down memory lane.' Alex continued packing. 'You always said you liked the place when you lived there.'

It was true that she did like Aldeburgh, but it was the trip down memory lane she didn't appreciate. Lili wasn't of a mind to revisit her past – what she knew of it, at any rate.

'I booked a hotel with sea views.'

Lili caught him checking his pocket again. She picked up her phone, climbed out of bed and into her clothes again, and nipped out of the bedroom on the pretext of making another cup of coffee. She didn't want him to overhear her conversation.

She rushed down the hall, made her way towards the compact kitchen and stepped inside. The grey tiled floor, a contrast to the white cupboard units, was cold underfoot. She closed the door behind her, switched the kettle on and put her phone on the worktop for a moment while she opened a jar of instant coffee. Lili spooned some into a mug and then picked up her phone. She had already told the news to the two friends she'd been out with the previous night, but she had yet to tell her best friend.

The call was answered on the second ring.

'Hannah, you'll never guess what?' she started before her friend could speak. 'I think Alex is about to—'

Before the word *propose* was out of her mouth, Hannah interrupted her. 'What perfect timing, Lili, I was about to call you. You'll never guess what!'

2

Lili sighed. Her best friend wasn't listening. She explained about the holiday, and Alex's plan to propose, but Hannah interrupted. 'Lili, I have a surprise for your birthday.'

'Really?' Her birthday wasn't until next month. Lili wondered if her day could get any better – she couldn't recall the last time her friend had remembered her birthday or attempted to buy her a present. Lili understood, though. Hannah's life wasn't like Lili's; she had responsibilities.

Lili poured boiling water from the kettle into her mug. 'Wow! Do you want to meet up, then?' she asked.

'Well, yes – I'm right outside,' Hannah replied.

Alex wandered into the kitchen. He'd heard the kettle boil. 'I wouldn't mind a cup of coffee, if you're making one,' he said.

Lili brushed past him in the confined space and pulled open the window blind. She waved at Hannah, who was in the street below.

Alex noticed that Lili was on the phone. He glanced over her shoulder. 'Who are you waving at?'

'It's Hannah.'

'Oh, hell,' Alex swore under his breath. 'What does *she* want?'

'She wants to give me an early birthday present.'

'Are you serious?' *I'll believe that when I see it*, he thought. In all the years he'd known Lili, Hannah had never once remembered Lili's birthday. She always made up some excuse or another after the fact.

Lili waved again. 'I'll be right down,' she said into her phone.

She rushed out of the flat, leaving Alex in the kitchen. He glanced out of the window at the taxi below.

Hannah was standing at the kerb with the passenger door of the taxi open when Lili arrived outside. She gave Hannah a hug. 'It's lovely to see you.' Hannah wasn't part of Alex and Lili's social circle that met at weekends; their friendship went way back to a time before Lili had met Alex or their mutual friends.

Lili glanced at Hannah's new partner, who was waiting in the taxi, looking bored. He didn't say much – just a perfunctory hello. Lili didn't see a package wrapped in gift paper that might be for her, even though Hannah said she'd brought her a present. Lili stood back and looked at her best friend. She had tied her blonde hair back in a ponytail. Like Lili, she was dressed in grey tracksuit bottoms, but in contrast to Lili's comfy old sweatshirt, she was wearing a black sweatshirt emblazoned with the logo *pretty woman* in gold lettering down one sleeve. Lili loved it.

'Why don't you come up for a coffee?'

Hannah shook her head. 'I can't stay long. We've decided to have a break. It's last-minute.'

Lili smiled. 'Talking of last-minute …' She was about to tell Hannah her news, when her best friend grinned and said, 'We're going to Barbados!'

'That's sounds wonderful, Hannah. Funny thing, Alex and I are about to go on a—'

'Problem is he booked an adults-only hotel by mistake,' Hannah interrupted, rolling her eyes in her boyfriend's direction.

Lili wasn't quite following, until Hannah added, 'Just this last time – I promise.'

Lili jumped at the sound of the boot slamming shut. A Trunki, the familiar make of children's hand luggage, appeared on the pavement.

'I'll see you in a week,' Hannah said before indicating to the driver that they were ready to set off. Before she got back in the cab, Hannah gave Lili a hug, whispering in her ear, 'It's a make-or-break holiday. We need this, just the two of us, to patch things up. He booked an adult-only vacation. Things haven't been going great.'

Lili sighed. *When were they ever?* she thought. Hannah hadn't been with her current partner long; he was one of so many over the years that Lili had lost count. Hannah seemed to lurch from one dead-end relationship to another.

When Hannah stepped back from their embrace, Lili saw Maisie standing on the pavement.

'Didn't I tell you I brought you a little present?'

'I am *not* little!' Maisie folded her arms and threw her mother a haughty look.

The sight of Maisie brought a memory instantly to Lili's mind: a three-year-old standing unexpectedly at her flat door with her suitcase five years ago when they had first moved into the area. Hannah had dropped her off on the way to the airport, promising to collect her in seven days. She hadn't returned for two weeks.

Lili stared at Maisie, wondering why she was at all surprised that Hannah had dumped her here with no advance warning. It had happened so many times in the past.

Maisie ran up to Lili and flung her arms around Lili's waist, hugging her close. 'I'm so happy I'm staying with you, Auntie Lili.'

'You're doing me a huge favour, Lili. Just this last time, I promise,' Hannah said again.

Hannah had been saying that since Maisie was tiny. Lili stole a glance up at the flat and caught sight of Alex standing at the kitchen window. She looked down at the blonde-haired girl in her arms and shook her head. She was about to say no. 'Look, Hannah, this isn't workable. We're going away on a—'

Maisie interrupted her. 'I don't want to go on holiday with them. I want to stay with you!'

'There you go.' Hannah smiled. 'I told you I'd brought you a present.'

Maisie whispered, 'I chose a *proper* present. I wanted you to have something to unwrap.'

'Oh, Maisie, that is so sweet of you.' Lili squeezed her tight and wondered how Maisie's mother, who could be quite selfish and immature, had brought up such a thoughtful child. That was the sad part; Maisie wasn't any trouble, and yet her mum always ended up in relationships with guys who had no time for her.

Lili glanced at Hannah's partner, who was still sitting in the taxi, avoiding eye contact. She didn't believe for a minute he'd booked an adult-only hotel by mistake. She wondered why Hannah couldn't find someone nice and kind, like Alex, with a decent job – someone who could give her and Maisie a good life.

Lili sighed. 'How long did you say you were on holiday?'

'A week.' Hannah grinned. 'You're the best, Lili.'

'I know.' She'd heard that before, too.

Lili waved at the taxi and turned around to pick up Maisie's case. She glanced up at the flat again, but Alex was no longer at the window. Was he coming downstairs to help her up with the suitcase? He didn't appear, so she guessed not.

Maisie ran ahead, up the stone steps to the front door. 'I'm super-excited about staying.'

Lili wondered what Alex would say when he found out.

3

Lili walked up the stairs to the flat. Alex was waiting at the door.

'Hi Alex.' Maisie ran straight past him into the flat and plopped herself down on the sofa. 'Can I watch TV?' she yelled from the lounge.

'Of course, sweetheart,' Lili called after her. She heard Maisie flicking through the channels.

Alex followed Lili down the hallway. 'What's going on?'

'Maisie is staying for a bit. Hannah and her partner are off on holiday, but he booked an adults-only hotel by mistake.'

'By mistake? How do you book an adults-only hotel by mistake?'

Lili caught the sarcasm in his voice. She knew what he was thinking. She did not add what Hannah had said about a make-or-break holiday – he'd heard that one before too.

'So, Hannah thought she'd just turn up here and dump her on us?'

Lili stopped outside the door to the lounge and turned around to face Alex. She wondered why he was acting all surprised, considering how many times it had happened before.

'Can we postpone our trip? With the start of the school

summer holidays, it will be crazy-busy on the roads. If we went another month, it might be quieter.'

'But I've made all the arrangements, taken time off work …'

Lili hadn't thought of that.

'How long does Hannah want to leave her with us this time?'

'A week,' Lili said in a small voice.

'A week?' Alex shook his head. 'Are you sure it's just *one* week?'

Lili noted the sarcasm again. 'What do you mean?'

'You know what I'm talking about.'

Lili avoided his gaze. Frequently, Hannah's one- or two-week trips away had ended up lasting the entire summer. Hannah didn't need childcare during the school break because she didn't work. Alex believed Hannah was lazy and just couldn't be bothered to entertain her own child during the holidays. Alex had often called Lili a soft touch for letting her best friend turn up on a whim to offload Maisie at their door.

'They've booked seven nights in Barbados.'

'How nice for them. But they could have given us some notice.'

Hannah isn't the only one giving short notice with holidays, Lili thought, but didn't speak the words aloud. Instead, she said, 'We can still go to Aldeburgh. I'm sure there will be another room available at the hotel. She's old enough to have a bedroom on her own – she *is* eight.'

Lili knew it wasn't what he'd had in mind. He was right though; she was a soft touch.

Alex frowned. 'This was a romantic break away for the two of us. I don't believe this!'

Lili's eyes darted to the lounge. 'Keep it down.'

Alex lowered his voice. 'Look, I get it. You think you owe Hannah. I understand.'

Lili looked at him. How could he put himself in her shoes? His comfortable middle-class upbringing was poles apart from her own start in life.

'You know I don't mind her staying, but this time … it's different.'

She knew what he was talking about, even though he wasn't aware she had overheard his conversation about what he was planning.

Alex placed his palms together and held out his hands as if in prayer. 'Please call Hannah and tell her to come back and pick up her daughter.'

Lili chewed her bottom lip.

Alex threw his arms up in the air when Lili didn't get out her phone or respond. 'I just want you, for once in your life, to tell her *no*. Can't you do that for me?'

Lili's eyes went wide. She started shaking her head. 'Alex, please don't make me choose. I want to go on the holiday.' *I want you to propose.*

'Maybe if you said no, Hannah would learn to grow up and take some responsibility.'

Lili eyed Alex. He had a point.

Alex sighed. 'Let me guess. She needs some space while she figures herself out, or is it another make-or-break holiday?'

Lili kept quiet.

He looked at her and shook his head. 'I've put up with this for years. Sometimes I feel there are three people in our relationship.' He said again, 'I just want you, for once in your life, to tell her no. Can't you do that for me?'

Lili still couldn't bring herself to do it. He was putting her in an impossible situation. 'She's my sister – I can't.'

'She is *not* your sister.'

Lili frowned at him. She knew it wasn't his fault – but talk about bad timing. If only the holiday Alex had booked hadn't coincided with the summer holidays. Lili knew that if she said that to him, though, he'd remind her that their lives – her life – shouldn't revolve around the school breaks of someone else's kid. *But Maisie wasn't just someone else's kid*, thought Lili. She was Hannah's, and by extension, she was family. Alex was right: they weren't related. But when you grow up without relatives of your own, your friends become your family. Alex didn't get that.

'You know my history. She's the closest person I have to family.'

Alex gaped at her. 'I thought, after all these years together, I was the closest thing you had to family?'

Lili pursed her lips.

'Fine, if that's the way it's going to be.' He got out his wallet and thrust an envelope at Lili.

'What's this?'

'There's the booking reference inside. Why don't you go – and take her with you? We've looked after her for years. I've had enough of the impromptu childcare.'

What does he mean, 'we' have looked after her? Lili thought. He was always busy with work; sometimes she felt he went out of his way to ensure he didn't have that much to do with Maisie.

Alex turned around, stormed into their bedroom and slammed the door shut.

Lili glanced at the piece of paper in her hand. 'Alex, it doesn't have to be this way.'

'That's right, it doesn't,' he shouted out from behind the door. 'We could go on holiday, just the two of us, if you would only do as I ask. I don't think I'm being unreasonable. I have my reasons this time.'

Lili scratched her chin, wondering if she should confess to him what she'd overheard in the pub. She eyed the door. 'Alex?'

'What?'

'I know what you were planning.'

There was a pause before Alex answered. 'What do you mean?'

'When we go on holiday, I know what you were planning to tell me … ask me. I overheard your colleague from work talking to you at the bar.'

'You did?'

'Yes.'

'Damn. I wanted it to be a surprise.'

'Well, you could do it here. We don't have to go away.'

Alex came closer. Lili could tell he was just on the other side of the door. He said, 'I wanted to make it a special occasion – you know, travel somewhere different.'

Lili smiled. 'I understand.'

'So, you're okay with everything, with what I was going to ask?'

Lili grinned. 'That's a silly question. Why wouldn't I be?'

'I am so relieved. I was worried you might have some reservations …'

Lili knitted her brow and stared at the door. 'What do you mean?' She had no reservations about getting married.

He opened the bedroom door and looked at her. 'I felt you would be reluctant to leave Kew, your friends and Maisie.'

Lili laughed. 'It's only a holiday to the East Coast.'

Alex frowned. 'I'm not talking about the holiday.'

'Then what are you talking about?'

'Our move to Washington, of course.'

Lili gaped at him. 'I'm sorry – what?'

'That promotion my colleague was congratulating me on in the pub. I'm managing the department in the Washington office in a month's time. That's why I have to take a break now; there is so much to arrange before we get over there, like where we live and …' Alex stopped when he caught the surprised look on her face. 'Wait, that's what you were talking about – wasn't it?'

Lili knew no such thing. She stood there, open-mouthed. She found her voice. 'I thought you were proposing, and we were getting engaged.'

'What?'

'I overheard your colleague discussing the surprise break you'd planned and congratulating you. I … I assumed …'

'Oh, crap.'

They stood there for a moment, staring at one another.

Lili spoke first. 'So, that's what the holiday was about, using up your leave?'

'And celebrating my promotion.'

'Celebrating your promotion,' Lili repeated, shocked that it wasn't what she thought it was, and very put out. They'd been together five years. When was he going to propose? 'Why didn't you discuss this with me first? You know I have a life here, friends – a job.'

'It's just a voluntary post, Lili.'

Lili was getting angry. 'I want to know when you intended to tell me that you'd accepted the position in Washington and that we'd be moving to the States? You watched me put in an application for my dream job at Kew – for goodness' sake.'

'There will be other jobs across the pond, Lili. And it's not like you've got any family to consider, whereas I've had my parents to think of. It's been quite hard for me to come to this decision and accept the new position, knowing I won't see them as often.' Alex looked at Lili, wide-eyed. 'God, I'm sorry. That was insensitive of me.'

'Yes, it was,' Lili said. 'And talking of family, what about Hannah and Maisie?'

Alex shrugged. 'What about them?'

'*What about them*?' Lili could feel her hackles rising along with her voice. 'You are joking! I won't see them if I'm thousands of miles away.'

Alex said under his breath, 'Maybe that's not a bad thing.'

Lili looked at him sharply. 'I beg your pardon?'

'Are you arguing?' said a small voice.

Lili whirled around to find Maisie standing in the lounge doorway across the hall from their bedroom, staring at them with her large round blue eyes. She was chewing a fingernail.

Maisie was dressed in her charity shop finest – she only ever had new clothes when Lili took her shopping on her birthday and at Christmas, and whenever she stayed. Lili recognised the little denim skirt she'd bought her, but not the multi-coloured woollen tights or the oversized red jumper. She still had the cute rucksack with the bunny ears that Lili had got her for a present a couple of years ago. 'Er, no – we weren't arguing.' Lili threw Alex a look.

He shut the bedroom door.

'Yes, you were. I heard you.'

Sometimes Lili forgot how old Maisie was. She hoped she hadn't realised they'd been rowing about her.

'Alex doesn't want me to stay, does he?'

Lili frowned. *Thanks, Alex.* The last thing she wanted was for Maisie to feel unwelcome here. Lili took her by the shoulders and steered her back into the lounge, out of earshot of Alex. She looked at the piece of paper with the booking reference for the hotel and wiped a few tears from her eyes as they sat down on the sofa.

'Are you crying?'

Lili sniffed. 'Of course not. I'm just so happy that you are here.' She leaned over and hugged Maisie.

'I'll take my Trunki into my room.' Maisie jumped up from the sofa. She had stayed so often that she even had her own bedroom.

Lili caught her arm. 'No – wait. I just want to have a word with Alex.'

Maisie's bottom lip quivered. 'I can stay, can't I?'

'Oh sweetheart, of course you can,' Lili lied. 'But I have a better idea. How would you like to go on a holiday to the seaside?' It was typical English summer weather, with rain forecast the next week, but with luck they might have one or two dry days to spend on the beach.

'A holiday to the seaside?' Her bottom lip quivered again. 'I don't want to go.'

Lili sighed. Whereas other children would jump for joy at the thought of a holiday, Maisie wasn't like other children. She found new situations difficult. Lili didn't want to blame her best friend, but she knew Maisie's upbringing must have created some insecurities. There had been different men in and out of her life and spells of homelessness when Maisie and her mother had sofa-surfed at theirs. She imagined that was why change made Maisie anxious.

Maisie stamped her foot. 'I don't want to go.'

Neither do I, thought Lili. Not if it meant leaving on this note, after a row with Alex. It didn't help that she now knew the holiday wasn't about getting engaged.

Alex appeared in the doorway, with his jacket on, looking contrite.

'Where are you going?' Lili asked.

'Out.' He turned to go, then did an about-turn. 'Look, I want this promotion, but I haven't signed the contract yet.'

Lili looked at him. 'So?' He had decided to take up the new post.

He held out his hand. 'We can still go on our holiday and talk things over.'

Lili stared at him. *What is there to talk over?* she thought. 'The holiday was a delightful surprise,' she said.

'Does that mean you're going to phone Hannah and tell her to come back and pick Maisie up?'

Lili heaved a sigh. 'Why can't we all go on holiday together?'

Alex gave her a look.

'What? Maisie won't be any trouble.'

'I said *I don't want to go*!' Maisie's voice made them both jump.

Alex winced at the sound of Maisie yelling. He looked at Lili. 'What was that you just said?' he asked Lili sarcastically. He left, slamming the door on the way out and shouting, 'And would you be so kind as to phone your best friend and make sure her daughter is not here when I get back!'

Lili turned around. Maisie burst into tears and ran down the hall, slamming the door to her room shut. Lili stood in the hall, looking from the front door to Maisie's bedroom before bursting into tears too. How had such a wonderful morning, with coffee and a croissant in bed and a surprise holiday booked, disintegrated into this? Her face clouded over. *Hannah*!

4

Lili picked up her phone and rang Hannah. It went straight to voicemail. Lili looked at her watch. Not much time had passed, so Hannah wouldn't have caught her flight yet. She sighed. How lucky for Hannah that over the years she'd had someone who would drop everything for her. Not anymore. Alex was right: this couldn't go on. Lili left a message. 'Hannah, it's Lili. Look, I'm sorry, but you will have to come and pick Maisie up. Now is not a good time – she can't stay. Alex and I are going on holiday. We have some things to iron out.'

When Lili ended the call, she saw Maisie standing at the bedroom door. 'I thought *we* were going on holiday.'

Lili didn't know what to say.

'You don't want me.' Maisie burst into tears and slammed the door to her bedroom again.

'Oh, Maisie …' Lili rushed forward and stopped outside her door. 'Can I come in?'

'No!'

'It's not true, you know. I want you to stay.'

'Then why did you phone my mum to pick me up? You've never wanted me to stay, have you?'

'Now, that's just not true.' Lili couldn't tell Maisie that, years earlier, she'd put her life on hold for her and her mother. She had planned to go to university straight after completing her A-Levels; she had been offered a place on a horticulture degree in Birmingham. It had been ideal; a cheap area to live and support herself as a student going through college. However, when Hannah had fallen pregnant in the last year before their exams, it had changed both their lives. Lili had known she couldn't turn her back on Hannah or her baby. Like Lili, Hannah had no parents to fall back on. But they had each other, and Lili had made a promise; Maisie would never end up in care.

The trouble was that Hannah wasn't ready for the responsibilities of motherhood. She wanted to go clubbing and have boyfriends. She still acted like the teenager she was. Lili lost count of the times the council gave her a flat – she often got behind with the rent or moved in with a new boyfriend, only to end up homeless again when things didn't work out.

Lili deferred her university place for a year and took a job at a firm of solicitors so she could help Hannah. She rented a room in a small flat share. Then Alex came along, and before she knew it, they had set up home together.

She had become Hannah's back-up plan when things went wrong – as they so often did.

But in the past year, since Hannah had moved in with her new partner, life had appeared more stable. There had been no more histrionics, no more walking out on boyfriends and sofa-surfing at Lili's. Hannah's life had turned a corner. Until now. Lili hoped she would not split up with this partner.

Maisie opened the door.

'There you are, sweetheart.'

'I want to stay with you.'

Lili's smile faltered, thinking of how many times Maisie had said that from a young age. Maisie loved her mum, but Auntie Lili offered the stability and normality she never had at home. Even though Alex didn't get involved when she stayed, he was still the same old Alex. There was no lurching from one boyfriend to the next for Lili.

It had crossed Lili's mind, when Maisie was younger, that Hannah should leave Maisie with her for a bit. It wouldn't be easy for Alex, she knew that, but Maisie would have benefitted from the stability. However, she didn't broach the idea with Hannah, after Hannah had thanked her for all she did for them both. It hadn't seemed appropriate. Hannah had said that although she knew she wasn't a good mother, the one thing she couldn't bear was the thought of losing her child. Lili knew that. That's why she'd always been there for her.

Lili got out her phone.

Maisie looked up at her with tear-streaked cheeks. 'Are you phoning Alex to tell him you changed your mind and I'm not staying?'

Lili stared at her. She'd heard more of their row than she realised. Lili had intended to do that; to let him know she'd contacted Hannah and told her to come back and pick Maisie up. However, after a few minutes of quiet contemplation, sitting on the floor by Maisie's bedroom door, Lili decided that Alex had no right to ask her to choose. So, he was disappointed about the week – she got that – but he could always book another time to go away. It wasn't the end of the world. Like Hannah, he just needed to grow up and stop thinking about himself for a change.

Lili was going over what he'd said about the imminent move

to Washington that she'd known nothing about. She wasn't convinced he'd intended to discuss it with her beforehand. Lili had been with Alex long enough to know when he had made up his mind. The holiday was all about convincing her to go. What if she didn't want to go to Washington? Lili stared at Maisie. What if she couldn't?

Lili punched in a number. It went to voicemail again. 'Hi Hannah, it's Lili again. Forget my previous message. Everything's fine. Alex was upset because he had something special planned. I'll tell you all about it when you get back. Have a great time. See you soon. Luv you lots.' Lili ended the call and turned to Maisie. 'There, you see. I want you to stay.'

Maisie glanced towards the door. 'What about Alex?'

The trouble with Maisie, now that she was eight, was that she didn't miss a thing. It was harder to gloss over arguments. 'Alex is always a grump in the morning – you know that,' Lili said, reaching for Maisie and tickling her.

Maisie giggled and tried tickling Lili back. They rolled on the floor, laughing. Lili turned on her stomach, chin in her hands. Maisie did the same, so that they were facing each other. Alex didn't want Maisie to be there when he got back. Lili didn't want to be there either. She was still mad at Alex for not forewarning her about his promotion. She decided that Alex's earlier suggestion, even if made sarcastically, would solve her problem. 'Now, what about this holiday? And before you say that you want to stay here, how would you like to see where your mum and I went to school?'

Maisie shrugged, looking disinterested.

Lili changed tack. 'Okay. I know you've never seen the sea before …' Maisie's mum had been to lots of places with her boyfriends – from Thailand to Cornwall – she just never took Maisie with her. Hannah was always jetting off here, there and everywhere, like she was a footballer's wife. That was what she aspired to be – not that she'd ever come close to meeting a famous footballer, let alone dated one. Lili thought of Hannah going on holiday yet again without Maisie. She sighed, thinking how some things never changed. In that respect, she could understand Alex's frustration.

'My friend at school finds shells on the beach when she goes away on holiday. They're beautiful.'

'Is that so?' Lili smiled. 'Would you like to find some pretty shells? We could be like the explorers I told you about who went in search of exotic flowers.'

'We can be explorers looking for seashells.'

'That's an excellent idea.' Lili stood up and looked at the reservation. Alex had booked the room for a week, starting that day. There were two train tickets in the envelope too – first class. Lili glanced at her watch. They might just make it to Liverpool Street station if they got a move on. Lili still had her case to pack. 'I will be as quick as I can. Where is your Trunki?'

'In my room.'

Lili walked into the spare bedroom to discover her suitcase open and empty. Maisie stood by the door, looking into the room. Lili glanced at her. 'Oh, Maisie – you unpacked.' Lili opened drawers and the wardrobe of the white children's furniture she'd bought, recalling Alex's annoyance that she'd kitted out the spare bedroom for Maisie instead of for their own kids – when they eventually had them. Lili had ignored that. Besides, she fancied bringing up her children out of London, somewhere in the country.

When Lili had finished packing Maisie's clothes, she returned to her bedroom and hastily packed her own. Heaving the suitcase out into the hallway, she placed it beside the little Trunki, thinking that the small ride-on case was a bit young for Maisie now.

'Right, let's go.' Grabbing her coat and handbag, Lili closed the front door and looked at her watch as she waited for Maisie to turn the key in the lock. Maisie handed the key to Lili.

'Are we all set?' Lili asked.

Maisie nodded.

'Okay, great.' She took Maisie's hand as they wheeled their suitcases to the top of the stairs. 'Let's go on our adventure.'

Maisie frowned at Lili. 'I'm not a little child anymore.'

Lili kept her expression in check in case she smiled. She didn't want Maisie to think she was poking fun at her. 'Of course not. But I think it is a big adventure.'

Maisie sighed. 'Fine.'

Lili smiled down at her. Sometimes when Maisie frowned it brought back that little toddler Lili had known, with those big blue eyes and round chubby cheeks. 'I wonder what else we might discover on the beach. Perhaps we could find a conch shell.'

'What's a conch shell?'

Lili explained that it was quite a large seashell.

'Do you think we might find some buried treasure?'

Lili smiled. 'You never know …'

They caught the tube from Kew, exited at Liverpool Street station and ran. Luckily for Lili, both their cases had wheels. They made it to the platform where their train was boarding. As the first-class carriage was at the front of the train, and empty, it didn't take them long to board and find their seats. Maisie insisted on an aisle seat in case she needed the loo. She put her pink headphones on and switched on the tablet that Alex had bought her for her last birthday.

'How long is the journey?' Maisie asked.

'About an hour and a half.'

'Okay.'

Lili watched her scroll through the tablet, looking for something to watch. As the train left the station, Lili stared out of the window. The overland stations passed in a blur until London and the suburbs gave way to open countryside.

Lili made the mistake of thinking about Alex. Tears rolled down her face at the thought of how they had parted.

She felt arms around her neck and Maisie's hot breath in her ear. 'Lili, is everything all right?'

Lili wiped her eyes dry before turning from the window. 'Of course it is.'

The expression on Maisie's face said she wasn't sure she believed her.

'We're going to have the most amazing time – you and me.'

Maisie brightened. 'I know. This is *so* cool.'

Lili smiled at her as she put her headphones back on. Everything was cool. It was her new catchphrase. She was right: this was cool. Lili was determined they would have a good time.

Lili's thoughts turned back to Alex's promotion. This might be the last opportunity she had to spend time with Maisie before Alex made his final decision. As he'd said, he hadn't signed a formal contract yet.

Her mind moved on to her best friend. She hoped Hannah's trip went well. Perhaps if the make-or-break holiday worked out, and the couple got married, then Maisie would have a new daddy. That would bring some stability for Maisie from now on, which meant Maisie wouldn't need Auntie Lili so much anymore.

She stared out of the window. A calm settled over her. Everything was going to be all right. She was looking forward to phoning Alex tonight and letting him know that this was most likely the last time Hannah would leave Maisie with them, so there would be no more arguments on that score. Now all she had to do was convince him *not* to go to Washington.

5

Lili leaned over and switched on the bedside lamp. It was no use; she couldn't get to sleep. Glancing across the room, she smiled at Maisie, who was fast asleep on the camp bed the concierge had set up. It had been embarrassing when they had turned up at the hotel and discovered that Alex had booked the honeymoon suite. There had even been a bottle of bubbly in a bucket of ice with two champagne flutes. It had made Lili wonder if there had been more to this holiday than just the news of his promotion. Had she been right all along? Had he been intending to propose?

Lili had told the concierge that her partner had been held up and would be arriving soon. It had been an outright fib to save her from embarrassment, although she had hoped he might change his mind and surprise her.

A little later, Lili had been lounging on the bed, reading a hotel magazine by the light of her phone, when she'd heard a knock on the door. It hadn't woken Maisie. Lili had leapt out of bed, thinking it was Alex. It hadn't been him. It had been the concierge with an enormous bouquet from a local florist, which had been delivered to the hotel earlier in the day. Alex had sent them. Lili had stared at the flowers and thought what a lovely gesture it was to send her a bouquet to make up for their row.

Now, unable to sleep, Lili picked up her mobile to see what the time was. As she did so, it rang. She got under the duvet to muffle the sound. It was Alex.

She was pleased he'd called – she had been debating whether to phone him since she'd got there. 'Oh, Alex – the suite is amazing,' she whispered. 'Can't you catch the last train down to Aldeburgh? I'll wait up.' Maisie was bedding down in their room for that night, but Lili thought that once she had settled in, she would be okay sleeping on her own. Lili didn't mind paying for another room if there was one available close by. She had some savings.

'The flowers are lovely, Alex.' She admired the bouquet she'd arranged in a vase from where she lay in the bed.

'What flowers?' He paused. 'Oh, I ordered them ages ago when I booked the hotel.'

'Oh.'

'Look, Lili, I suggest we take a break.'

She sat up. 'What do you mean – *take a break*?'

'Just that.'

'You mean *us*,' she said in shock.

'The lease is up on the flat soon.'

'What are you saying – we're breaking up?'

Alex was silent on the phone.

Lili scrambled out of bed and walked into the bathroom, closing the door behind her. She perched on the edge of the sunken enamel bath. 'You can't be serious.'

'I need some time to figure things out.'

'Figure things out? What's that supposed to mean?'

Alex heaved a sigh. 'I don't know yet.'

'Is this because of Maisie?'

There was a long silence.

Lili guessed it wasn't just that. He was a careerist and very driven. He knew she didn't want to move to Washington. Was he thinking she was going to hold him back? Is that why he wanted a break – to decide which came first, her or his career? Lili had it on the tip of her tongue to say she'd come with him to the States, but the thought of leaving Maisie made her stop.

Lili hadn't outright decided she wouldn't go to Washington. She had to concede that Alex was right; her life, their lives, shouldn't revolve around Hannah and her whims.

'If this is about the move to Washington …'

His silence said that it was.

Lili's mind was racing. 'Look, I'm sure we can work things out. I'll be back in a week. Let's not make any rash decisions, okay?'

'Sure,' Alex replied, although the tone of his voice didn't sound convincing.

'You've already decided. You're moving without me.'

Once again, he was silent. She wondered why he'd bothered making the call.

'What will I do?' Although Lili had put in an application for the job at Kew, the position wasn't guaranteed, and she couldn't afford to take on their rental flat on her own. And it wasn't as though she had parents who could help.

She could almost see him rolling his eyes if she mentioned her past. He often said, 'How many times do I have to hear about Malory Towers?'

Lili didn't appreciate it when he referred to her boarding school as if it were something out of an Enid Blyton novel, and all such fun, *tally ho*. It certainly hadn't been like that for Lili – not with her background. The only person she'd made friends with was Hannah, another girl who, for all intents and purposes, had no relatives either; Hannah had been a misfit, like her.

In that moment, Lili realised she was still looking for somewhere to belong. She'd thought it was with her partner and that they would have children. She didn't want to break up with Alex. 'What's going to happen after next week if you haven't figured things out?' Lili needed to know if this was it. Where would she go after that? 'I have no family to fall back on,' she said, thinking aloud.

'Yes, you have. You're always saying how Hannah is like a sister to you – the closest thing you have to family. You could stay with her. God knows it's about time she returned the favour.'

'That's not fair!'

'Isn't it?'

Lili shut up. She knew he had a point. How many times had Hannah stayed with them over the years as she'd lurched from one relationship to another? Alex had often said in the past that he'd had enough of her turning up at all hours, dumping her child on them – yet again – and flouncing off to go clubbing. Rocking up in the small hours, she'd often disturbed his sleep when he hadn't long gone to bed and had an early start for work the following day.

Alex obviously resented Maisie too. Lili had told herself that having someone else's youngster around must be different. But there was always that niggle at the back of her mind – what sort of family would they make? Once children were on the scene, would he discover it wasn't for him? Would she find herself in Hannah's shoes – a single parent?

Alex was still at the end of the line. 'What will you do?'

Did she detect some concern in his voice? Perhaps she did, but what did it matter? It sounded as though he didn't need time to figure himself out; he'd already made up his mind. Lili stared miserably into space. 'I don't know.'

She felt like slamming the phone down. She couldn't, though, because she was on her mobile. Instead, she tapped the 'end call' button.

'Shit!' she whispered to herself, shocked that it had come to this. Six years together. They'd met when she was twenty-one. She perched on the cold enamel bath, feeling her thigh going numb as she imagined what she'd be doing right now if Maisie hadn't turned up like that. She'd be soaking in a luxurious bath before dressing for dinner. Instead, here she was, close to tears, in her PJs, in bed, getting an early night. Except she would not sleep tonight.

She took some deep breaths. 'Everything is going to be okay,' she told herself. It didn't help. At least she knew that in a week, when Hannah was due home from her holiday, she could move in with her for a little while. She wouldn't expect to stay for free; she had some savings, so she'd pay her way until she found a job and a place to live. Alex was right on one score; it was time Hannah returned the favour. Lili could feel the tears welling up. She called another number. 'Connie?'

'Lili? Is that you? I haven't heard from you in a while. How are things, sweetheart?'

Lili burst into tears.

'Oh, Lili. Has something happened?'

Lili nodded her head up and down. 'Alex and I have split up. Well, Alex has dumped me.'

'Oh, dear. Look, why don't you come round?'

'I can't. I'm in Suffolk.'

'Suffolk?'

'Yes, Aldeburgh, would you believe?'

'What are you doing there?'

Lili was on the verge of tears again. 'It was Alex's idea. He booked a surprise break away. He knew I went to school here and thought I'd like a trip down memory lane.' Lili walked over to the bathroom door while she was talking and opened it a crack to check Maisie was okay. Although she had turned over in bed, she was still fast asleep.

Lili closed the door again. 'I had thought he was going to propose.' Lili caught sight of her face in the mirror, her eyes puffy where she'd been crying, her short, blonde-bobbed hair escaping from the hairband she'd tied it back in. 'I can't believe he broke up with me.'

'Do you want to talk about it? You can come to me any time. You know there's a spare room – well, several since my girls left home.'

Lili managed a smile. 'That's kind of you, Connie.' She would have liked nothing more than to see Connie just then, but she couldn't – not with Maisie to care for. It wasn't that Connie wouldn't let Maisie stay over; of course she would. But although Lili trusted her, Connie was still a registered social worker. She had been Lili's social worker since the day Lili had stepped off the plane from Corfu as an orphaned toddler to start a new life in England. But ever since Hannah had got pregnant in her last year of sixth form, Lili had kept the two people she was closest to in the world in separate compartments.

Lili's secret fear was that one day, Hannah would mess up

too much and social services would take Maisie away. With no biological dad in the picture – Hannah refused to divulge who he was – Maisie would end up in the care system.

Lili suspected that the reason Hannah hadn't revealed who Maisie's father was that she didn't know herself. She'd most likely got stoned at a party and slept with someone. She could probably barely remember that night, let alone who she'd spent it with.

Connie interrupted her thoughts. 'You know I'm here for you. If you change your mind and decide you want to come over, just call me. I'll pick you up from the station.'

'Thanks, Connie.'

'In the meantime, I suggest you recharge your batteries, try to make some plans for the future. I realise that won't be easy but have a go. One day at a time, remember.'

Lili glanced at the bathroom door. This wasn't how the week was meant to pan out, but she wasn't sorry that Maisie was there; she would provide a distraction from Alex and the sudden, unexpected breakup of their relationship. 'Okay, Connie.'

'What will you do next week? Have you got somewhere to stay?'

Lili was still thinking about Maisie when she said, 'Yes, my best friend's place.'

'Good. Good.' Connie went quiet. 'You know you are welcome here any time, so if things don't work out with your friend, I'm just a phone call away.'

Tears ran down Lili's face. 'What would I do without you, Connie?' she said. They were words she had spoken many times before.

'Don't be silly, it's what—'

'Social workers are for,' Lili finished her sentence, something she had heard Connie say to her and other looked-after children in the care home before Lili went to boarding school.

'I was going to say *friends*, Lili. It's what *friends* are for.'

Lili grinned. That's what they had become over the years – firm friends. She guessed there weren't many people who stayed in contact with their social workers once they left care, but it was Lili's good fortune to have a person like Connie who went above and beyond. She was lucky. Without her, she didn't know where she would have ended up.

'Now, Lili, remember to breathe. And don't forget …'

Lili smiled and said Connie's oft-quoted mantra, 'Only ever look back to see how far you've come.'

'Good girl. Now get some paper and start thinking about your future. It will not be easy. Your future was with Alex. Who knows – that may still be the case? You might find your way back to each other.'

Lili managed a smile. *Perhaps he'll discover how much he misses me while I'm gone*, she thought. Of course, agreeing to move thousands of miles away with his job would help.

'How long have you been together?'

'Five years.'

'Well, there you go. It might be the five-year itch.'

Lili hoped so.

'In the meantime, use this time to have a think about yourself, Lili. What do *you* want? You will walk out of this stronger and wiser.'

Lili sat there listening to Connie's soothing Irish brogue. She was to Lili what Lili knew she herself was to Maisie – that calm island in the storm. She only had to think of Connie and it calmed her down. 'Thank you, Connie.'

'Don't thank me – find that pen and paper and get cracking with your plan.'

'I will.'

'Good. Now call the concierge and have them bring you up a nice hot cocoa before bedtime or, better still, a large glass of wine.'

'Do you want me to contact you tomorrow morning, see how you are?'

Lili thought of Maisie. It would be hard to miss a chattering eight-year-old in the background asking who she was speaking to on the phone. 'No, that's all right.'

'Well, if you need anything, Lili, anything at all, just call me. And if you need a place to stay, you know where I am.'

'Thank you, Connie.'

'Goodnight, sweetheart.'

'Night, night, Connie.' Lili sat staring at her phone. It had been good to hear her voice. She regretted not having got in touch more often, rather than just when she was having a bit of a crisis. Although she imagined Connie didn't mind. At least if she didn't get in touch, Connie knew things were okay.

Lili walked out of the bathroom and considered calling the concierge to send up a hot chocolate to her room, but she decided against the idea; Maisie was sleeping, and she didn't want to wake her. Instead, Lili dimmed her lamp and climbed into bed. She couldn't remember the last time she'd retired this early. There was a small jotter pad courtesy of the hotel and a biro pen. She started by planning the week ahead and made a short list of the things she could do with Maisie to make sure she had a good time. After all, this was meant to be a holiday, and Lili wanted it to be memorable – for all the right reasons.

She decided to look on the bright side. What had Connie said? This might be the five-year itch. Maybe this was just a blip. Maybe by the end of the week, he would be calling or texting to have her back.

On that happy thought, a relieved Lili started writing her list, determined she would enjoy their holiday. Perhaps this time apart would only go to show Alex how much he missed her and would strengthen their relationship. Lili smiled. After three lines, the pencil slipped from her fingers as she fell asleep.

She dreamed of Malory Towers. That wasn't the name of her boarding school but, as with most dreams, it was all mixed up. She was walking through the school with Hannah, and then she was in a big house with high ceilings and velvet curtains at the old sash windows. In her dream, a feeling of déjà vu settled over her. Stepping inside another room, she felt she had been in that place before, many years ago, and this was one of her earliest childhood memories.

And she wasn't alone. A young woman with big brown eyes and long blonde hair held out her hand as though beckoning Lili to follow her out of the house to the bottom of a garden where a summerhouse overlooked a lake.

In her sleep, Lili called out, 'Mum?'

6

Lili woke after a restless night's sleep. She reached for the other side of the bed, for Alex. Instead she found the notepad and pen. She opened her eyes and remembered where she was. She wasn't surprised she'd had a fitful night after the phone call with Alex, but it was more than that; she had dreamed about her school and some strange old house. She sighed. She'd rather not remember her dreams. It didn't help that, in the cold light of day, she wasn't feeling optimistic about this being just a blip in their relationship. What if this really was it?

Despite speaking with Connie, which had cheered her up last night, Lili felt so alone. Her thoughts turned to practical financial matters. She knew Connie would put her up at her house for as long as she needed, but she couldn't live on her or Hannah's hospitality indefinitely. She would need to find a job and a place of her own.

There was that new position at Kew Gardens. Lili had been refining her application, anxious about submitting it. She had intended to send it off the previous day before they set off on holiday, but with all that had gone on, she had forgotten all about it. She made a note in the little notebook to use the hotel computer to log in and ping over her application. The job couldn't be better, although even working full time, she wouldn't be able to afford the London rents on her own. She'd have to find a bedsit or a flat share. From experience, they weren't easy to come by.

It helped if you were a friend of a friend and could secure accommodation that way. Otherwise, you had to go through marathon interviews with a close-knit group who demanded to know every detail about you to see if they thought you'd get on in their household, if you were a good fit, if you would be the sort of person they wanted – *their* sort of person.

Before meeting Alex, she'd had to start looking for another house share when her landlord at the time had asked them all to vacate so that he could sell his property. During interviews, the moment she'd mentioned she was an orphan, her potential flat mates had looked uncomfortable. They always chose people from ordinary backgrounds, people who had grown up in families; people to whom they could relate.

She got that, even though she found it upsetting. After all, in many ways she was just like them – young, starting out in life – but in other respects she wasn't like them at all. No one with parents could understand the deep, bottomless pit of loneliness that orphans carried around with them all their lives. Marilyn Monroe, Lili's idol, had once talked about it in an interview. She had been an orphan too, but despite such a huge disadvantage, the film star had made something of herself in her short life. She had made Lili determined to do the same.

Lili knew there would always be setbacks in life, no matter what background a person came from, but if she heeded Connie's advice about only looking back to see how far you'd come, everything would be all right in the end. She hoped so, anyway. Besides, she wasn't alone – not anymore. Not since meeting her best friend at school. Lili smiled at Maisie across the room. Although she was lying in bed, under her covers, Lili could hear her Nintendo game. She wished Alex hadn't put her in this position – forcing her to make an impossible choice. It wasn't fair. She wondered too what it said about the strength of their relationship, about their future together, that he would consider a new job thousands of miles away without discussing it with her first.

The covers that were piled on top of Maisie like a tent moved, and her head appeared from under the duvet. 'You're awake!' she said.

Lili smiled. 'I am. That is so sweet of you to let me lie in.'

Maisie raced over to the king-sized bed. She crawled under the blankets next to Lili.

Lili snuggled down too, her head on the pillow facing Maisie as she tucked in the covers round her. They were almost nose to nose. Lili tweaked her nose. 'Did you have a good night, sweetheart?'

Maisie put a finger to her lips, a thoughtful expression on her face. 'Um, kind of. I heard strange noises.'

'Did you, now?' Lili grinned. She had an idea what that had been. Unfortunately, they had lost a good part of the day travelling. They should have had an enjoyable hour on the train before catching the bus from Saxmundham to the English seaside resort of Aldeburgh. It had turned out to be anything but enjoyable, though. They'd had a frustrating journey, with long delays due to works on the line which meant several changes en route. Why did maintenance have to be done at the weekend?

They should have arrived at the hotel well before dark, in which case Maisie would have seen the sea from her window and realised that those strange noises were waves crashing on the shore across the road from the promenade. Lili had planned to take Maisie to explore the beach before teatime and had been looking forward to exploring the little shops behind the promenade, interested to see what had changed in the years since she had last been there.

But Lili's plans were not to be. Instead, they'd arrived in Aldeburgh after dark. The bus driver had dropped them as close to their hotel as possible. They had both been tired, and all they'd wanted to do was get their room key, unpack and have some dinner.

Lili recalled their arrival at the hotel. It had not started well.

'I don't like it here,' Maisie had said, refusing to enter the lobby of the hotel. 'I want to go somewhere else.' She had put her Trunki down on the pavement and refused to budge. To add to Lili's already rubbish day, it had been pouring with rain.

There had also been a power-cut in the town. Maisie had freaked out upon seeing the old hotel building unlit. It had only been the concierge appearing at the door with a candle that had persuaded her to go inside. She had wanted one too. It had been quite a novelty for Maisie to find their room by candlelight.

The hotel had once been a coaching inn, with dark wood, creaky floorboards and narrow, winding passages that had seemed to extend up steps, down flights of stairs and around hidden corners before leading to their bedroom.

Lili had fancied dinner in the restaurant. However, Maisie hadn't wanted to venture out again, down those dark, scary corridors, so they'd enjoyed room service instead. They'd had a picnic on the bed and watched cartoons on the massive wall-mounted TV.

Lili smiled. It had turned out to be a lovely evening, despite the phone call with Alex. Maisie loved the suite with its duck-egg blue walls and its enormous bed with an old-fashioned iron bedstead, white linen and a throw to match the colour of the walls. There were lots of pillows and cushions, a large sofa and a flat-screen television. Alex had booked a suite. It was cosy, and appeared newly decorated, with cream architraves and Georgian sash windows that let in plenty of light. The room had kept some features that Lili imagined had been here when it was a coaching inn two centuries ago – the old fireplace, picture rails and the wooden doors to the bedroom and en suite bathroom. It was very tasteful.

Lili smiled. What Maisie didn't know was that they'd arrived at the rear entrance to The Harbour Inn, but their room was at the front. Lili had always thought it was a strange name for a hotel, given that it wasn't near a harbour. There was no harbour in Aldeburgh. The hotel sat on a long promenade lined with an eclectic mix of pastel-coloured holiday villas. Some were quite small, like cottages, while others were grand townhouses built in the nineteenth century.

When she was growing up, Lili had often come here with the girls from school who didn't go home for the Christmas holidays. They would sit with glasses of warm mulberry wine outside on a bench in the cold, along with half the town, and sing carols. Lili smiled at the memory. She had liked the feel of the small community, where everyone knew everyone else; it had been so different from her early years spent in London in care before she moved to Aldeburgh.

'Maisie, why don't you open the curtains and I'll make us both a cup of tea?' There was a tray on the dressing table with a teapot, kettle, two cups and saucers, tea bags, coffee, small bags of sugar and sachets of milk. Lili put the kettle on, waiting for Maisie's reaction when she opened the drapes.

Maisie screamed, but it wasn't in fear – it was delight.

Lili's immediate impulse was to chide her with the words *indoor voices, please*, but on this occasion she didn't. Maisie couldn't contain her excitement; this was the first time she'd seen the sea. Lili joined her at the window. Seagulls were making a racket with their distinctive call outside on the low wall that separated the wide promenade from the beach.

Maisie pointed at a seagull. 'So that's where the strange noises I heard last night were coming from.' She pressed her nose up against the windowpane. 'And that funny whooshing sound …'

Lili joined her, casting her gaze down to the pebble beach where the waves were lapping on the shore. Lili noticed that unlike the previous day, the sky was blue, with hardly a rain cloud in sight. Not that it wouldn't change. With that thought, Lili forgot her cup of tea and decided to head down to breakfast instead. She didn't want to lose the pleasant weather.

'Come on – let's get dressed and have breakfast. Then we can go to the beach.'

Lili ran over to her suitcase. She was getting out some clean clothes when she noticed Maisie was still at the window.

Maisie turned around. 'Why do you think Mummy never takes me on holiday?'

Lili stared at her. Maisie was still standing there in her pyjamas, waiting for an answer.

'Well, they are staying in a hotel just for adults.' She hadn't told her a lie, but it wasn't an explanation, and Maisie wasn't stupid.

'I know, but Mummy is always booking adults-only holidays. My friends at school go on holiday with their parents. Why doesn't she go somewhere that allows children?'

Because she doesn't want you there, Lili thought. It was much easier for Hannah to leave Maisie with her best friend and go away to party until the early hours and to have romantic candle-lit dinners and late-night walks with her partner before sleeping in the following morning. Children could really cramp your style. If Alex had come with them, Lili realised it wouldn't have worked. In fact, it would have made things worse because nobody would have got what they wanted out of the break – least of all Alex.

Lili sighed. 'Perhaps Mummy thought you wouldn't want to fly. You know she goes on foreign holidays a lot.'

'Why can't she go on holiday to Aldeburgh?'

'When you get home, you can tell her all about it and perhaps she'll book her next break in this country.'

Lili knew her best friend aspired to a jet-set lifestyle. She couldn't imagine Hannah taking her daughter to the Suffolk coast for a holiday. When she thought about it, Hannah had done very little with Maisie over the years; she was always too preoccupied with her relationships. Lili was the one who had taken Maisie to London Zoo and the museums.

Lili walked over and handed Maisie her phone. Even though she knew it wouldn't persuade Hannah to return here, Lili said, 'Let's take some nice photos – show her what's she's missing.'

Maisie said, 'I wish I had my own phone.'

'Do you?' It was Maisie's birthday soon, and she'd just given Lili a gift idea.

Lili noticed the sky clouding over already. She sighed, thinking it was turning out to be a *typical British summer.* 'Come on, let's get cracking before the rain sets in.'

Before she got dressed, Maisie took some photos of the beach from the window. 'This is *so* cool.'

Lili smiled. She wasn't sure whether Maisie was referring to her phone or the views. A little of both, she suspected when she looked through the photos while Maisie dressed.

7

Maisie walked out of the bathroom looking downcast.

'What's the matter?' Lili asked, noticing the change in her mood.

'Do we have to go down to the dining room for breakfast?'

Lili looked at her. She guessed that it wasn't just how gloomy it had been downstairs the previous night that was putting Maisie off; it was that the people they had seen on arrival were all a certain age.

Lili thought she might find it a bit stuffy herself. She also imagined that with waiter service, the idea was to have a leisurely meal – which was fine if you didn't have children with you. She had thought to suggest they had breakfast in their room, but she was unsure how long they would have to wait.

She had an idea. 'How about we eat outside on the beach?'

Maisie jumped up and down and raced to the door. 'What are you waiting for?'

Lili grabbed her raincoat – just in case.

'Maisie – what about your coat?'

'I don't need one.'

'But it might be cold first thing in the morning.'

Maisie rushed out the bedroom, eager to get going. Lili walked out, arms laden with their coats, and handed Maisie the room key. 'Would you be a sweetheart and lock up?'

Maisie had just locked the door when she said, 'I need a wee.'

'Can't it wait until we get downstairs? There are toilets in the lobby.'

'No!'

Lili sighed while she unlocked the door and Maisie ran inside. At this rate, they'd miss the sunshine.

When they arrived downstairs, Lili left Maisie sitting in the old-fashioned foyer scrolling through her photos and walked into the dining room. The restaurant was in a small conservatory tacked on to the side of the Georgian building. She walked in and saw couples sitting at tables by the windows, enjoying the view of the promenade and sea beyond. She couldn't help thinking that the couples should include her and Alex, relaxing after a good night's sleep in the honeymoon suite, taking their time over breakfast.

'Madam, can I help you?'

Lili wiped a tear away from her face before turning around. 'I wondered if it's possible to have breakfast to go?'

He raised an eyebrow. 'Breakfast – to go?'

Lili reminded herself this wasn't London. 'Never mind.' She walked out of the diner and collected Maisie from the foyer. 'I'm hungry,' said Maisie. 'Where's my food?'

'In the restaurant,' Lili quipped, thinking it might persuade her to have something to eat in the hotel. No such luck. Maisie was still heading for the door. 'I want to see the beach.'

Standing on the promenade, Lili spotted an old forties-style van parked up ahead with one side propped open. Lili could see a small queue forming and a man serving hot drinks and snacks. *Perfect*, she thought.

'Come on.' She took Maisie's hand.

'But I want to go to the beach.'

'We will, but first let's get a cup of tea and a hot chocolate and something to eat.' Lili thought they were bound to have some snacks, even if it was just some crisps or perhaps a bacon butty. Not a healthy breakfast, but they were on holiday. Lili took her hand, and they walked along the promenade.

Ten minutes later, they stepped on to the pebbly beach, Lili with a cup of tea and a cheese bagel, Maisie with a hot chocolate covered in whippy cream and sprinkles and a large chocolate muffin.

'What are they?' Maisie asked, noticing the black wooden single-storey shacks sitting on the beach as she took another bite of her muffin. Beside one hut was a fishing boat. 'That's where the fishermen sell the catch of the day.'

There was a sign outside the huts. Maisie read out loud, 'If it was any fresher, it would still be swimming.' She wriggled her nose. 'What does that mean?'

Lili laughed and tried to explain the joke, but it was lost on Maisie. Lili smiled. 'It's a grown-up joke.'

'This beach isn't sandy,' Maisie said, disappointed.

Lili knew Maisie wanted to bring back some seashells. 'Let's try nearer the shore.' They walked over a large mound of pebbles and made their way towards the sea. 'This is so cool,' Maisie said, her disappointment evaporating as they crunched over the small stones. There, on the strip of sand where the sea was lapping against the seashore, were the shells she was looking for. Maisie ran over and picked some up, putting them in her pocket. As they strode along the shoreline, and Maisie realised there were enough shells to fill hundreds of pockets, she became a bit more discerning. Then she had an idea. 'I'm going to look for treasure.'

Lili smiled at her. Although some children her age were perhaps more worldly and had grown out of make-believe play, Maisie had not. Sometimes she was a spy or an explorer. Just then, she was a treasure-hunter.

Lili stopped to breathe in the sea air. The easterly wind that the Suffolk coast was renowned for was bracing, but that didn't seem to bother Maisie as she picked up seashells. Lili stood at the water's edge, drinking her tea out of a takeaway cup and staring out to sea at the distant horizon, trying not to think of the end of the week and Alex.

Maisie came running over. 'Look what I've found. What is it?' She opened her hand to reveal a honey-yellow stone.

'Oh wow, Maisie! You found some amber.'

'Amber? What's that?'

'It's a gemstone.'

'You mean I discovered some treasure after all?' She looked at Lili, wide-eyed.

'You might uncover some more if you look closely. That's why this stretch of coastline from Felixstowe to Southwold is called The Amber Coast. People collect these gemstones and make jewellery out of them.'

Maisie held up her precious stone to examine it. 'This looks like the one in your ring. Is that amber?'

Lili put her hand to her chest, where the ring hung on a necklace. She clasped it between two fingers and held it up. Inset in the circle was a stone with a reddish-orangey hue. When the light caught the stone, it glowed yellow. Lili looked again at the gemstone Maisie was holding up. It looked remarkably similar. 'You know what? I think you're right,' said Lili in surprise.

She didn't know whether amber would be classed as precious; it was a gemstone, but not in the league of diamonds or sapphires. Lili had never taken her ring to a jeweller to find out how much it was worth because she would never part with it. It was all she had to remember her parents by. Apart from the clothes she had been wearing when she was found wandering on a beach in Corfu, this ring – which she kept on a chain – was all she'd had.

Connie had made sure to keep it somewhere safe until Lili was old enough to take care of it herself. Lili recalled that back when Maisie was small, and she could carry her in her arms, little podgy inquisitive fingers had often latched on to the pendant. When she was teething, it had often ended up in her mouth. That was the only time Lili took the necklace off.

'Do you think the amber in your ring came from here, on this beach?'

Lili smiled at Maisie. It was a nice thought, but they could find amber anywhere in the world. She imagined this ring was most likely purchased by her parents in a tacky backstreet tourist shop in Corfu or somewhere else on their travels.

'What does the writing say?' asked Maisie.

Lili looked at her, bemused. 'What writing?'

Maisie reached up and held the ring for a moment. 'There's writing on the inside. It isn't French. I'm learning that at school. Listen …'

Lili listened to Maisie recite one to twenty in French while she turned the ring over and studied the inside. Could Maisie be right? Could it be a language and not just decorative squiggles to embellish the piece of jewellery and make it look more attractive, as Lili had always thought?

'Let's find some more treasure,' Maisie called out as she ran along the beach.

Lili followed her, joining in with the amber hunt. She was thinking about her ring, wondering if the markings were an inscription and who might be able to decipher for her what language it was.

8

Maisie got the amber out of her coat pocket and spread the pieces on the table in front of her. 'Do you think we could make some jewellery with my precious stones, like your ring?'

'I don't see why not,' Lili replied. 'We could do a necklace too. I'm sure we could look up how it's done and find out where to buy the materials.' Lili picked up a menu. 'What would you like for lunch, Maisie?'

They were sitting in the window of an old-fashioned café. Small and cosy, it had chintzy tablecloths and curtains, and a cabinet displaying a variety of homemade cakes. Behind the counter, two middle-aged ladies were making sandwiches and pots of tea and coffee for their customers. The café was busy, which didn't surprise Lili, given that it was the school holidays.

'Ah, I see you've found some amber,' said the woman who had walked over to their table to take their order. She smiled at Maisie. 'That's quite a find. I can't remember collecting that amount when I went foraging with my children.' She glanced at Lili.

Lili shifted in her seat. People always assumed Maisie was her daughter.

'I have nine pieces,' said Maisie, looking pleased with herself.

'You must have been on the beach a long time.'

When Lili had woken up that morning, she had been wondering how to fill the days. She didn't have a car, which meant that unless they caught a bus, there were limited places they could go and things they could do during the week. This wasn't London, where there was always another museum with activities for children or the zoo or a variety of parks to run around in and explore.

Lili had looked up the weather forecast; it was going to be cloudy with rain showers interspersed with a few sunny spells. That meant they couldn't spend long, lazy days at the sandy coves along the coast that they could reach by bus, building sandcastles, swimming in the sea and having picnics.

She'd thought she'd be lucky if Maisie spent even an hour on Aldeburgh's beach, but she'd had such a good time collecting seashells and amber that the morning had flown by, and it was soon lunchtime. They'd walked from the beach along the promenade and down a little lane between the villas with sea views. They'd emerged on the main street and had found the café they were now seated in.

Lili ordered two sandwiches.

'Can I have some cake?' Maisie asked.

Lili followed her gaze – she had spotted the cakes on the counter. 'You can have a slice after your sandwich.' Lili glanced at the menu and handed it to the lady. 'Can we have an orange juice and a pot of tea as well, please?'

'Certainly. Are you here on holiday?'

'Yes,' Maisie replied. 'We're staying in the hotel.'

'Which one?' she asked.

'The Harbour Inn.'

'Fancy,' the woman said, smiling at Maisie. 'Have you been here before?'

Maisie shook her head, no. 'I've never been to the seaside.'

'We live in London,' Lili said, even though it didn't explain why a girl Maisie's age had never visited the coast. She caught the lady glancing at the empty seat. The table in the window was for three. 'Will anyone else be joining you?' She looked towards the door expectantly.

Lili shook her head, no.

'Your other half has to work?'

Lili smiled and nodded. That was the trouble with small towns. Lili wouldn't get asked that sort of question sitting in a café in London. She'd just be another anonymous customer. Even though she didn't appreciate the question, and didn't want to be reminded of Alex, she wasn't sorry she'd come here with Maisie on her own.

Maisie was still busy rearranging her amber and seashells on the table, creating a pattern.

Lili held the ring on her necklace between her thumb and forefinger. It was such a pretty ring, with its amber stone; she had considered whether she might use it as a wedding ring. She hadn't told Alex. She had been waiting for the right moment, for when he proposed, as she'd always assumed he would – eventually.

'What's the matter?'

Lili looked across the table at Maisie. 'Oh, it's such a windy day – I had something in my eye.' Lili wiped her eyes with a tissue and tried not to think about the end of the holiday. It made her stomach churn at the thought that this might be it; that they'd split up. After almost six years, surely it wouldn't be over just like that? The conversation with Connie the previous night came to mind. Connie hadn't felt that would be the case either. The trouble was that Lili hadn't mentioned the imminent move to Washington and the problem she had with leaving the country to live abroad.

Lili decided that her time away with Maisie was for the best. Perhaps at the end of the holiday, with Maisie back home, the argument about looking after Hannah's daughter would have blown over. Lili felt Alex had overreacted. However, it was his promotion that was bothering her. She still believed her reticence at the news had precipitated this so-called *taking a break*. She knew that if she decided not to go with him, their relationship would be over.

Lili placed the tissue in her bag, determined to put a brave face on the events of the previous day and not spoil the week, even though she had an awful lot on her mind.

Maisie ate her sandwich while eyeing the cakes.

Lili smiled at her as she picked up a sandwich. 'Slow down, Maisie, there are plenty of cakes to go round.'

'So, what are we doing next?' Maisie asked, her mouth full.

Lili stared through the little panes of glass in the window. It was now lashing down with rain. They'd had the best of the weather that morning; there had only been light showers. Lili was trying to think up things to occupy Maisie after lunch. She was sure there would be a bookshop in the town and hoped there might be an art and craft shop too. Perhaps there would be a book on making jewellery. She imagined you would need some specific implements or tools to create necklaces out of raw amber, but they could look for a toy shop with a crafts section which stocked jewellery-making kits for children. She'd had an idea to get Maisie one for her birthday, but it would give them something to do this afternoon instead. 'I thought we'd visit some shops.'

Maisie's face fell.

The lady serving at the counter came over to clear away their dishes. 'Would you like some cake?'

Maisie nodded her head and cheered up. 'I like chocolate cake.'

'Me too,' the lady said, smiling at Maisie. She commented, 'I love your hat.'

Maisie said, 'It's a beret. It's French. Mummy got it for me when she went to France with her boyfriend. We're learning French at school. I can count all the way up to twenty. Listen …'

The lady's eyes roved to Lili while Maisie counted in French up to twenty.

Lili wanted the ground to swallow her up, but she didn't let on that she wasn't Maisie's mother. Even now, after all these years, Lili still had a secret fear that Maisie would be put into care. It was irrational. She was paranoid about it. It was perfectly okay for Maisie's mum's best friend to take her on a brief trip during the school summer holidays.

It wasn't as though Hannah had left Maisie home alone. She would never do that. And it wasn't as though Hannah was homeless. Those days of sofa-surfing were behind her. In fact, now Lili thought about it, if things didn't work out with Alex, it was she who, for the first time since leaving care, might be homeless.

Lili tried to shrug that thought aside as the lady came with two generous slices of cake – chocolate for Maisie and vanilla sponge with jam and cream for Lili. She smiled. If anything could cure her of a large dose of feeling sorry for herself, it was a slice of homemade cake.

Maisie didn't bother with the delicate fork wrapped in a serviette. She picked up the whole slice in her hands and took a big bite; chocolate frosting covered her lips and cheeks and the tip of her nose.

Lili was about to pass her a serviette. Instead, she picked up her slice and took a big bite. She could feel her cheeks slathered with cream.

Maisie giggled. 'You've got cream on your nose.'

Lili smiled. 'And you've got chocolate on yours.' She wondered why cake tasted so much better eaten this way, sticky fingers and all.

Lili wiped her nose with the serviette and licked her fingers. She glanced around the room, feeling self-conscious, and caught the eye of an older lady who was sitting at a nearby table with a boy of about Maisie's age. Lili guessed she was in her late fifties or early sixties and was looking after her grandchild during the holidays. They had also just been served cake.

The lady put down her fork and picked up her slice, smiling at Lili as she took a large bite. The boy sat there, holding his fork, with a delicate morsel suspended in mid-air.

'Grandma!' Lili heard him exclaim, throwing her a questioning look as he put the fork in his mouth. She overheard the woman's reply. 'Why don't you put your fork down,' she said, licking her fingers. 'Cake tastes so much better eaten this way.'

Lili smiled. They were precisely the words she had thought to herself.

He furiously shook his head. 'No, I'll get all sticky.'

Lili noticed he had a serviette tucked in his shirt collar to catch any crumbs, unlike the wild child sitting opposite Lili. The tangled mass of Maisie's blonde hair under her hat fell about her shoulders, looking as though it needed a good brush. She was also dressed in clothes that didn't match. She wore different coloured socks, a denim skirt, and a plain tee-shirt two sizes too big with a round smiley face on the front accompanied by a few stubborn stains. The boy on the adjacent table had his short black hair neatly combed, and he wore chinos, a white shirt and a navy jumper.

He said, 'We don't eat with our fingers. It's not the done thing.'

'Well, it might not be the done thing in London, sweetheart, but here in Suffolk we can please ourselves.'

Maisie overheard the conversation too. She rolled her eyes, which made Lili smile. 'We live in London, but we don't eat cake with a fork. He's weird,' said Maisie.

Maisie had spoken her mind a little too loudly. The boy shot Maisie a look. 'Who are you calling weird?'

'William, don't be rude.'

'But she's the one being rude, Grandma. She started it.'

The boy's grandmother told him to shush and turned to Lili. 'Sorry, he didn't mean to be rude.'

Have you been amber-hunting?'

Maisie turned around. 'Yes, I found lots on the beach.'

'Ah, Aldeburgh is one of the best places to find them.'

'I want to make jewellery out of them.'

'That's stupid,' William said under his breath as he sliced a bit of cake with his fork, glancing at his grandma to see if she'd heard. If she had, she didn't let on.

'What a marvellous idea. You know, I used to look for amber

with my son years ago, but my grandson doesn't want to play on the beach.'

'You could come with us,' suggested Maisie. 'We could go amber-hunting together. I'm sure there's lots more.' Maisie stole a glance at the boy. So did Lili. She caught him sticking his tongue out at Maisie when his grandmother wasn't looking.

Lili expected that, as with the lady serving here, the grandmother would assume that Maisie was her daughter. Although she seemed nice, Lili preferred to spend the day with Maisie – just the two of them. However, the weather was not on their side, which meant nobody was going to the beach. 'It's pouring with rain now, Maisie. Perhaps another time.'

She doubted they'd run into the lady or her grandson, William, again. However, noting that the lady sounded as though she lived in Aldeburgh, Lili did say, 'Do you know of a bookshop or an art and craft shop?' The town wasn't very large, comprising a high street dotted with little independent shops a stone's throw from the promenade and the beach. It wouldn't have taken long for Lili to find out for herself, but with the weather as it was, she imagined that if they walked in the wrong direction, they'd get drenched.

The grandmother smiled. 'I know the perfect place.'

9

Lili and Maisie stepped into the courtyard. It was called Cobblers Yard. Although Lili remembered the town from her school years, she didn't recall venturing down the narrow alleyway which opened out into this small, cobbled square. Several independent stores fronted the square. William's grandmother had been correct; there was an art shop – although looking in the window, Lili got the impression from the paints and canvases for sale that it was aimed at adults.

Lili had wanted an art and craft place geared toward children. There was a toy shop next door with wooden crafted toys on display. She doubted they sold the sort of jewellery kit she was after for Maisie. Lili glanced across the courtyard at a second-hand bookshop with peeling paint and a rundown exterior that had seen better days. The books appeared dusty and old, as though stuck in a time warp. She guessed it had closed down. There were no lights on inside.

In contrast, the music shop appeared bright and welcoming. There were violins and guitars on display. On her way to the art shop, she glanced inside and thought it resembled someone's sitting room, not the interior of a store. There was also an old antique shop, with gold lettering above the door; it was called George and Son Antiques. Across the yard was a charity shop, next door to a shop called The Potting Shed which sold handcrafted bouquets and potted plants. This completed the small group of shops in this hidden corner of the town.

Cobblers Yard reminded Lili of a Dickensian Christmas scene. The old-fashioned storefronts had their original leaded windows, and some were painted a vintage green. There was even a streetlight that had once been a gas lamp.

In the gloom of the overcast afternoon, it flickered on, casting an eerie glow. Lili was drawn to the flower shop. She crossed the courtyard and stood outside, admiring the window display. It was laid out like a small garden; there were pretty pots filled with seasonal summer flowers sitting on a bed of artificial grass. She liked the imaginative combinations, especially the lilies and lavender. There were also colourful bouquets and intricate wreaths for sale.

She tried the door, thinking she'd just pop inside on the off-chance and see if they had any vacancies. Not that she was looking for a job there. She was still holding out for her dream position at Kew. However, it couldn't hurt to make inquiries in case she and Alex really had split up for good. The rental properties were far cheaper in Suffolk than in London.

Lili found herself thinking about Alex again. Had the worst happened already, and she just couldn't accept it? She wished he wasn't on her mind most of the time.

Alex. Lili sighed. It hadn't been love at first sight. She had grown to care for him. When he'd asked her for a date, she'd accepted his invitation to dinner. She hadn't been seeking Mr Right, but Mr Dependable. After years of witnessing her best friend in and out of so many relationships with losers, Lili had wanted a nice guy with his head screwed on; someone who would provide stability and security for their family when they had children. All that falling in love, that instant can't-get-enough-of-one-another attraction, was for teenagers.

Alex had been perfect.

The flat he'd been able to afford to rent in Kew had been a bonus. It had enough room to accommodate the two of them – and her best friend along with Maisie when they came to stay, which in the beginning had been often.

Just before she had met Alex, Lili had been voted out of her house share. Her house mates hadn't thought it was fair that she'd kept having her friend to stay with her infant – rent-free – and they hadn't appreciated being woken at all hours by a screaming baby.

Lili had been on the verge of homelessness before Alex had walked into her life. Had it been serendipity? Had they been destined to be together?

If things had been different, if she hadn't assumed responsibility for her best friend and had left London for college instead, she and Alex would never have met. It had only happened through circumstance.

Don't most relationships happen through fate, though? thought Lili. You were in the right place at the right time to meet that special person. Or the wrong place at the wrong time, meeting someone you weren't destined to be with. She frowned. She knew why she was thinking this way; if Alex dumped her, then the only course to mend her broken heart would be to make the excuse that they were never meant to be together anyway.

She wondered why stepping into the flower shop was

making her speculate about all this. Perhaps seeing all these beautiful flowers was making her think about how her life might have turned out if only Hannah hadn't got pregnant at eighteen. Lili still wondered who Maisie's father was.

A little bell tinkled above her head as she opened the door and stepped inside. She cast her gaze around the cosy interior. A funny thought came out of nowhere: how lovely it would be to run her own flower shop. *What happened to your dream job at Kew?* she asked herself.

Lili made her way toward the counter. A young girl was writing a message on a card. She placed it in a bouquet for her customer, a gentleman of retirement age who was dressed in casual jeans and a sweater. He turned to leave, and Lili stepped aside. He smiled at her as he passed.

'Can I help you?'

Lili stared at the bouquet. 'They're beautiful.'

'Aren't they? He is our biggest customer, in here every other day to place an order.'

Lili glanced over her shoulder as the man strode out of the shop. 'He must be so in love to send so many flowers.'

'I guess.'

Lili smiled. 'She will receive such a lovely surprise when you deliver them.'

'Oh, we don't need to deliver these,' said the young woman.

Lili looked at her. Had she missed something?

The assistant saw Lili's bemused expression. 'The flowers are for the shop owner.'

Lili giggled. 'Sorry, let me get this straight. He buys flowers *from* the lady who owns the flowers shop *for* the lady who owns the flower shop?'

'That's right.'

'How romantic,' mused Lili. 'They must be very much in love.'

'Well, that remains to be seen.'

'What do you mean?'

'They're separated. He's trying to win her back.'

'Oh.' That wasn't what Lili had expected to hear.

'What happens to the flowers?'

She shrugged. 'I don't know. I only work here part time for a few hours each day.'

That answered Lili's question about job vacancies. She asked anyway.

The teenager shook her head. 'I don't think so, although you could come back when the owner is here. I'm off to university next year, so there might be an opening then.'

Lili smiled. 'That's okay.' Besides, she couldn't live on a few hours' work a week, even if the rents were cheaper than in London.

With a start, Lili suddenly realised she was missing something. She'd assumed Maisie had followed her into the store, but she was nowhere to be seen. Lili ran outside, her heart pounding. 'Maisie?' She'd lost her. How could she have let her out of her sight?

Frantically looking around the cobbled courtyard, Lili didn't know where to turn first. It was still lunchtime, and some shops were closed. Lili ran towards the toyshop, but she could see through the window that Maisie wasn't inside. The antiques shop was closed for lunch. Maisie wouldn't have ventured in there anyway, with the old antique furniture from another era.

Lili didn't bother looking in the windows of the bookshop

or the music shop as she raced by. That left the art shop. She knew Maisie was hoping to find materials to make amber necklaces, so it was the most likely place. She rushed up to the window and spotted her. Lili breathed an enormous sigh of relief. 'Thank God!'

Lili realised that the shop owner Maisie was talking to was the same older gentleman who had just left the flower shop. Maisie must have waited outside until he returned. Lili entered the shop and walked up behind Maisie, clasping her by the shoulders. 'Oh, Maisie! I thought I'd lost you.'

Maisie turned her head and glanced at Lili. 'I was right here the whole time.'

Lili realised she had been in her own little world from the moment she'd spotted the flower shop. She hadn't even told Maisie she was going inside. 'So, did you find some things to make amber necklaces?' she asked.

'Amber necklaces?' the owner of the shop said in surprise.

Maisie replied, 'Oh, I forgot about that.'

Lili was surprised. She'd been talking about it non-stop all morning, and through lunch. She wanted to create and sell jewellery. Lili would be the first to encourage her if that was what she was interested in doing.

'I'll see what we have in stock. I might have something for you.'

'Great! Isn't it, Maisie?'

'I guess.'

Lili looked down at her. 'Why the glum face?' She wondered what Maisie had been discussing with the shop owner; it clearly wasn't the amber she'd found on the beach.

He soon returned, carrying a box – a children's kit for

making jewellery. 'It's the last one. Do you want to take it as well?'

'As well?' Lili glanced at Maisie, who was uncharacteristically quiet. On the counter in front of them there was a large sketch pad, some paints and crayons, and an easel. Lili looked at Maisie in surprise. 'You paint?'

She shrugged.

Lili said, 'I guess we'll have those too.'

He cashed them up on the register. He'd just reached for the last item when Lili stopped him. 'Not the easel.' She'd caught him in time before he added it to the bill.

Maisie stamped her foot in frustration. 'But I *need* that.'

Lili pointed at the easel. 'It's not a toy, Maisie.' She had no intention of paying a lot of money for a passing fancy. It was a proper full-sized wooden easel for adults, and she imagined it had a price tag to match. The paints were expensive too. She couldn't really afford it all.

'I know it's not a toy! I really need it.'

Lili sighed. 'Can you excuse us a moment?'

The shop owner smiled and said, 'Of course.'

Lili preferred to avoid a tantrum in the middle of the store. She took Maisie to one side. 'Look, I thought you wanted to make jewellery using your amber?'

'I do. But I need those things too. I keep asking Mum, but she says it's silly. She bought me a Nintendo instead. She doesn't want paint or crayon marks on her walls. You haven't seen our house yet, have you?'

Lili shook her head. Hannah had moved into a brand new detached place with her current partner. Lili eyed the materials; she was surprised that little Maisie was interested in painting.

'Please can I have them?' Maisie's large blue eyes peered up at Lili, tugging at her heartstrings.

The shop owner interrupted. 'You know what? I'll do a special discount in exchange for one of your paintings, young lady.'

Maisie nodded. Lili sighed. They both returned to the counter. 'Thank you, that's very kind of you,' Lili said. 'All right. Yes, I will take those.'

'Do you still want this?' He held up the jewellery-making kit.

Lili glanced at Maisie, who nodded her head to have that too.

'I'll take all of it.'

He rang up the items on the till, giving a generous discount of thirty percent. Lili was delighted until he said, 'That will be two hundred.' She thought there must have been some mistake. Then she caught sight of the price tag on the easel. It was a lot of money to pay for something that, at Maisie's age, was probably a phase. But Lili couldn't back out now.

'Oh, wait. I have a book around here somewhere that's all about famous paintings. It might give you some inspiration. Would you like that too?' Although he directed the question at Maisie, he eyed Lili.

Lili shrugged. 'Okay – why not?' She'd spent this much already. What difference would a book make? Lili watched as he handed Maisie a large volume about artists. She thumbed through it. 'This is *so* cool.'

'I guess we'll be taking that too.' Lili got out her bank card. She had some savings, so she didn't need to put it on a credit card. Lili turned to the door. It was still pouring down outside – not the best time to walk back to the hotel carrying Maisie's painting equipment and easel.

The shop owner saw them hesitating. 'I can drop them off later, after I close.'

Maisie moaned, 'But I want them now.'

'I know, sweetheart, but look at the weather …'

'Can't you call a taxi or something?'

Lili didn't want to add the expense of a cab coming from goodness-knows-where just to take them down the road to the hotel. She retraced her steps, depositing the carrier bag and painting easel on the counter. 'Yes please, that would be helpful, thank you. We're staying at The Harbour Inn. We're on holiday.' Lili turned to go. 'Now, what are we going to do this afternoon?'

'If you're at a loose end because of the weather, there's always The Picture House.'

'The Picture House?' Maisie repeated excitedly. 'Can we see it? Will there be paintings to look at?'

Both Lili and the chap serving in the shop looked at Maisie. 'What do you mean?' Lili asked.

'I always wanted to go to an art gallery.'

'Really?' Lili made a mental note that when they returned to London at the end of the week, she'd take her to a gallery. That was when she understood. 'Oh, sweetheart, The Picture House doesn't have paintings. It's a cinema.'

Maisie looked crestfallen.

Outside the shop, Lili was too busy trying to open her umbrella against the rain that she didn't notice an old man in the antiques shop. He was putting a clock in the window display when he looked up and caught sight of the pair. Although he could barely see them with the rain lashing against the windowpane, he felt there was something familiar about her that made him pause. By the time he had reached over to wipe the condensation from one of the small panes and had shifted his half-moon glasses on his nose to get a better look, she had gone.

Lili held Maisie's hand, trying to keep her umbrella up against the wind and rain as they made haste toward the cinema, a short distance along the high street.

'I don't want to go,' yelled Maisie, yanking her hand out of Lili's so hard that she nearly careered into a lady who was walking by. 'I want to go back to the hotel!' Maisie stood on the pavement and stamped her foot.

Lili looked at her. She was acting like a two-year-old about to throw a tantrum. Lili had no intention of returning to their lodgings and sitting in their room for the rest of the afternoon, waiting for Maisie's stuff to arrive from the art and craft shop. She now wished she'd returned to the hotel with them – at least Maisie would have been occupied and they wouldn't be standing on the pavement in the pouring rain arguing about it.

But it was too late for that now. Lili tried to put on a stern voice, although she never seemed to be able to pull it off. 'We are not going back to the hotel, so either we spend the afternoon standing here in the pouring rain or we go to the cinema, buy some popcorn and watch a movie. Well, what is it to be?'

Maisie threw Lili a dirty look and set off for cinema.

Lili took off after her. The first day of their holiday had not turned out how she'd envisaged. She sighed as she caught up with Maisie. She wondered what she'd be doing with Alex right now if Hannah hadn't interrupted their plans. What would they be doing with themselves on a wet afternoon? Lili thought of the large king-sized bed in their hotel room. It *was* the honeymoon suite, after all.

10

'Where now?' Maisie shouted, coming to a stop where the high street forked. Lili caught up. She knew that if they branched down the street to their right, it would lead to a small parking area fronting the promenade and the beach with the little black huts where the fishermen sold their catch of the day, and then on to their hotel. If they kept going along the main road, which narrowed into a terrace of cottages, the cinema was on the left. They could see it from where they were standing.

'Is that it?' Maisie pointed toward a mock Tudor building with dark leaded windows. 'I don't like it.'

Lili took her hand. 'You'll love it when you get inside. I promise.'

There were double doors leading into the foyer, just as Lili remembered. It looked bright and welcoming. Lili encouraged Maisie to put her nose up against the door and look through the glass. Lili did the same. Her first impression was that it hadn't changed a bit. It was one of the few independent cinemas that still existed in the country, and it was especially rare to find an old picture house in a small seaside resort like Aldeburgh. Lili drew back as a family with two children approached. She stepped aside, letting them pass. Maisie watched them walk inside.

'How about we go inside out of the rain and have a look around?'

Maisie thought about it for a moment. She was shivering with cold. Lili noticed. At least she had something to thank the weather for. 'Okay,' said Maisie, pulling the door open. They both stepped inside. The family were buying sweets at the counter.

'Can I have some sweets?' Maisie asked.

'I don't see why not, but only if we are going to watch the film.' That was a bit of a fib. She imagined they could buy sweets and walk out. 'Shall I get the tickets for the movie?' she asked.

Maisie thought about it for all of two seconds, her eyes fixed on the sweet counter. 'Yes.'

'Great!' Lili sighed in relief. She walked over to the man in an old-fashioned blue uniform with red braiding, trying to keep her face expressionless. His outfit would not have looked out of place on a bell hop in a grand hotel.

Lili asked for the tickets. She paid with her bank card and got two ticket stubs in return. Back in London, she always purchased seats online for the local multiplex cinema and scanned the barcode on her phone into a machine to confirm her seat. The only human contact at the multiplex happened when buying a ridiculously overpriced soft drink and popcorn from a bored teenager. Soulless, charmless places, they weren't a patch on these small independent cinemas housed in unusual buildings. Lili had always loved coming here when she was younger.

Lili searched the man's face as he handed her the tickets, wondering if he remembered her from ten years earlier. She recognised him. He had seemed ancient back then. She couldn't believe he was still here.

'Would madam care for some refreshments?' he asked.

'Yes please.'

'I want some Smarties.' Maisie stood on tiptoes to look at the sweets on the counter. Although she was eight, she was petite like her mother and could pass as a six-year-old until she opened her mouth. 'Please,' she added as an afterthought, throwing the old man a shy smile.

Lili glanced at the jug of juice on the counter. It was freely available for customers. She poured some juice into a polystyrene cup for Maisie and some coffee into a takeaway mug for herself. She paid for the coffee and Maisie's Smarties.

'You forgot the popcorn,' said Maisie.

'I thought you were having Smarties?'

'Yes, but you said we could have popcorn.'

Lili rolled her eyes. Maisie didn't miss a trick. 'Okay.'

'Sweet or salty?' the man asked.

Maisie couldn't decide. She liked both, so Lili bought a small tub of each.

Lili carried the tubs of popcorn and her drink through the foyer. The old man held the thick blue drapes open for them to walk inside. Maisie hesitated.

'Just hold on one moment,' he said. He let the drapes drop and disappeared. A minute later, he opened the drapes again. The auditorium's lights weren't dimmed anymore; the room was brightly lit for Maisie to choose her seat.

Lili thanked him as they walked inside. Where in London would someone adjust the lighting for a hesitant child to enter the auditorium?

'Is there only one screen?' Maisie asked.

'Yes. There are blankets to cosy up under, and booster seats.'

Maisie grabbed two blankets, even though Lili thought they wouldn't need them.

They looked around, deciding where to sit. Apart from the family who had taken seats in the last row, right at the back, the auditorium was empty. Lili had just sat down next to Maisie when in walked the old man wheeling a trolley loaded with confectionery and soft drinks. Maisie spotted the ice cream. 'I want some ice cream.'

'Not now. Perhaps in the intermission.'

'What's an intermission?'

Lili smiled. She'd seen the white banner across the film poster saying, *please note this performance has an intermission.* She guessed that the gentleman who had served them was the projectionist too. She assumed the intermission wasn't for the benefit of the viewing public but so that he could have a break and sell more food and drinks. Independent cinemas relied on the income they brought in from food sales. It didn't bother Lili. She thought it was lovely to preserve some old-fashioned traditions. She intended to buy some ice cream during the interval to support the cinema.

As the lights dimmed, Maisie fidgeted. Lili whispered, 'Your mother and I used to go to this cinema at the weekends.' Their school had been along the country road that led into Aldeburgh, set back from the road so that you couldn't see the Edwardian building and its grounds as you went by. A bus route ran past the entrance, and their teachers had regularly given them passes to visit the town.

'Did you sit right here in these seats?' Maisie whispered.

'It's possible.' What hadn't seemed likely back then was that almost a decade later she'd be sitting here with Hannah's daughter. *It just goes to show*, thought Lili, *that you never know where life will take you – or with whom.* She hadn't expected to return in a hurry. As Connie had impressed on her over the years, there was little point in looking back – although sometimes it was nice to reminisce.

Lili smiled. 'I first met your mum at boarding school.'

Maisie nodded. 'I know. What's boarding school like?'

Before Lili could answer, Maisie said, 'Does it cost a lot of money? Mummy said her grandparents paid for her to go because her mummy and daddy didn't want her. That's why we don't see them. They sent her away.'

Lili had always known about Hannah's background. Hannah had told Lili that she had been a bit of a handful, and that her parents hadn't been able to cope with her behaviour, so they had placed her into care. Her grandparents had stepped in and paid for her to go to boarding school, which is how she had arrived at the school at thirteen, five years after Lili had started.

Lili didn't know why they had become best friends; they were so different. Lili was shy, and not the rebellious type, but Hannah had brought Lili out of herself. Lili, for her part, had tempered Hannah's wild streak.

Hannah had often stayed with her grandparents during the holidays. Lili had always gone with her. Best friends forever. Sisters. Before Lili had met Hannah, she'd spent the holiday periods at school. She had desperately wanted to go home like most of the other children, although there had been some students with parents in the army or the diplomatic service who'd had to stay on too. But Lili's father and mother weren't in the military or the diplomatic service. As far as she and everyone else knew, her parents were dead. Hannah and her elderly grandparents had become Lili's pseudo-family. Lili smiled at Maisie. Hannah's grandparents had been the nicest couple she could ever have hoped to meet. It was sad that Maisie would never know her great-grandparents; they'd died when Lili and Hannah were seventeen. She had fond memories of the rambling old house they'd lived in, in the Kent countryside, with an Aga in the kitchen and their dogs, who always seemed to be under her feet, vying for attention.

Hannah had thought that when her grandparents passed away, they would leave their home to her in their will. If only they had. But it was not to be. The property had been left to their two children, Hannah's mother and uncle, who were free to decide whether to share that inheritance with their offspring. The only provision the will made for Hannah was the money set aside to fund her school fees so that she could finish her education at the school.

Hannah had remained estranged from her parents. It was the only thing she and Lili had ever argued about. Lili understood how Hannah felt – or tried to, at least; Hannah's mother and father had given up on her. But Lili thought Hannah was so lucky that she still had parents. Surely, she could forgive them and find a way back to them?

Lili often wondered if that was why she and Hannah had been drawn to each other at school and had become firm friends; even though Lili didn't know the circumstances surrounding her own parents' disappearance, she had been abandoned too.

She glanced at Maisie. That was the other ongoing disagreement between them. Maisie had grandparents and an aunt – Hannah's sister. Cousins, perhaps. There was a family out there who might dote on her and love her as much as Lili did. If

Hannah didn't want to mend bridges for herself, then at least she could do it for her daughter. That was what Lili had said. Her opinion had fallen on deaf ears.

Lili thought back to her early years with Hannah. As time had gone by, Hannah's behaviour had changed from that of the rebellious thirteen-year-old who had started at the school. As she grew older, and with Lili's influence, she had matured, settled down and studied – but the death of her grandparents had been her undoing. That was when she had rebelled once again.

Lili recalled that Hannah had started smoking, then drinking, then dabbling in drugs and sleeping around. If only Hannah's grandparents had known how much leaving their house to Hannah would have meant to her and her child. Lili knew it would have been very unfair of them to do that – they had their own children to consider – but what a difference it would have made to Maisie to have a home to grow up in, stability. Perhaps Hannah wouldn't have burned through relationships like some people burn through money – although she was pretty good at that too. She had often asked Lili to lend her cash.

Lili smiled at Maisie. 'Did I ever tell you that your mother's grandparents, your great-grandparents, were the nicest people I've ever met?'

'Yes,' Maisie replied, rolling her eyes.

Lili knew it didn't mean much to an eight-year-old who was more interested in whether she'd be getting an ice cream in the intermission. Maisie stopped eating Smarties and looked at Lili. 'Did your grandparents pay for you to go to boarding school? Mummy says your parents are dead.'

Lili's smile faltered. She didn't know that her parents were dead. Not for sure. But that's what she'd told Hannah in the beginning. She knew it might surprise some people if she told them that she hoped her parents *were* dead. The reason was simple; she was protecting herself from the possibility that they had abandoned her on that beach in Corfu because they hadn't wanted her. When a passer-by had found her, she had been old enough to talk, say her name – *Lili*. She had an English accent, blonde hair and brown eyes, so it had been deemed unlikely that she was from Greece.

Social services in the UK had flown her to England in the care of Connie. Lili smiled. Luck had been on her side. Connie had been holidaying on the island and hadn't long qualified as a social worker. It had been big news at the time; children went missing all the time, but both parents going missing was practically unheard of. The authorities had tried to find them, but with no luck. Connie had come forward to see how she could help the little English child. She'd been helping Lili for her whole life since.

Maisie was still staring at Lili, waiting for her to reply.

Lili managed a smile. Despite the police and social services looking for her relatives at the time, none had been found. It had been a mystery – as though Lili didn't exist. She didn't have grandparents to step in and take her, give her a home. Nobody who would have paid for boarding school. But she had Connie. 'I had an assisted place.'

'What's that?'

'You sit an entrance exam and, if you pass, a government scheme pays all your fees.' Luckily for Lili, she had been a bright child who enjoyed schoolwork. Connie had put her name forward for a place, and it had changed the course of Lili's life. 'If it hadn't been for my lovely social worker, I would have grown up in a care home and I would never have met your mother.'

'Or me,' Maisie added.

Lili smiled. 'Or you.'

'I hope I don't end up in care.'

Lili looked at her in disbelief. She couldn't believe what Maisie had just said. 'That's a strange thing to say, Maisie …'

'Mummy says if I'm not nice to my new dad, that's where I'll end up.'

'Your new dad?'

'Yes, Mummy thinks he's going to propose.'

'Really?' Lili was surprised Hannah hadn't mentioned it.

'I don't like him.'

This wasn't news to Lili; she was aware that Maisie didn't like any of the men who had been in her mother's life. But it shocked her to hear that Hannah had threatened to put Maisie into care. How could she even say that to her daughter – let alone think it?

Lili had always worried what might happen if Hannah had another child. Maisie would feel left out of a new family unit. Hannah vowed she wouldn't have a baby unless she married; so far, she had stayed true to her word. Now, by the sound of things, she had finally met Mr Right.

Lili stared at Maisie and thought *how dare she say that to her.* Hannah had no idea what it was like, being passed from one foster carer to another, moving in and out of care homes when the foster carers didn't work out. She'd had doting grandparents who had paid for her private education. Maisie didn't have anybody else.

Yes, she does, thought Lili. *She has me.* Maisie was the reason that Lili couldn't remain without a job or a stable place to live for long. If the worst happened and Hannah could not or would not look after Maisie, Lili knew she'd step in and take care of her. Lili chewed her bottom lip. She didn't want to think about Alex right now and his stupid move to Washington. She knew that for her, it was a no-win situation; she was going to have to lose either Maisie or Alex. All Alex had done was make the decision easier by ending their relationship himself.

Maisie stared back at her, the cartoon running before the film all but forgotten. Her bottom lip quivered. 'What's it like in care? Mummy said that's where you used to live.'

Lili put her cup of coffee down in the holder by her chair and turned to Maisie, taking her little face in her hands. 'Listen to me. That's never going to happen to you. Do you hear?'

'But Mummy said—'

To hell with her mother, thought Lili. She said, 'Mummy didn't mean it.'

'Then why did she say it?'

Lili breathed a sigh. 'Sometimes we say silly things we don't mean. Besides, you've always got me. So, if anything happens …'

Maisie's eyes went wide. 'What might happen?'

Lili realised too late she was digging herself a hole. Maisie was looking more anxious by the second.

'Nothing – nothing at all. What I meant was, we all have arguments and squabbles sometimes, so if you fancy another holiday with your auntie Lili then—'

'Can we come to Aldeburgh again?'

Lili thought *don't make promises you can't keep*. She didn't know if she'd even be able to afford a holiday without Alex around. 'Perhaps, or we could see some galleries in London.'

'That would be awesome too.'

'Cool,' said Lili, smiling at her and borrowing Maisie's catchphrase.

Maisie happily settled down as the movie started.

Lili sat back in her seat, not feeling happy at all. She glanced at Maisie, who appeared to be enjoying the film about a dragon. Lili couldn't focus on it herself; her mind was going over and over what Hannah had said to Maisie. She was still quite shocked that her friend could say such a thing to her own daughter.

When Maisie had finished her Smarties, Lili handed her the juice. Maisie reached inside the bucket of popcorn on Lili's lap and took a handful, her eyes never leaving the screen.

The intermission caught Lili by surprise. She felt like the film had just started when the lights went up and the old man was back with his trolley.

'Hey, where's the popcorn gone?'

Lili looked down at the bucket and thought *good question* when she discovered Maisie had chomped her way through most of it. Lili held up the pot. 'I don't know. I imagine a little goblin gobbled it all up when I wasn't looking.'

'Oops,' Maisie giggled. 'It wasn't a goblin. I ate it.' She spotted the old man. 'Can we have an ice cream now?'

'I think you've eaten enough.' Lili eyed her, anxious she would get a stomach ache.

'Oh please – you promised!'

Lili didn't mind spending the money. In fact, she had intended to, but that was before Maisie had scoffed all the popcorn. 'How about tomorrow we visit the ice cream parlour instead?'

'What's an ice cream parlour?'

Lili had spotted the parlour on the way to the cinema. She

was pleasantly surprised that it still existed. It had been where they had always gone for a knickerbocker glory at the weekends when she was younger. The interior resembled an American diner, with pastel-coloured stools and a counter serving the most amazing ice cream. She described it to Maisie. 'There wasn't just strawberry or vanilla or chocolate,' she added, 'but almost any flavour you could think of.'

Maisie had a thought. 'Do they have bubble-gum flavour?'

Lili didn't know. 'They might have.' She could tell Maisie still wanted her ice cream tub.

'Wait here.' Lili got out of her seat and approached the trolley. She waited behind the other family as they chose their ice creams. She stepped up when it was her turn but didn't ask for ice cream. Instead, she purchased a soft purple dragon; she'd noticed merchandise related to the movie for sale in the foyer.

Lili returned to her seat empty-handed.

Maisie looked disappointed. 'I thought you were getting me an ice cream?'

Lili smiled as the old man reappeared from behind the curtain and walked up the steps to where they were sitting. He was carrying the dragon. Lili stifled a smiled. He was not doing a particularly good job of keeping it hidden; Lili could see the purple tail peeping out from behind his back.

Maisie hadn't noticed. She was too busy sitting there, arms folded, in a grump. The old man shuffled along the row, and with a flurry, the purple dragon appeared. He presented it to Maisie. 'I believe this belongs to you,' he said.

'For me?' Maisie gasped.

'Yes.'

Maisie grabbed the toy before he changed his mind and sat it on her lap, its bright blue eyes staring up at her. 'I love it,' she gushed.

Lili overheard one of the girls from the family sitting on the back row asking if she could have one too. Then the other girl joined her. A moment later, their dad walked down towards the stage and exited through the velvet curtain. He reappeared a few minutes later with a dragon tucked under each arm.

Lili turned in her seat when she heard the girls squealing with delight as they spotted the cuddly toys. Lili smiled. Maisie wasn't the only one who had not grown out of soft toys yet.

Maisie turned to Lili with a question. 'Can I keep it?'

'I bought it for you. It's all yours.'

'Josh says I'm too old for Cuddlys.'

'Josh?'

'Mummy's boyfriend.'

Cuddlys. They were what Maisie called her cuddly teddies and fluffy toys. Lili raised an eyebrow. 'Well, you know what I think?'

Maisie shook her head, no.

'No one is ever too old for a cuddly or a cuddle,' Lili said playfully, putting an arm around Maisie's shoulders and pulling her close. 'Oh, look, the lights have dimmed.' The film was about to restart. Lili smiled at Maisie, who was cuddling her new toy, and settled down in her seat for the second half. This time, she was going to enjoy the show and put all thoughts of Hannah and Alex to one side. Lili wanted to do what children did so well, which was to enjoy the moment.

11

Lili woke to find Maisie already seated at her easel by the window, painting. The hotel staff had found a padded chair. Over the past few days, since they'd visited the art shop and Maisie had had her easel and paints delivered, they had fallen into a comfortable routine. Lili saw an advantage; she got a lie-in every morning – and some peace and quiet.

Maisie had, to Lili's surprise, swapped her Nintendo for her paints and easel. Sometimes, Maisie would balance the art book of famous paintings on the window seat, trying to copy her favourite artists. At other times she would paint the view from the window.

Lili had sneaked a peak at the work one evening when Maisie was asleep. She was taken aback. For someone so young, Maisie was surprisingly gifted. Maisie appeared self-conscious about her artwork, as though prepared for criticism. Not that Lili would criticise – she had nothing but praise for Maisie's paintings.

The child had an incredible natural talent. Lili knew very little about art and painting, but anyone could see that Maisie's work had maturity beyond her years. You could imagine that an adult had painted these, not a precocious eight-year-old whose favourite food was pizza, who had discovered boy bands and who loved bubble-gum ice cream. Lili smiled at that thought. They'd had a lovely time in the ice cream parlour a few days earlier. God, it had taken her back. Maisie was growing up to look just like her mother, and she sounded like her too.

For the next couple of rainy days, they'd spent most of the time holed up in the hotel, Maisie painting and Lili enjoying reading a novel from the hotel library. They'd had all their meals in the restaurant, so they hadn't had to venture outside. Maisie had been keen to get back to her art.

The previous day, the storm clouds had disappeared, and it had been sunny. Lili had persuaded Maisie to put her paint brush down and venture out. She'd had somewhere special to take her. They'd turned left out of their hotel, heading away from the town toward Thorpeness, another small town just a mile from Aldeburgh.

They'd walked along the concrete pathway next to the beach. At the end of the path, their route had continued across the shingle. They'd come across a row of detached wooden houses with wraparound verandas, sitting on the shore.

Maisie had never seen a house on a beach before; this trip to Aldeburgh was the first time she'd visited the coast. Lili recalled that she'd stopped to stare at them as they passed by. A lady who had been watering one of her flowerpots outside had given them a friendly wave.

Lili had waved back. *If Maisie finds this amazing*, she'd thought to herself, *just wait until she sees Thorpeness*. As they'd continued along the beach, Lili had said, 'Do you see it?'

'See what?' Maisie had replied.

Lili had stopped and pointed. 'Look up.'

'What is that?' Maisie had asked, squinting as she looked up at the blue sky. 'Is that a house?'

Lili had wanted Maisie to see the House in the Clouds, and she had Googled some information on the place before they'd left the hotel. She'd known Maisie would ask her questions.

Built in the early 1920s as a water tower, the building was disguised as a weatherboarded building to fit in with the mock Tudor properties in the locality. However, in the late 1970s, once the village had a mains water supply, the water tower was completely converted into a house. It was now a self-catering holiday property seventy feet in the air.

From a distance, the House in the Clouds lived up to its name. Thorpeness fulfilled its creator's dream, a quintessentially English coastal holiday village with a mix of detached and semi-detached mock Tudor red brick properties and a large boating lake, all within a short stroll of the beach. Maisie hadn't wanted Lili to hire a rowing boat; she'd been quite content to sit on a bench with an ice cream and watch other people rowing on the lake.

A family of swans had waddled along the path and stopped in front of their bench waiting to be thrown a crumb or two. Maisie wanted to take a photo for her mum – she had never seen swans up close before. Lili had got out her phone and after Maisie had licked the remaining ice cream from her fingers, she'd stood up and taken photos. Lili had asked Maisie if she remembered when she took her to see Peter Pan at the theatre in Richmond. 'Some of the little islands surrounding the boating lake were given names by the author who wrote Peter Pan – isn't that amazing,' Lili had said. That's when Maisie had asked, 'Can we go and see the house in the clouds now?'

Later they'd stood together gazing up at the magical house

that Maisie had seen from the distance on their walk. Maisie had got out a small notebook and pencil from her pocket and made a rough sketch of the house. Lili smiled thinking of the perfect day they'd had. She stretched in bed and sat up. Maisie had started another painting the previous afternoon, as soon as they'd arrived back at the hotel. Lili had taken a peek that night, after Maisie had fallen asleep, and had discovered a wonderful landscape – Maisie's first from memory – of Thorpeness and the House in the Clouds. This morning, she was putting the finishing touches on it.

'That looks amazing,' Lili commented.

Maisie glanced over her shoulder, pointing her paintbrush at Lili. 'You're not meant to look until I'm finished.'

Lili smiled at her. She was still in her pyjamas, but she had her painting apron on. Lili reached over and checked the time on her mobile. It was still early. She scanned her phone for messages. There weren't any from Alex. She'd thought he might have been in touch to see how the holiday was going, or even to tell her how much he missed her or to wish her a happy birthday. Lili would not contact him first, but she hadn't heard from him all week, and the last day of their break had arrived – along with her special day. That day, Lili was turning twenty-seven.

Lili hadn't done what Connie had suggested, which was to make some plans for the future. She knew Connie was trying her best to be helpful, encouraging her to figure out what she was going to do if it turned out she and Alex had split up.

Lili didn't want to consider the possibility and found she would rather bury her head in the sand, thinking that if Alex needed more time to figure himself out, at least she could stay with Hannah for a few days when they returned to London the next day. She could meet up with Alex in a café and they could talk things through once Maisie had gone home. That seemed reasonable.

I have a plan, thought Lili. She smiled across the room at Maisie. She still didn't regret taking her on holiday one bit, even though she wouldn't be celebrating her birthday with Alex.

After a bad start with the weather, they'd made the best of it, thanks to meeting the lady with her grandson in the café on their first day. If it hadn't been for her, they might not have discovered the art and craft shop in Cobblers Yard. Lili wouldn't have bought the painting set which had kept Maisie occupied on the rainy days. Maisie's talent, and where it came from, intrigued Lili.

She had promised Maisie that she wouldn't peek, but of course she did, every evening. The paintings were something quite wonderful. Lili enjoyed flicking through the book, seeing which masterpiece Maisie had tried to copy, or looking at the pictures she had done of the different views from the windows. The staff had got wind of their resident artist and had let her sit in the hotel restaurant on the days with inclement weather. The restaurant looked on to the beach, and Maisie enjoyed painting the fishing huts and a small trawler perched on the shingle beach.

It was money well spent, Lili decided, as she sat in bed with a cuppa and watched the morning news on the TV. She wondered what they should do on their last day. She was just pondering this, wishing the week hadn't gone by quite so fast, when her phone rang. She jumped in surprise. 'Alex!' Lili grabbed her mobile and discovered it wasn't Alex on the line. It was Hannah. Lili guessed she must be home from her holiday.

Just the person, thought Lili, glancing at Maisie as she got out of bed and walked to the bathroom before answering her phone.

Lili was not a confrontational person by nature. On her return to London, Lili intended to speak to Hannah about what she'd said to Maisie – her threat to put her into care. Lili closed the door to the bathroom and answered the phone.

'You'll never guess!' Hannah said. Before Lili could speak, Hannah exclaimed, 'We got engaged!'

'What?'

Hannah screamed in excitement. Lili had to hold the phone away from her ear. 'It was just so unexpected, Lili. We had talked of marriage, the subject had come up before, but I didn't expect him to propose. I had no idea that was the reason he was taking me to Barbados. He proposed on the beach as the sun set. It was so romantic.'

Lili sat on the edge of the bath thinking of Alex. Shouldn't she be the one phoning her best friend to say, *guess what – he proposed?* With the break coinciding with her birthday, she had assumed that it would be that particular day that he chose to propose.

'Aren't you going to say something?'

'Congratulations,' Lili said flatly.

'I keep looking at the engagement ring on my finger and having to pinch myself. By the way, we're having such a good time, we extended our stay. We're going to another island. The mobile reception isn't particularly good there, so I thought I'd better phone you now before …'

'Wait – what? Did you just say you've extended your holiday?'

'Yes, for a week. I knew you wouldn't mind. You love spending time with Maisie.'

Lili guessed Hannah had forgotten it was her birthday. 'I

don't know what I'm going to do with her,' she said to Hannah.

'Oh, you'll figure something out. There's so much to do in London. She kept asking me to take her to an art gallery. Not my thing, but there's an idea for you.'

That wasn't what Lili had meant. She couldn't turn up at the flat with Maisie in tow – assuming, that was, that Alex had climbed down, and they weren't splitting up for good.

'I must ring off now, the plane is boarding, sweetie. Love ya.'

'Wait, Hannah. I can't—' Lili halted when she realised her best friend had rung off. She frantically tried to dial her number, but it kept going straight to voicemail.

There was a loud knock at the bathroom door, making her jump. 'Lili, I need a wee!'

Lili opened the door. Maisie barged passed her. Lili glanced at the television as she stepped out of the bathroom. She'd left the TV on, which meant Maisie hadn't heard her on the phone. She stared at the mobile in her hand. 'Now what am I going to do?'

'I want to go back to the art shop.'

Lili turned around. 'I'm running out of paint,' Maisie said, returning to her easel.

Lili sat on the end of the bed. She had three choices. Phone Alex and let him know what had happened. Don't contact Alex, catch their return train home, and just turn up with Maisie. What could he do? She still had a key. If he hadn't changed his mind, she would have to sleep on the couch for a week until Hannah returned from abroad and picked Maisie up.

The flat was still her home too, for now. The alternative was to stay with Connie. That had been her original fall-back plan for if she wasn't able to crash at Hannah's place. Connie would be able to accommodate both her and Maisie. She had more than enough room. All three of her daughters had left home – two married, one at university. Maisie's situation was the problem. Lili sighed. Connie was her friend, but she was still a social worker. Although Lili trusted Connie, it worried her that she might deem Hannah an unfit mother and they would take Maisie away.

Maisie stopped what she was doing and stared out of the window. 'I wish we didn't have to leave tomorrow.'

'I know.' They were Lili's sentiments too. She felt she had no home to go back to. She knew it wouldn't be pleasant if she just turned up at the flat, unless Alex rang before then and apologised. Even if he did, she could imagine his reaction when he found out she would have Maisie for another week.

Lili didn't like any of the choices she'd come up with. There was an alternative. Lili switched off the television.

'What if we stayed a little longer?'

Maisie turned around so fast that she almost dropped her paint brush. 'We can stay here on holiday?'

Lili nodded, although she didn't know where she would find the money to remain in the honeymoon suite with the marvellous views.

'Yippee!'

'We might have to change rooms, Maisie.'

'That's fine.'

Lili added, 'Mummy is staying in the Caribbean for another week, so I thought we could stay on holiday too. Are you okay with that?' Lili asked softly. She worried how Maisie would feel when she found out Mummy wasn't coming home. During their phone conversation, Hannah hadn't once asked to speak to her daughter to find out how she was or let her know her plans.

Maisie shrugged. 'Oh, yes. I'm okay with that.'

Lili bounced off the bed. 'Great.' A saying came to mind. *Every cloud has a silver lining.* Lili didn't want to go home right then either, especially as she hadn't heard from Alex. *Perhaps in another week, when he discovers how much he misses me …*

A text message interrupted her. Lili grabbed her phone. *Alex?*

It still wasn't Alex. It was the hotel reminding her about the check-out time the next morning.

'Maisie, I'm just getting dressed so I can go down to reception.' Lili wanted to see if she could get a deal to stay another week and change rooms. She imagined the honeymoon suite was costly. 'Do you want to come with me?'

Maisie shook her head, no. 'Can we have breakfast in our room?'

'Yes.' Lili had already arranged room service the previous night.

She changed out of her pyjamas into a pair of jeans and a cosy chenille jumper. She brushed her hair and dabbed a bit of lipstick on her lips and some blush on her cheeks. She then made a quick call to Kew Gardens, wondering what the reaction would be when they found out she wouldn't be returning to her voluntary role the next week as planned.

Lili breathed a sigh when a friendly voice from Kew told her not to worry, and that they looked forward to seeing her when she was able to return. Lili rang off, relieved that her job was voluntary, otherwise she wouldn't have this flexibility.

'I'll be back soon,' she said before closing the bedroom door behind her.

Lili skipped down to reception, hoping they had vacancies,

until something occurred to her. How much had their suite cost? She had no clue. Lili reached the bottom of the grand staircase and hesitated. She only had so much money in her account. To save her the embarrassment of finding she couldn't afford it, Lili Googled the hotel on her phone, found the room rates and gasped.

The concierge spotted her standing on the stairs. 'Can I be of help?'

'Er, no … um, I'm fine.' If an ordinary room cost in the region of two hundred and fifty pounds a night, which Lili had just discovered, then how much was the honeymoon suite? Little wonder Alex was pissed off that Maisie had scuppered his holiday plans.

Lili returned to the bedroom. Maisie was busy getting dressed. 'I finished my painting if you want to look?'

Lili walked over to the painting and stared at the house peeking out above the treeline, with its red roof that looked like something out of a fairy tale. Down below was a windmill, a street of mock Tudor houses, and a boating lake. The sea was in the distance with those pastel-coloured clapboard beach houses they'd passed by sitting on the shore.

Lili smiled. 'This is amazing.' She noticed two people sitting eating ice cream on a bench skirting the lake. Lili pointed. 'Is that you and me?'

Maisie nodded. 'I called the painting, Auntie Lili and Maisie by the lake.'

'I love it.'

'You can keep it.'

'Oh, Maisie. Are you sure?'

She nodded. 'It's for your birthday.'

Lili looked at her and felt quite overwhelmed. 'You painted this just for me, for my birthday?'

Maise nodded her head and put her arms around Lili. 'I love you, Auntie Lili.'

'I love you too, Maisie.' When she drew back, Lili asked, 'Will you sign it for me?'

Maisie knitted her brow.

'All great painters sign their work. Look …' Lili picked up the book containing works of the eminent artists and pointed. 'See here …'

Maisie went over to take a closer look.

'That is the artist's signature.'

'It is?' Maisie grasped a very thin paintbrush, dabbed it in a beaker of water, chose a colour and wrote her name, *Maisie,* in the lower right-hand corner of the painting.

'Perfect.'

Maisie swirled the brush in the water. 'Can I be an artist when I grow up, Lili?'

'I don't see why not.'

'Can I go to an art school?'

'When you leave school, you can go to university and study fine art.' Lili felt excited at the thought of telling Hannah about Maisie's gift for painting. It was quite extraordinary at her age. But then her heart sank. She remembered what Maisie had said about Hannah's attitude to taking Maisie to galleries. She imagined that Maisie wasn't going to get much encouragement from her mother. Lili would give her plenty of encouragement, though. 'Did I hear you say that you were running out of paints?'

Maisie nodded. 'Can we go back to the art shop?'

'We most certainly can.' But first she needed to sort out their holiday accommodation. They couldn't stay there – unless Alex paid for it.

Lili bit her lower lip and eyed her phone, which she'd left recharging on the dressing table. Would she have the cheek to tell Alex that she had Maisie for another week, and ask him to pay for the hotel? No. She didn't think pouring salt into the wound was the right approach. But she was going to ring him and let him know she was extending their holiday in Aldeburgh.

Maisie interrupted her thoughts. She had been rummaging in her Trunki. She ran over to Lili with something behind her back.

Lili smiled at her even though the look on Maisie's face said she was up to something. 'What are you up to?' Lili asked in a playful voice.

Out from behind her back, Maise produced a small, gift-wrapped box. She held it out to Lili. 'I got you a present and I wrapped it myself.'

Lili remembered when Hannah had turned up outside the flat and told her she had a birthday present for her. Lili hadn't expected the present from Hannah to be Maisie. That was when Maisie had said something about a present that she'd gift-wrapped so that Lili had something to unwrap.

'Oh, Maisie, that is so thoughtful of you.'

Maisie frowned. 'I didn't have any money to buy you something, so I made it.'

Lili reached out and put a hand around Maisie's shoulders, pulling her close, giving her a hug and a kiss. 'Hey, this is turning out to be the best birthday ever. I wouldn't swap your hand-made present for all the money in the world, or all the gifts money can buy. And do you know why?'

Maisie shook her head.

'Just like your painting, Maisie, this is priceless because you made it and there won't be anything in the world like it. Do you understand?'

Maisie grinned. 'It's priceless.'

Lili looked at the little box in her hand. 'Shall I unwrap it?'

Maisie gave her a big nod, and a big smile.

She carefully undid the little ribbon and unwrapped the parcel. Inside was a large matchbox. Lili pulled the sleeve of the matchbox to reveal what was inside.

'It's a friendship bracelet.'

Lili stared at the multi-coloured bracelet that must have taken Maisie hours to thread together. 'It's beautiful, Maise – thank you. Will you help me put it on?'

Maisie put it around Lili's wrist and pulled the two cords to tighten it. 'I made you a card too.'

Lili watched her go to the pad of paper beside her easel. She flicked through the pages and found what she was looking for within the pages. She handed it to Lili.

Lili opened the hand-made envelope. Inside was a folded piece of paper. She had used her paints to produce a beautiful Suffolk coastal scene on the front of the card, with a shingle beach, blue sky and sea, and a little fishing boat in the distance, bobbing on the water. She'd written the words Happy Birthday Auntie on the front, just like on a traditional card.

Lili opened the card and read the birthday message she wished Maisie hadn't written. 'I'm sorry that I spoiled your birthday because Alex isn't here. Hope you have a nice day. Luv Maisie.'

'Maisie, you haven't spoiled a thing. I don't want Alex here.' It was true; right now, she didn't – not one bit. 'And I'll tell you another thing: this is the best birthday ever, being here with you on holiday. I shall treasure these, Maisie, truly I will. They're the best birthday presents ever.' Lili wasn't exaggerating. She looked at the painting and the friendship bracelet and knew she would always treasure them just as much as she treasured the little ring on the necklace around her neck – her only link to her parents. She pulled Maisie close. 'Come on, go and get dressed. We are going to have the best day.'

12

'Okay, not a problem.'

Lili couldn't have been more surprised by Alex's response when she told him her plans. Had he really just said *not a problem?* There wasn't an offer to pay for the hotel, but he did say, 'Let me know where you're staying.'

Lili smiled. Was she imagining things, or was that concern in his voice? 'Okay – will do.'

'How was your week?'

'Great.' Lili said. 'I miss you,' she added hastily, not wanting it to sound as though she didn't want him to be there. She had intended to ask him to join her for the weekend, but Maisie interrupted her. 'I want to go to the art shop,' she whined.

'I won't be long, sweetheart, I promise.'

After breakfast, they'd been on their way out of the door when Lili had realised that she'd forgotten her phone. They were planning to do more than visit the shop; Lili needed to find some alternative holiday accommodation. On the spur of the moment, she had rung Alex. She'd thought he might not take her call, but he'd answered straight away, not sounding at all annoyed – until he heard Maisie's whining voice interrupting their conversation.

'I've got to go,' he said. 'Remember to let me know where you are next week – there's something I want to send you.'

Lili got off the phone, smiling. Although he hadn't offered to pay for her accommodation or ask her to return home, he *was* going to send her something. Lili thought of the local flower shop and glanced at the bouquet. Would it be flowers again? She grinned. Of course it would.

'Come on, Maisie.' Lili almost skipped out of the room. Like Connie had said, everything had a way of working out in the end. Although Alex hadn't responded when she'd said she missed him, she reminded herself that it was just at that point that Maisie had interrupted them. *There's nothing to worry about*, Lili told herself as they walked out of the hotel. 'Now, I must look in some holiday rental agents.'

'No, I want to go to the art shop.'

'We *are* going to the art shop, Maisie, but we need to find somewhere to stay. We've only got one more night in the hotel.'

'I want to stay at The Harbour Inn.'

'It's expensive, sweetheart.'

'But we're already there.'

'I know, but it will be fun staying in a cottage. You can have your own bedroom and set up your painting easel.'

Lili could tell by the look on Maisie's face that she was warming to the idea.

'Okay.'

On the way to the art shop, Lili visited every holiday let agent in the town. All the holiday cottages in Aldeburgh were already booked. Why was she surprised? Despite the changeable weather, it was the school summer holidays, and not everyone wanted to go abroad.

Lili walked out of the last holiday let agent in the town with nothing arranged. There was a property available further afield in the Suffolk countryside, but it was not practical without a car.

Lili sighed as she stepped outside. She glanced at Maisie.

'Did we get a cottage?' Maisie asked.

'No, sweetheart, they are all booked.'

'Can we pick up my art stuff now?'

Lili sighed. 'Okay, we might as well.' It was looking more than likely that they would have to use their return train tickets and go back to London the next day. Alex would not be pleased one bit when she turned up with Maisie in tow. But what choice did she have?

'Come on.' Lili took Maisie by the hand. They turned around and retraced their steps along High Street, passing some boutiques, a bakery, two fish-and-chip shops, a bookshop and another craft shop. When Lili saw the craft shop, she suggested they look inside, but Maisie insisted she wanted to go to Ray's.

Lili looked at her. 'Who is Ray?'

Maisie rolled her eyes at Lili as though she'd asked a stupid question. 'The man who owns the art shop, of course.'

'Ah.' Lili hadn't known his name was Ray. 'Let's go, then.'

Walking into Cobblers Yard, they soon discovered most of the stores weren't open yet.

The art shop had a sign reading *Closed* in the window. Maisie tried the door handle. It was locked. 'Why aren't they open?'

Lili glanced at her watch. In London, the shops opened early and closed much later; some were open twenty-four hours. This wasn't what they were accustomed to.

'We will have to wait.'

Maisie stamped her foot in frustration.

Lili thought she felt a spot of rain on her nose. She looked up. Although it had started out as a lovely, sunny day, like the previous day, the sky had clouded over. She got out her umbrella, anticipating a downpour. She'd just opened her brolly when it poured. 'Talk about déjà vu.' They had been there at the start of the week, and it had been raining then too.

Lili checked the opening and closing times displayed in the front window. They had ten minutes to wait. When Lili turned to Maisie, she was no longer there.

'Can we go in here?' Maisie called out. She was standing outside George and Son Antiques across the courtyard, looking in the window. The lights were on in the old-fashioned shop front, throwing out an eerie glow. Lili didn't know why Maisie would want to go inside, unless it was to get out of the rain. She decided it was a good idea – rather than getting wet, they could browse in the warmth. She had no intention of buying anything, but there was no harm in browsing.

Lili walked over to see what had caught Maisie's eye.

She pointed. 'Look.' There, on the wall, was a painting. Maisie turned to her. 'Is this an art gallery?'

'No, sweetheart, this shop sells antiques.'

'What's an antique?'

'Something that is quite old.' *Speaking of which*, Lili thought. She was looking through the windowpane when she spotted an old man, presumably the owner, sitting behind a wooden counter which had an old-fashioned cash machine. As though sensing someone was staring at him, he looked up. Their eyes locked for a moment as he slowly rose from his chair.

Lili checked the sign, which said *Open*. She took Maisie's hand and opened the shop door. 'Come on, let's get out of the rain – then you can have a closer look at the painting.' Lili lowered her voice. 'But only a look, mind. We're just window shopping. Remember I explained what window shopping was?'

'Yes,' Maisie said, her voice resigned.

What Lili hadn't told Maisie about antiques was that they weren't just old; they were expensive – and that went for paintings too.

As she stepped into the shop, the old man was already on his feet. He rounded the wooden counter in a hurry, exclaiming, 'Alena!'

Maisie looked up at Lili. 'Who is Alena?'

Lili shrugged. 'I don't know.' She smiled. 'I think you have me mistaken for someone else.'

He slipped on his half-moon glasses as he approached. 'Sorry. Of course you can't be her.' he said. He peered at her. 'Remarkable,' he added quietly.

Lili was about to ask him what he'd meant by that comment when Maisie let go of her hand and ran over to the painting. 'Maisie – watch where you're going and don't touch anything!'

Lili turned back to the old man. 'She's fascinated by your painting.'

'It's for sale. Would you like to know the price?'

Lili decided she would rather not. 'I think I'll just browse, if that's okay.'

'Of course, be my guest.'

Maisie ran over to Lili.

'Maisie, stop running in the shop!' Lili winced at the thought that she'd knock something over.

'Sorry.'

'Are you here on holiday?' the old man asked.

Maisie answered first. 'Yes, we were only going to be here for one week, but now we're staying another whole week.' Maisie's face fell. 'There are no cottages left, and the hotel is too expensive, so we've got nowhere to stay.'

'Is that a fact?' the man replied, staring at Lili.

Lili said, 'I'm sure we'll come up with something.' She glanced out of the window and saw the lights on in the shop across the yard. 'Maisie, the art shop is open.'

'Yippee!' Maisie skipped to the door.

Lili was about to follow when the old man said, 'Wait!'

Even Maisie turned at his insistent voice.

'I know of a place you could stay.'

Lili eyed him. 'You do?'

The old man, who was leaning on a walking stick, was impeccably dressed in a tweed suit from another era. He nodded. 'It's not a cottage, I'm afraid, but my daughter and son-in-law are always on at me about renting it.'

'Where is it?' Lili asked. 'I haven't got a car, you see.'

'Oh, you won't need a car.' He raised his eyes heavenward. 'It's the flat upstairs above the shop.'

'A flat?' She was thinking about the lovely hotel they'd stayed in over the past week. A flat above a shop didn't sound all that inviting for a holiday. Lili's expression must have given her away.

'I can assure you it has lots of character. There are beams, a wood burner, and sloping ceilings in the eaves. Would you like to take a look?'

Maisie appeared by Lili's side, hands tugging on her arm. 'Oh, please say yes.'

'How much is it?'

'Oh, I'm sure we can work something out.'

Lili wouldn't commit to looking unless she had a firm price. She turned to leave. 'I'll think about it.'

He followed her towards the door. 'How about a hundred for the week?'

That stopped Lili in her tracks. 'A hundred pounds?'

'Too much?'

'No, not at all.' Lili looked at him curiously. Either he had dementia – you couldn't get anything under at least five hundred pounds hereabouts in the summer – or he had never rented out the place before. Something told her he wasn't losing his faculties. Even so, Lili didn't feel inclined to take advantage of an old, possibly naïve, man. 'Look, I'm sure your flat is lovely, but for a place right in the town you should charge a lot more than that.'

'Well, in that case, if I charge you a hundred and fifty, will you accept?'

Lili didn't know what to make of the conversation. She got the impression that he was trying to convince her to stay. Was it because she reminded him of someone from his past?

He was staring at her again. It was making Lili feel uncomfortable.

He pointed at a wooden door toward the back of the shop. 'At least pop upstairs and look around.'

Despite Maisie's protestations, Lili decided against the idea. She knew that if she went upstairs, from his description, she'd like the place. Lili didn't want to commit. 'Thank you for the offer. I will think it over.'

'Wait. Before you go …' He produced a small business card and a pen from his jacket pocket. He wrote something down, then handed it to Lili.

Lili took the card. Printed in a flourish was the name of the shop along with the phone number and address. He'd written the price he'd quoted for the flat and signed it.

'But why can't we go up there and have a look?' Maisie whined as they walked out of the shop.

Lili cast a backward glance as she stepped outside. She caught the old man standing in the window staring after her. 'Like I said to the gentleman, I want to think it over.' Lili was keen to change the subject. 'Let's sort out your materials – shall we?'

Maisie entered the art shop ahead of Lili. She ran over to Ray and told him all about the man in the antique shop allowing them to holiday let his flat above the shop.

Lili frowned at Maisie. She had made it sound as though that was what they were doing when she hadn't decided yet.

As she turned around to close the door, she saw him standing at the window across the yard looking in her direction. Lili stood for a moment, staring back. There was something about him she couldn't put her finger on.

Lili shut the door and called Maisie over. 'Look, when we return to the hotel I will get online and find somewhere we can stay next week.'

As they walked up to Ray, who was sitting in an easy chair with a novel in one hand and a cup of coffee in the other, Maisie said, 'But you've already found something. I like Cobblers Yard.'

So did Lili. She just wasn't sure yet what to make of the old man across the yard.

13

Lili reached out for his arm to steady him, but he was already falling, taking her with him. They collapsed in a heap on the floor. 'Oh, hell!' she exclaimed.

Lili had known this was a bad idea before she stepped inside the shop. She'd had no joy finding a holiday property online the previous evening. Now they'd had to vacate their hotel, and they either had to go home to London or take up the old man's offer of the flat. Maisie had refused to get on the bus to the train station, so they'd returned to Cobblers Yard that morning with their suitcases, not long after the shop had opened. As soon as they entered and he saw their cases, he'd rushed forward, intending to greet them, arms extended in a welcoming gesture, offering to help. But the silly fool had forgotten about his walking stick. He'd tripped on his way to the door, and now they were in a heap on the floor.

'Alena!' he murmured.

'Who's Alena?' Maisie asked, remembering that the old man had called Lili by that name the day before, when he first saw her.

'I don't know, sweetheart,' Lili replied as she got to her knees and took his hand in hers. His eyes were closed. 'Joseph?' she said. That was the name he'd written on the business card.

To Lili's relief, he opened his eyes. Looking straight at her, he said, 'You came back!' Then he was gone.

'Is he dead?' Maisie asked.

'No, no.' At least, Lili hoped not – but this time he wasn't coming round. 'Oh, God, I'll have to ring for an ambulance.' Lili frantically got out her mobile phone and dialled 999, noticing a sharp pain in her wrist as she did so. She tried to ignore it, guessing she must have sprained it in the fall.

Maisie found a newspaper somewhere and started flapping it over the old man. 'What's wrong with him? Why won't he wake up?'

'I don't know, sweetheart. I expect he's had a funny turn.'

'What's that?'

'Like a dizzy spell. Maybe he hit his head on the way down.'

Maisie knelt to take a closer look. 'I don't see any blood.'

Neither did Lili. In no time at all and she could hear a siren.

'Is that the ambulance?' Maisie asked.

'I hope so.'

Lili heard heavy footfalls running down the alleyway. Three people wearing green uniforms burst into the shop. Friendly faces from the ambulance crew greeted Lili and Maisie, putting them at ease. Lili recounted what had happened. One of the team had a portable crash cart. 'Doesn't sound like a cardiac arrest.'

'He fell over,' Maisie said.

The paramedic smiled at Maisie. 'Thank you, young lady – that is most helpful.' He patted her head. 'I will make a note.'

Lili took Maisie's hand and led her away from the old man to give the paramedics space to work.

'Is he going to be okay?' Maisie asked.

'Of course he is,' Lili reassured her. 'The paramedics will make him all better, I'm sure.'

One of the team collected a stretcher from the ambulance. Lili raised an eyebrow. 'Or they might take him to hospital.'

'Will the doctors and nurses in the hospital make him better?'

Lili nodded. She stepped forward and asked if he was going to be okay.

'He's got quite the bump on the head, so he might have a concussion. The fall has knocked him out and we can't bring him round – that's why we're taking him in. He may have a fracture, so they'll be able to assess that.' The paramedic saw Lili cradling her arm. 'Talking of which, may I see your arm?'

'Oh, it's nothing. I stupidly grabbed him as he fell and he took me with him, I'm afraid.'

'It might be broken,' Maisie said, sounding worried.

'Well, if it is,' the paramedic said, leading Lili over to an antique chair to sit down, 'Then she will need a cast and you, young lady, can decorate it.'

Maisie grinned. 'I'm really good at drawing.'

'Well, there you go. Every cloud has a silver lining.' The young man winked at Lili, making her feel a little embarrassed at the attention. 'Now, let's have a look.'

'I'm sure it's just a sprain,' Lili said hopefully.

Five minutes' later, Lili and Maisie were sitting in the back of the paramedic's car. The old man was gently lifted on a stretcher into the ambulance parked in front of them. A nurse climbed inside and closed the doors. The other member of the crew jumped into the driving seat and started the engine.

Lili sat with her arm in a sling. The paramedic couldn't say if she'd broken her wrist or if it was just a sprain. The only way to know for sure was to have an x-ray.

He put the indicator light on and moved away from the kerb, following the ambulance in front. 'The shopkeeper regained consciousness for a bit and asked after you. He said, *where's Alena*? I told him you were in the car.'

Lili leaned forward in her seat. 'Look, the old man is confused. I'm not Alena – my name is Lili.'

The paramedic nodded. 'I see.'

Maisie asked, 'Will you have a cast – do you think?'

'I don't know.' Lili hoped not. Her friend at work had broken her wrist once, and it had taken a long time to mend. She'd had to have surgery too.

Surgery! Lili's mind was racing. She hadn't thought of that possibility. A sprain was one thing. If her wrist was broken, it could end her gardening career – or at the very least put it on hold for several months. Lili thought about her application to Kew. She'd heard nothing, but if they offered her an interview, she didn't really want to turn up with her arm in plaster. *Please, please, don't let it be broken,* she prayed.

They arrived a few minutes later outside Aldeburgh Community Hospital. The paramedic told Lili she was lucky; the minor injuries unit had just reopened after a long campaign.

Lili wasn't feeling particularly fortunate.

'You and Joseph will be among the first patients.'

Lili rolled her eyes and murmured, 'Lucky me.'

The cottage hospital looked like a country manor. The paramedic told her the building had been rebuilt after being bombed during the war.

Lili was familiar with the place. She was fortunate that she hadn't had to visit the minor injuries unit when she was at school, apart from that one time with Hannah. Her best friend had fallen over during a netball game and twisted her ankle. She had needed an x-ray. The nurse had asked her routine questions while filling out the paperwork. It had turned out that for Hannah, one of the questions wasn't routine at all – *are you pregnant?*

Lili recalled Hannah hesitating, until she whispered, 'I don't know.'

Lili also remembered her own response. She had barked at Hannah, 'What do you mean, *you don't know*? Are you saying you might be?'

That was when they had given her a pregnancy test. Ten minutes later, after a trip to the loo, she had been back with the nurse, who had ticked the box marked *yes* – with two stunned teenagers sitting in front of her.

Lili glanced at Maisie. She wondered if the hospital had changed all that much inside. It hadn't on the outside.

She guessed it was one of the few cottage hospitals left in the country. She couldn't imagine it had the means to perform surgery, but at least it had x-ray facilities. She was relieved she didn't have to travel further afield to find out whether she had a break.

'Right, here we are.' The paramedic pulled the car up behind the ambulance, parking on a paved courtyard outside the hospital. He turned in his seat and smiled. 'Lili, we will take you to the minor injuries unit and from there you could be sent for an x-ray.' There was no hanging around after that; he got straight out of the car and opened the door for her. Joseph was already being wheeled inside.

'What about—?'

'Ah, the porter will take him straight to the ward, where a doctor will see him.' He held the door open for Lili and Maisie. They followed the paramedics, who were wheeling the trolley.

'The duty nurse will tell you when you can visit him.'

A nurse standing by the reception desk overheard the conversation. 'Ah, a relative.' She offered Lili a warm smile. 'Don't worry, we will let you know what's happening as soon as the doctor has examined him. Come, come …'

'I'm not—'

The nurse was already walking along the corridor, heading towards the minor injuries unit.

Lili followed, holding Maisie's hand. They passed the paramedics who had brought Joseph in. She overheard them giving his details to the admitting staff. Eighty-two years old, he lived at a property called The Summerhouse in Thorpeness. She saw them with a wallet they must have found in his pocket. They knew his surname. It would have been no good asking her; she hadn't a clue.

'The doctor will look at your arm. He's new. Hope you don't mind.'

Lili didn't object to seeing a newly qualified doctor. She said as much.

'Er no, that's not what I meant. He's a locum who has just started work here this week. Some people like to see the same physician, but you haven't been here before – have you?'

Lili had been there before, but that had been years earlier. She shook her head.

'This way.'

Lili held back. 'Can Maisie come too?'

'Of course, but I'm afraid your daughter will have to stay behind in the waiting room if you need an x-ray.'

Lili didn't bother mentioning that Maisie wasn't her daughter. Maisie was too busy taking in her surroundings to respond either. She clutched Lili's other arm, not wanting to leave her side.

'Maisie – what a pretty name. Everything is going to be fine.'

Maisie managed a smile.

'Right, if you'd like to take a seat, I'll leave you in the capable hands of the triage nurse.'

Lili took a seat in the small waiting room. Maisie sat down on the plastic chair next to her. Lili noticed that, apart from the posters on the wall, the room had changed little since her last visit. Her gaze settled on the paramedic who had brought them in. He was having a chat with the nurse, although Lili couldn't hear what he was saying.

Lili noticed that his hand brushed the nurse's arm. She got the impression that the conversation wasn't about work. The nurse smiled at him, gave him a quick peck on the cheek, and said, 'I'll see you tonight after work.'

Maisie saw that too. 'Ugh, she kissed him.'

The paramedic threw Lili a disarming smile before he left.

The triage nurse called Lili over to a small cubicle, where she asked her what she was there for.

Lili did her best not to roll her eyes as she held up her arm in a sling. After briefly explaining what had happened while the nurse took notes, Lili was dismissed back to her hard plastic chair with a couple of painkillers to wait for the main event – seeing the new doctor. Lili glanced at the young nurse as she called another patient. The nurse and paramedic had seemed besotted with one another. She couldn't help thinking about Alex. What did it say about their relationship that he had not responded when she told him how much she missed him? She tried to sweep that thought aside.

'Lili Skye.'

Lili turned in her seat to see another young man, this time in a white coat, holding a clipboard, standing outside the door to another cubicle.

Maisie put her hand up.

'Um, that's me.' Lili rose from her seat, her stomach churning at the thought she'd broken her wrist. She walked over and stepped inside.

The doctor closed the door behind them. Maisie took a seat in the corner. Lili sat down in front of a desk. She felt like she was in a doctor's surgery, not a hospital.

The doctor glanced at the notes and summed up, 'So, your friend had a fall. You tried to break the fall and ended up …' he trailed off, pointing his pen at her sling. 'Yes or no?'

'Well, the thing is, he's not my—'

'Yes, or no. Is that how it happened or not?'

Lili glared at him. She did not like his tone. He was acting as though he didn't want her to be there. Lili frowned. She didn't want to be there either. 'Yes,' she said curtly. His bedside manner left a lot to be desired. She imagined that with a face like that – brown eyes, slicked-back black hair and gorgeous cheekbones – he'd have the junior nurses falling at his feet. Lili was still glaring at him as he examined her wrist. 'Ow, that hurt!' Lili pulled her hand away.

'Hmm.'

Lili watched him pick up a pen and make a note. 'Is it broken?' she asked.

He didn't answer. *How rude.* She noticed there was no ring on his finger. That didn't surprise her, given what she'd seen of his personality. Is this how he treated all his patients? Is this how he treated everyone – like he had a prickly pear stuck up his backside?

'Did you hear what I just said?' Now he was getting irritated.

'Sorry – what?' Lili hadn't been paying attention. She was thinking that, for such a good-looking guy, he had zero charisma.

Maisie piped up, 'The doctor said you need an x-ray. What's an x-ray?'

To Lili's surprise, rather than brushing her off for interrupting him and wasting his time with silly questions, he rummaged in his drawer and found something. He walked over to where Maisie was sitting and showed her a 3D image of a hand which lit up so that Maisie could see the skeleton beneath.

'That is so cool,' exclaimed Maisie.

'So that's what your mum is going to have in a minute, if that is okay with you?'

Maisie was so absorbed in the x-ray that she hadn't taken in what the doctor had just said – but Lili had. She was aware of the medical profession's duty of care towards children, and the role of social services. Although there was nothing wrong with looking after her best friend's daughter, Lili once again kept her mouth shut and did not correct the misconception. She didn't want to risk it.

The doctor was still kneeling beside Maisie's chair. 'My name is Nathaniel, but everyone calls me Nate.'

'I'm Maisie.'

'Maisie, I'm afraid you can't come along to the x-ray, but don't worry, the receptionist will look after you. Would you like to choose a chocolate bar and a drink from the vending machine while you wait?'

Maisie said, 'Yes, please.'

'And I have something else for you.' He was back in his drawer, rummaging for something else.

Along with Maisie, it also intrigued Lili as to what he had in that drawer. This time he found a notepad and crayons, a sticker that said, *I'm a brave heart,* and a toy stethoscope.

Although Maisie took the toy and the sticker, Lili could tell she was more interested in the notebook and crayons.

Lili's smile faded when she saw how attentive the young doctor was to Maisie. It brought Alex to mind. She understood that Maisie was someone else's child, but Alex had barely ever given her the time of day. Why couldn't Alex have been half as nice to her as the doctor? He'd started to grow in her estimation until he said brusquely, 'I haven't got all day.' He stood by the open door as Lili stepped out of the room. 'The x-ray department is that way.' He pointed a rude finger for Lili's benefit and then clicked his fingers at the triage nurse. 'Hey, you.'

Lili caught the exasperated look on the nurse's face as she walked over. Lili sympathised. She wouldn't want to work alongside him either.

As Lili took a seat close to the reception desk, the receptionist came over with a packet of chocolate buttons and a soft drink from the vending machine. 'The doctor asked me to get these. I believe they're for you.' She handed them to Maisie and offered Lili a reassuring smile. 'She's going to be fine here while you go for your x-ray.'

Lili still didn't feel comfortable leaving Maisie. Lili turned to her. 'Maisie, I want you to stay right here until I get back.'

She opened her notepad and was busy choosing which colour crayon she was going to start her artwork with.

'Maisie, look at Auntie Lili.'

Maisie sighed and made a show of looking at her, her big round eyes moving closer until their noses were almost touching.

'What did I say?' Lili asked.

'To stay here until you get back.'

'Do you promise?'

'Yes.'

'Good girl. I won't be long.'

'Can I decorate your cast?'

'I don't know if I'm getting one yet.' Lili hoped not.

'Okay.'

'Well, here goes …' Lili stood up. She was about to go, when Maisie asked, 'How come the man has the same ring as you?'

Lili stopped and turned around. 'What man? What ring?'

'The man in the shop, the old man, Joseph. He had a ring on his finger, just like yours.' Maisie was busy drawing a picture. She finished and held it up. 'See.'

Lili lowered herself into the seat next to her and took Maisie's drawing. Lili didn't remember a ring, but then she'd been preoccupied trying to bring the old man round and then calling for an ambulance.

'Are you sure you saw this ring, Maisie? Did it look like mine?' Lili got out her necklace, even though she didn't have to show Maisie; she knew what it looked like.

Maisie nodded.

Lili rose from her seat. She was about to take Maisie with her to see Joseph when the doctor walked out of his room and spotted Lili about to walk out of the minor injuries unit without having had her x-ray. 'Where are you going?'

Lili glanced at the drawing in her hand. 'Something came up. Can the x-ray wait?'

'No. If it's broken, it will need to be in a cast, otherwise you will just have more issues down the road. Do you understand?'

Lili wished he wouldn't treat her like a five-year-old. 'Yes, I understand.' But she wasn't happy about it. All she wanted to do right now was to see the ring for herself. Lili sighed. 'Maisie, are you going to be okay while I have an x-ray?'

She nodded but didn't look up. She'd turned to another page in the notebook, busy drawing.

Nate glanced at the little slip of a thing. Although Maisie looked around six, he realised she was older, perhaps seven or eight. 'What are you drawing, Maisie?'

'An outline of a painting I saw this morning. I'm doing it from memory. It's a bit tricky. Then I'll paint it later.'

'An outline?' Nate looked at her in surprise.

'Yes, that's what all the great artists do first before they paint. It's in my book about them.'

'Is it?'

'Yes.' She looked up. 'I want to be an artist.'

His smile faltered. He knew two artists. 'Let me give you a piece of advice,' he said. 'Art is a pointless waste of time.'

14

Lili had been in and out of the x-ray department in double-quick time. There had been only one other patient they were waiting for from the ward. She'd overheard them talking about a hip fracture. Lili thought of Joseph. She was relieved they'd seen her first, as she hadn't wanted to leave Maisie on her own for too long in the waiting room.

Lili caught the look on Maisie's face as she approached her. 'What's the matter, sweetheart? Did something happen while I was gone?'

'The doctor told me that art is a pointless waste of time.'

Lili stared at her. 'Are you sure that's what he said?'

Maisie nodded. The doctor opened his door and noticed his patient had returned. Lili saw him walking across the room toward her. She couldn't believe he'd said that to an eight-year-old.

'So, how was the x-ray? Anything broken?'

Lili rounded on him. 'What do you mean: *art is a pointless waste of time*?'

Nate looked at her in surprise and glanced at Maisie. 'Just what I said.'

'Well, that's your opinion, but keep it to yourself. Someone with Maisie's talent, with her gift, should go to art school, no question, and I'm going to encourage her all the way.'

Lili could tell by the look on his face what he was thinking; he assumed she was Maisie's mum, and of course any mother would think their child was talented. 'Come on, Maisie, we can leave now.'

'But aren't you getting a cast?'

Lili looked at her wrist. It was good news – kind of. She *had* broken her wrist, but it was a hairline fracture. She didn't need an operation, but she would have to wear a wrist support for six weeks to immobilise her hand while it healed. The support was secured with Velcro fastening straps, which meant she could take it off. Not that she should. But if an interview at Kew came up, she could slip it off. She'd be able to do some types of gardening, although nothing too strenuous that required both hands.

However, doing something like typing for hours on end was out of the question. At the back of her mind, there was a worry that if things didn't work out with Alex, and she didn't get the job at Kew, she would need to return to working in an office. What was she going to do for the next few weeks if she couldn't type? How was she going to earn a living?

Lili held up her wrist and told Maisie about the hairline fracture, but that it was all perfectly fine. She wasn't speaking to the doctor, but she noticed out of the corner of her eye that he was writing something down, taking note.

'Come on.' Lili stood up.

Maisie was about to close her notebook when Lili had a thought. She turned around looking for the doctor and discovered that he was still standing there. Good. She was about to prove a point. 'Maisie, sweetheart, I know you don't like anyone to see your work until you're finished, but would you mind showing us the outline?'

Nate shook his head. He was just about to say, *she doesn't have to do that, I'm not interested,* when Maisie turned her notepad around to show them.

'And that …' said Lili glancing at the drawing and smiling smugly at the young doctor, whose face was full of surprise, 'is why Maisie is going to art school.' She took Maisie's hand and walked out of the waiting room, leaving him staring after them, stunned.

He had known someone, years ago, with that capability; someone whose parents had wanted him to go to art school. They had been failed artists themselves, who hadn't had their son's raw talent, and their obsession with finding missing artefacts had always taken precedence over their only child. That was why he'd abandoned his gift; to get back at them. He had wanted nothing to do with the art world and had become a doctor instead.

A nurse saw him staring into space, lost in thought. She asked, 'Is everything okay?'

He growled at her, 'Yes, why wouldn't it be?'

The nurse, no stranger to the new locum's taciturn manner, was hoping he didn't get a permanent job here. He'd only been at the hospital for a week, but he already had a reputation for all the wrong reasons; he was an arsehole.

She shook her head and returned to her work. He was a good-looking guy – it was just a shame about his personality. Rumour had it that he was bringing up his young son on his own. It wouldn't surprise her in the least if his wife had left him. She wouldn't have been able to live with someone like that either. It sounded as though that was the reason for his move out of London; he had family here. She imagined there were grandparents who could look after his child while he worked. That meant he was likely to be after a permanent position. She didn't fancy working with him for the foreseeable future, but at least she would only see him at work. The nurse thought of her fiancé, the paramedic who had also started a new job here. Glancing at the doctor as he walked back into his consulting room, she was grateful she had met someone so lovely.

The door slammed shut. A moment later, it flew open. He barked at her, 'Have I got another patient or what?'

'What a twat,' she said to herself as she looked at her notes. 'We've admitted a man in his early eighties after a fall. He's just come out of x-ray.'

'Well, don't stand there – give me the notes.'

She frowned at him across the room. *Come and get them yourself,* she felt like throwing back. She wasn't the only nurse working in the minor injuries unit who was now seriously thinking about a transfer to another department or, better still, another hospital. If he wasn't careful, he'd have no one to bark orders at.

15

'I wonder where they took Joseph?' Lili looked at Maisie. 'I want to see him before we leave. You don't mind – do you? It's about my ring.'

Maisie shrugged. 'That's okay.'

The cottage hospital wasn't that big, but Lili didn't feel inclined to wander the corridors looking for him in case she bumped into that horrible doctor again.

They returned to the entrance where the reception staff sat. Lili asked about Joseph's whereabouts.

'Are you a relative?'

Lili hesitated.

'Oh, hello.' The nurse, who had been on duty when the paramedics brought Joseph in, had recognised her. 'Come with me.'

'Sorry, I don't know where they took him.'

'No problem. These old buildings are a bit of a maze.'

Lili followed the nurse, but this time she felt compelled to own up. 'Look, I'm not a relative.'

'Don't worry. You came in with him. He knows you, so we make allowances if we can't get hold of relatives straight away.'

Knows me? He doesn't know me – he's just mistaken me for someone else, thought Lili. She about to correct the misconception when she remembered the ring. She decided to keep quiet and followed the nurse.

'Here we are. There's only one ward at Aldeburgh, but we have a side room.' The nurse stopped at the door. 'A doctor will be visiting. Joseph has just come back from x-ray.'

Lili was about to step into the room.

'It's a broken hip, I'm afraid.'

'Oh dear.'

'It could have been a lot worse.'

How so? thought Lili. The poor man was concussed and had a damaged hip.

'If you hadn't been there, he might have been waiting for hours until someone found him.'

That didn't make Lili feel any better. In fact, she was the reason he was here. If he hadn't been so excited to see her, perhaps he wouldn't have taken a tumble. Lili was having second thoughts about visiting. 'Should I wait until the doctor has been?'

'Not at all. Go right in.'

'I'll make it quick.'

The nurse smiled. 'Don't worry, it will be fine. The doctor won't mind.' As she said that, she wondered who was still on call down in the minor injuries unit. If it was the good-looking new guy, with the irritable, short-tempered disposition, then the young woman might wish she hadn't stayed.

'How's the hand, by the way?'

Lili glanced at her wrist. 'Hairline fracture, but I don't need surgery or a cast.'

The nurse nodded. 'Well, that's good news, isn't it?'

Not if I have to go back to admin work soon, thought Lili. She said, 'The doctor who saw me was …' Lili searched for the right word. None of the ones she thought of were very flattering: *irritable, abrupt, bad-tempered …*

'He's an arsehole.'

'Maisie!' Lili turned to look at her, suppressing a smile. It summed him up perfectly. Maisie stared back at her, wide-eyed. 'Wherever did you hear that language?'

'That's what the other nurse said.'

Lili glanced at the nurse standing in front of her. 'So sorry – she doesn't normally use those words.' Lili caught the nurse suppressing a smile too.

The nurse looked around before leaning towards Lili. 'I'm afraid that's the consensus about the new locum. I hope he won't be here long.' She wanted to add that if Lili didn't want to bump into that arsehole again, she had better make her visit short. However, her pager went off, and she had to run. 'Oh, before I forget – here.' She handed Lili a set of keys. 'These were on a chain attached to Joseph's trouser pocket.'

'What are these for?' It was a stupid question. Why had the nurse given them to her?

'I know he's in and out of consciousness, so what he said could be utter nonsense …'

'What did he say?'

'Something about forgetting to lock his front door.'

Lili looked at the keys. 'The shop!' she exclaimed. 'He runs a shop full of antiques.'

'Oh, dear.'

She didn't know if anybody had closed the door when they had left in the ambulance, let alone if anyone had been along and locked up. *What if an opportunist thief has found it open?* she thought. The other shops hadn't been open when they left, which meant nobody would be around to see a dodgy van loading up stolen goods.

The nurse looked at the keys. 'Perhaps you should cut your visit short and lock up the shop.'

Lili had intended to move into the flat that day, so she needed the key anyway. She sighed. What a start. That was the other reason she had to meet Joseph. Although he had appeared thrilled to see her, she hadn't signed anything official or paid him for the week. He didn't even know her name.

'We need to see his ring first,' Maisie said, a little too loudly. Lili needn't have worried that the nurse would overhear. She was already striding down the corridor.

Lili stepped inside the room. Maisie ran over to the old man's bed and reached for his hand.

'Maisie – wait!' Lili joined her at the bedside.

'See.' Maisie pointed.

Lili gaped at the ring on his finger. 'Joseph – are you awake?'

He didn't respond.

She picked up his hand and examined the ring. It looked similar. However, Lili didn't want to read anything into it. She fingered the ring on the chain around her neck. It was just a coincidence – wasn't it? She imagined there were plenty of these items to be found in shops and market stalls.

Amber wasn't particularly precious or expensive – unless you had the blue stone. Lili had read about it in a magazine once. Natural amber came in a variety of shades, although there was a rare colour that looked quite normal, but in certain lights had a blue hue.

Lili had one such gemstone in the ring that hung around her neck. *Was his the same?*

'Is it the same?' Maisie asked, as if reading her mind.

Lili beckoned her closer. She gently turned his hand this way and that. 'Tell me what colour you see.'

Maisie concentrated, 'Yellow, orange, brown …'

'*Blue*!' they said in unison. It was only a flash as she turned his hand over. Lili did it again. There it was. 'You see it, don't you, Maisie?'

'It's blue, like yours.'

Lili put his hand down and stared at the ring.

'See, I told you he had one just like yours.'

But is the ring really just like mine? thought Lili. The only way to know for sure was to take the ring off and see if there was in inscription on the inside, like hers. She wouldn't find a piece of jewellery that was inscribed like that in a typical shop or street stall.

'I'll have to remove it and take a closer look,' she said out loud.

'I'll do it.'

'No, Maisie, I need you to do something else for me …'

A moment later, Maisie was standing by the door on lookout duty.

Lili was just taking a breath before she attempted to take the ring off Joseph's hand when Maisie said, 'Oh, no. There's that arsehole …'

'Maisie! I told you before we don't use that sort of lang—' Lili jumped out of her seat when she realised what Maisie was saying. Someone was coming, and worse still, it was that horrible doctor. She rushed to the door and grabbed Maisie's hand.

Peeking outside the room, she could see him strolling down the corridor, looking at some notes.

Lili pulled Maisie behind her and trotted in the other direction. She approached the helpful nurse, who was walking towards her.

'Gotta go.'

She smiled knowingly. 'A wise decision. The doctor has just arrived.'

Lili breathed a sigh of relief when she saw him walk into Joseph's room. He hadn't seen her. She turned to the nurse. 'I'd like to visit again. Can you tell me the visiting hours?' Lili assumed Joseph wouldn't be released from hospital soon; not if he needed surgery.

'You can come each evening after teatime from six to eight.'

'Perfect.'

The nurse smiled. 'I'm sure he will be more responsive soon.'

Lili looked at her blankly.

'More with it.'

'Oh, I see.' It occurred to her that once he was awake, she could just ask him if there was writing on the inside of the ring.

'I'm sure he will appreciate seeing a friendly face.'

Lili managed a smile, which dropped off when she turned to go. She and Joseph weren't friends. She didn't even know him; she had just been there when he'd had his accident. She told herself as she walked out of the hospital that he could have slipped and fallen at any time; she tried to ignore the thought that it was all her fault.

She glanced at the keys in her hand. The least she could do for the old man was to make sure his shop was locked and secured.

'Can we go to the art shop now?'

For a moment, after all that had happened, Lili didn't know what Maisie was talking about.

'I need another sketch book and some watercolour paints.'

Lili remembered that Maisie had asked if they could visit the art shop again that morning. They were becoming regular customers. Lili had decided to drop off their suitcases first and check the old man had had no second thoughts about letting the flat.

Although it was now only mid-morning, that conversation in the hotel a couple of hours earlier seemed a distant memory.

16

They were making their way back along Park Road towards the town centre, heading for Cobblers Yard. It wasn't far. Lili had been taking note while they were being driven to the hospital in the paramedic's car. Although it was only a short drive, it took fifteen minutes on foot to reach the High Street.

Maisie enjoyed the walk. She was getting what she wanted at the end of it: another visit to the art shop. Lili was partly regretting bumping into the woman and her grandson in the café at the start of the holiday. Although Maisie's artwork had kept her occupied for hours during the bad weather, and Lili had discovered the little girl had quite a talent, the cost of the materials was adding up.

Although her savings were dwindling, and she could do with the cheap rent offered on the flat, Lili thought of Joseph in hospital and didn't want to take advantage of an old man. She'd had a feeling it was a bad idea when she'd turned up with her suitcases that morning – and that was before he'd had his fall. She had already decided she would pay for a night or two in another hotel in the town and then head back to London.

She wasn't looking forward to turning up at home with

Maisie in tow, but it couldn't be helped. She wanted to speak to Alex and find out what was going on; they had barely spoken since that row over Maisie and his imminent move to Washington. There was also the fact that Alex had said he had something to send her; she wanted to tell him there was no point sending it when he could give it to her in person.

When they arrived in Cobblers Yard, Lili sent Maisie into the art shop to choose her materials while she dealt with Joseph's shop. Lili opened her purse and found a twenty-pound note. It wouldn't be enough. She gave it to Maisie anyway, telling her she'd be along in a moment with her bank card to settle up. She watched Maisie walk into the shop before turning on her heel and crossing the cobbled courtyard. Lili noticed the door to the antique shop was closed, but as expected, it wasn't locked.

Lili stood on the doorstep, looking at the different keys on the chain and wondering which key fitted the lock. Then she spotted that the lights were on. She opened the door and stepped inside. She'd forgotten all about their cases, which they'd brought with them that morning. She was just reaching for the light switch, intending to take the suitcases outside, when the little bell above the door tinkled. 'I'm sorry, we are closed,' she barked.

'It's only me,' said Maisie as she entered the store.

'Oh! Did you find what you were looking for?'

'Yes.' She smiled as she held up a paper bag with her materials inside.

'Didn't you need some more money to pay for those?'

Maisie shook her head. 'I had enough.'

Lili doubted that. She guessed Ray had let her have what she needed regardless of the cost.

'I'm just turning the lights off, and then we can go.'

'Wait – I want to see the painting again.'

Lili glanced at the large watercolour that Maisie had first spotted when she'd looked in the window the day before. She frowned. 'Let's be quick. I've got things to do.'

Maisie walked up to the canvas hanging on the wall.

'Careful …' Lili warned Maisie as she skirted an antique side table. The expensive-looking vase resting on the top tottered. Lili reached to steady it.

'Oh, sorry,' Maisie said, skipping right up to the picture. She stared at it. 'Was it painted by a famous artist? Do you think it's for sale? Can we buy it?'

'I don't know who painted it, but if it is for sale, sweetheart, I'm sure it will be a lot more money than I can afford.' Noting Maisie's look of disappointment, Lili had an idea. She knew what to say to perk Maisie up. 'Now you've got more painting materials, if you like it so much, why don't you paint one for yourself?' She could tell that hadn't occurred to Maisie.

'Okay, I will.'

'Great – time to go.'

Maisie looked at their suitcases. 'But I thought we were staying here?'

'There's been a change of plan. Joseph is in hospital, so I don't think we can stay here.'

'Why not?' Maisie ran off.

'Maisie, come here right now, young lady.' Lili was getting cross. Her heart rate shot up at the thought that Maisie might knock something over, leaving her with a huge repair bill.

'What's up there?' Maisie opened a door and found a flight of stairs. 'Do you think it's the flat?'

'Maisie!'

It was too late. Maisie ran up the stairs.

Lili walked over and glanced up the narrow flight of stairs. 'What are you doing up there?'

'I found another painting.'

'Maisie, I want to lock up the shop. Come down this instant.' Lili rarely raised her voice, but when she did, Maisie always did as she was told.

'Come and see.'

Lili sighed. 'All right, but only for a minute – then we must go.'

Ten minutes later, Lili was still upstairs, exploring the flat in the eaves. There was a short hallway with a kitchenette off it, then a door to a spacious but cosy double bedroom with a bedstead and mattress, an inbuilt wardrobe and a dressing table. The end of the hallway opened into a sitting area with an inglenook fireplace, a wood burner, and an old sofa with two matching chairs.

There was another bedroom off the lounge with a small single bed. Between the lounge and bedroom was a wet room which had been updated at some point. It had a toilet, sink and large walk-in shower with stone-effect brown tiles and chrome fittings. Lili thought the entire flat could do with a freshen up. She imagined repainting the walls and brightening up the place with some new curtains, some flowers in the windows, and perhaps a painting on the wall – or several.

'What's the matter, Auntie Lili?'

Maisie had caught her standing there, lost in thought.

'I like it,' Lili commented.

'So do I. Can we stay, Lili? Please. Joseph said we could.'

Lili chewed her bottom lip. It wasn't what she'd been

intending to do. She would have to buy some bedclothes and towels, but that wouldn't be half as expensive as staying another couple of nights at the hotel in the town – if there were vacancies.

Lili looked at Maisie. Staying there would get around the complication of going home to Alex. She knew that would not work – not if she wanted to return and have time with Alex sorting out their relationship. She didn't want Maisie hearing them arguing over her. That wasn't fair. It wasn't Maisie's fault her mum had jetted off on holiday without her.

'Did you say you'd found another painting?'

Maisie nodded her head. 'It's over there under a dustsheet.'

They both walked over to the canvas on the floor. Someone had left it propped against a wall in the lounge. Maisie lifted the corner of the sheet. Lili sneezed. So did Maisie.

They both laughed, and each of them grabbed one end of the dustsheet. They pulled it away together to reveal a gorgeous picture by an unknown artist. There appeared to be no signature on the painting. Lili smiled. 'This would look perfect hanging over the fireplace.'

Maisie agreed.

Lili walked over to the window in the eaves with the little panes of glass that looked over the cobbled square. The single old-fashioned streetlamp was illuminating the yard; it was still switched on even though it was mid-morning. She wouldn't know until this evening whether there were any other flats over the shops that were occupied. Lili tried the lights upstairs. The electricity and gas were working. In that instant, she made a decision.

'Shall we bring our cases up?'

'Does that mean we're staying?'

All it took was a smile from Lili and Maisie was in her arms giving her a big hug as a thank you.

Lili followed Maisie back down the stairs to collect their suitcases. She had just stepped off the bottom stair when she heard Maisie say, 'There's some people in the shop.'

'What?' She saw a couple who appeared to be retirement age browsing. Lili realised too late that she hadn't locked the door or put the *Closed* sign in the window.

She was about to tell them the shop was closed when the woman approached. 'I love this. How much is it?'

Lili stared at her. She had no idea.

Maisie saved the day by walking over and checking the price tag. 'That's one hundred and fifty pounds.'

Lili did a double-take. *One hundred and fifty pounds for a lamp?*

'Well, aren't you the cutest thing?' the lady said to Maisie. Her husband murmured something about the price tag, but she told him to be quiet. Lili suppressed a smile.

The woman offered Lili her bank card.

Lili approached the desk and stared at the old-fashioned cash register, wondering what to do with the lady's card.

Maisie saved the day, yet again, appearing by her side with an electronic payment gizmo of the type that Lili had seen in most shops. Maisie pointed at the shelf below the counter where she had found it. She seemed to know how to work it; Lili didn't have a clue. She asked the lady to insert the card and put in her PIN while Lili grabbed some white crepe paper and a large bag from underneath the counter. Lili wrapped the small lamp and handed the bag and the receipt to the lady.

She'd just sold her first item.

'This is such fun,' said Maisie.

'Yes, it is, isn't it?'

Perhaps it wasn't a bad thing if they stayed on the premises while Joseph was in hospital. At least there would be someone around to keep an eye on the shop. She was holiday-letting his flat at a knock-down price. It was the least she could do. *Who knows*, she thought, *I might sell a few expensive antiques while I'm here.* That would mean he wouldn't lose money. Lili thought of the lamp she'd just sold. That was a start.

Lili glanced at the door behind her that led to the flat. She imagined that after a little spring clean to remove the dust and cobwebs, Maisie could set up her painting easel upstairs. It would keep her occupied while Lili minded the shop.

Lili intended to visit the cash machine in the High Street later, withdraw the holiday rental and put it straight in the shop's till – if she could work out how to use it. Otherwise, she would leave the money in the flat. By the sound of things, Joseph wouldn't be out of hospital before they left at the end of the week.

She still had his business card in her purse. At least she could prove he had agreed to let the place to her. Explaining why she was running the shop in his absence might be tricky. Lili wouldn't worry about that right now; if anyone asked, she was an old family friend doing Joseph a favour. It seemed like a reasonable explanation.

Lili had zero experience of being a shopkeeper. She took a deep breath and closed the door behind her first customers, leaving the sign that read *Open* in the window.

17

Nate had been making his way to see his next patient, an elderly gentleman who had been taken back to the ward after visiting the x-ray department, when he was called to an emergency; someone waiting in the minor injuries unit had collapsed. He returned thirty minutes later, feeling run off his feet. It was a small cottage hospital but having only one doctor on call was ridiculous.

He picked up the notes again from the nurses' station, not bothering to read the name on the form before familiarising himself with the condition. The nurse walked along with him, giving him the patient's vital statistics and blood pressure.

Nate barely looked up until he arrived at the door to the side room. He halted in the doorway. 'Joseph?' He rushed over to the bedside.

'You know him?' the nurse said in surprise, following him in.

'He's my grandfather.'

'You missed the friend who brought him in.'

Nate spun round and snapped at her, 'What friend? He doesn't have any friends!'

The nurse looked him up and down. *Why am I not surprised?* she thought. She turned on her heel and walked out.

Nate had already been over the notes. Joseph had had a fall. It had happened that morning in the shop. Nate frowned. *Silly bugger.* How many times had he told him he should retire? Joseph now needed a hip replacement. Normally, patients weren't kept in until their date for surgery, but Nate decided that he would make sure Joseph wasn't sent home before his operation so that he could be looked after properly. His grandfather would remain in hospital for some time.

He sighed. If he'd known the patient was his grandfather, he would have seen him first before that annoying woman with the fractured wrist and her precocious offspring.

Nate shook his head, smiling despite himself when he thought of Maisie. The child's mum had been quite right when she'd said her daughter had talent. She'd known he'd get a shock when he saw the sketch the little girl had drawn in her notebook. Maisie wasn't just talented; she was gifted. *A child like that comes along once in a lifetime*. He stared at his grandfather. That was what his grandfather had told him when he was a small boy.

Nate put the medical notes to one side and sat down on the edge of the bed. 'Joseph?'

The old man shifted but didn't respond. Nate leaned over and opened each of his grandfather's eyelids in turn, shining a light in one eye and then the other before making some notes. The old man had an IV drip and was on painkillers.

'Joseph!' Nate said.

His grandfather's eyes flickered open.

Nate sighed in relief. 'There you are.'

His eyes darted around the room. 'Alena?'

He was still concussed. Nate didn't know who Alena was; he'd never heard his grandfather speak that name before. 'No, it's

Nate – your grandson.'

Joseph focused on the young man in front of him. He raised a shaky hand and touched his face. 'Nathaniel, what are you doing here?'

Nate smiled at him. 'More to the point, what are *you* doing here, you daft fool? Do you know where you are?'

Joseph looked around the room with a vacant expression.

'We're in the hospital. I work here – remember? I started my new job this week. That's why I came back to stay with you while I sorted out a place. You remember that too – don't you?'

Nate watched his grandfather, who was nodding his head. Nate hadn't told Joseph he wanted to look at the flat above his shop. He wanted his own place. He didn't want to hurt his grandfather's feelings, but it wasn't ideal, living under someone else's roof. He had planned to ask him if he could move in, but he hadn't got round to it. He'd pay rent, of course. The flat was in a perfect location, right off the high street, within walking distance of his new job. And it was just sitting there, vacant.

He knew that his grandfather had always been reluctant to let the flat; that was understandable, considering the antiques shop downstairs. But his own grandson wasn't just anybody – he was family.

Thinking of the shop, Nate took Joseph's hand. 'Joseph?' He was about to ask him if someone had locked it up but held his tongue. According to his medical notes, Joseph had been out cold when he reached the hospital; he wouldn't know if the shop had been locked. The last thing Nate wanted to do was worry him.

'Joe, have you got your keys?'

It was a daft question; Nate knew he always had them

attached to his trouser pocket by a chain. He looked in his grandfather's pockets and then searched the bedside cabinet. 'Where are they?'

'What are you looking for?' Joseph asked.

'Nurse!' Nate called out.

The nurse on duty appeared, eyeing him coldly. 'Yes?'

'A word.' As Nate got off the bed, Joseph reached for his hand. 'I'll be back in a minute, I promise.' Nate walked over to the door and whispered, 'Where are the keys?'

The nurse looked uncomfortable. She'd given them to Joseph's friend. Now she wondered if she'd done the right thing. How was she to know the patient was related to the new locum doctor? They didn't have the same surname. She presumed Joseph must be his maternal grandfather.

Nate stared at the nurse. 'Well?'

'I gave them to his friend who said she'd lock up his shop,' she replied in a small voice. 'She'd called the ambulance for him, so I thought …' she trailed off, expecting him to lift off because she hadn't waited for a relative to turn up.

To her surprise, Nate said, 'Okay.' He didn't know who this friend was, but if they were going to take advantage of an old man and steal stuff from his shop, they wouldn't have called an ambulance and accompanied him to hospital. Nate didn't have time to leave the ward and go to check on Joseph's shop. At least he knew that someone had – but he wanted to know who it was. 'If this friend returns to visit Joseph, you are to inform me straight away.'

Nate walked back into the room, unaware that the nurse was glaring at him. *He didn't even say please*, she was thinking. It was like an order. She decided she'd do no such thing.

Nate sat down on the edge of the bed. 'Joseph, can you tell me what happened?' Although he had already read the account given by the paramedics who'd attended the scene, he still wanted to hear it from Joseph before the porter took him down to the x-ray department again. After an examination, Nate had concluded he might have fractured his forearm too. If it was a bad break, he'd need a cast.

Joseph glanced around the room. 'Where is she?'

'The nurse will be back. She's getting a porter to take you down to have another x-ray.'

Joseph shook his head from side to side. 'Not the nurse. Where's Alena? She was here, I saw her.'

Nate looked at him, mystified. He had no idea whom he was talking about, although that wasn't a surprise. They weren't close; Nate had hardly visited in the years since he'd left school and started his career; he'd settled in London straight after medical school. He felt guilty that he'd only come back to see Joseph when he needed somewhere to live – albeit temporarily. Perhaps that was why Joseph had been reluctant, at first, to let him stay. His grandfather hadn't changed; he still kept himself to himself. He didn't have friends and wouldn't socialise. Living in that big old house on his own, Nate knew of his reputation as the town's recluse. So where had this friend come from? It was puzzling Nate.

Nate was about to ask him who Alena was. Was that his friend – the one who had called the ambulance? Nate lost his moment to ask when the porter walked into the room. He stood up and watched as the porter wheeled the bed outside.

'Joseph,' the porter said jovially, 'a little bird tells me you had a bit of a mishap this morning.' The porter's colleague had made the trip downstairs with Joseph not that long ago. 'How about we take you down to x-ray again, check those old bones are still intact – eh?'

Joseph didn't have a choice. The porter was already wheeling him toward the lift, which took them down to the x-ray department on the ground floor.

Joseph held up a shaky hand. 'Nathaniel?'

'I'll be here when you get back,' Nate reassured him, even though he knew he'd have to return to minor injuries. But first he had a phone call to make.

He had just got out his mobile when he heard a familiar voice outside the ward.

18

'I'm Joseph's daughter, Sarah. I want to know what happened!'

Nate walked out of the room to find the porter waiting by the lift, explaining that Joseph had had a fall.

'You silly man,' Sarah said to Joseph, echoing Nate's sentiments.

Nate stepped forward. 'Mum?'

She turned around. 'Nathaniel! Why didn't you let me know Joseph had had an accident? A lady in the co-op said she'd seen the ambulance outside Cobblers Yard – she thought I already knew …'

He held up his mobile phone. 'I haven't long found out myself. The paramedics took him straight up to the ward before he went to x-ray. I was about to call you.'

'Why is great-grandad in hospital?' came a voice.

Nathaniel knelt in front of his son. 'Joseph had a fall, sweetheart. He'll be fine, though, I promise.'

Sarah glanced at her father. 'What about the shop?'

'Don't worry – a friend took the keys and locked up the store,' said the nurse.

Nate scowled at the nurse for volunteering that information.

He saw the confused expression on his mother's face as she looked from the nurse to Nate.

'What friend?' Sarah asked.

The question did not surprise Nate. He had no idea, but he didn't want to worry her further, so he said, 'It's a long story …'

Nate's pager went off. He sighed. 'Duty calls.' He glanced at the porter manoeuvring the bed into the lift. 'Look, he might be quite a while in x-ray. Why don't you go home and come back for visiting hours this evening? Then you can spend time with Joseph on your own.'

Sarah looked at her grandson. 'All right.'

'Are you sure he's going to be okay, Daddy?'

Nate turned to his son. 'I'm sure.' William appeared tired. He hadn't been sleeping well this past week. Too many changes all at once, thought Nate. He missed his friends. If it wasn't for needing childcare, Nate wouldn't have moved away from London, although he did see advantages for a child William's age growing up on the Suffolk coast. But The Summerhouse was part of the problem. Joseph's rambling house was too large, with old-fashioned wallpaper from another era on the walls and dark oak everything. From the doors to the floors, to the skirtings and dado rails, and the impressive staircase rising from the first floor. It was all too much for a boy with an overactive imagination.

Nate had lost count of the times his son had heard a creak and imagined ghosts on the stairs and ghoulies in his bedroom, and of the number of times William had woken him up in the middle of the night, crawling into his bed and shivering in fright. This was the reason the flat appealed. It did not have a garden, which William would miss, but the place was small and cosy. It was just what Nate felt his son needed, and it was close to his grandparents. That was what he needed too. Joseph was not a hands-on great-grandparent. In fact, Nate knew his son was a little afraid of the old man with few words who would sometimes wave his walking stick at him in frustration. It didn't surprise Nate that a young boy in the house, with the noise and disruption, would be a nuisance to someone Joseph's age.

Nate recalled his own childhood. He was no stranger to the place; he had been sent away to live with Joseph in The Summerhouse. Although his grandfather had obviously been younger back then, he had always seemed to walk around in a black mood, as if he were carrying the weight of the world on his shoulders. However, Nate's experience of The Summerhouse as a young child had been quite different to William's, and that was because of Joseph's father, George, who had still been alive when Nate had lived there – it had been his house before he passed away of old age. Nate had had the pleasure of knowing him for a short time. He had fond memories of long afternoons spent playing chess or poker with lots of sweets and fizzy drinks.

The housekeeper had often been very cross, scolding Great-Grandpapa George for feeding Nate rubbish in between mealtimes. Then there were the times the crazy old man had pulled him up onto his lap, in his wheelchair, and had made Joseph whizz them around the house, pushing his wheelchair at breakneck speed.

Nate wished William had been able to meet George. A more jovial, larger-than-life character, you couldn't hope to meet.

The lift doors closed. Nate turned to his mother. 'So, what are your plans for this afternoon?' he asked.

'I might call into my shop, see how things are going.'

Nate sighed. 'You're meant to be on holiday.' Nate did feel

guilty, wondering if perhaps she would prefer to be spending her time in The Potting Shed rather than looking after a six-year-old. 'I'm sure Zoe can run the flower shop.'

'I know, but I thought I'd pop in, all the same. While I'm there, I'll nip next door and check Joseph's shop is locked and the lights are all switched off. Oh, I forgot – a *friend* has done that already.'

Nate didn't want to get into that again, but his mother changed the subject. 'Shame you haven't moved into the flat above the shop. Then you could have kept an eye on the place while Joseph is in hospital.'

Nate hadn't thought about that; it was another valid excuse to move in without asking Joe first. Nate grinned. 'What a good idea.'

William stamped his foot. 'I don't want to move into that horrible flat.'

Nate raised his eyebrows. 'How do you know it's horrible? You don't even know what it looks like.'

'I don't care. I want to stay at Great-Grandpa's house.'

'Since when? I thought you didn't like The Summerhouse?'

'Not true!'

Nate understood. Moving again just meant more change. He exchanged a glance with his mother and turned to his son. 'We talked about this, William. We need a place of our own.' It wasn't exactly a place of their own, but it wasn't living with the old man either. The trouble was that there was a shortage of rental properties in the local area. Until the house sold in London, Nate was stuck when it came to buying his own home. Besides, he'd need a permanent job for that. He was hoping to get one here.

This was quite a change, moving to a small town. His career

had been going places in London. Not anymore. This was the price he was paying for being a single parent. He'd lost his reliable au pair, who had returned abroad, and the agency hadn't been able to come up with anyone else he felt confident with to look after his son. He damned well wasn't going to repeat his parents' mistake – sending their only child to live with a grandparent while they focused on their careers. William would remain living with him, even if it was in a flat – to begin with.

'But there are lots of bedrooms,' William whined. 'Why can't we stay?'

Because Great-Grandpa does not like little kids running around his house, snooping in his stuff, causing a nuisance, Nate thought. He knew this all too well. Nate didn't want to think about the past. Right now, he had to earn a living, so here he was, back in Aldeburgh, the last place he'd expected to return to – and all because his parents had moved here.

He glanced at his mother. Joseph was getting on in years, so she'd retired here to be near her father. But who would have thought she'd set up a business? After the sort of career she'd had, Nate would never have imagined she'd open a flower shop. Although Aldeburgh was the last place Nate wanted to be right now – he'd had a life in London, a career, friends – becoming a widower had shifted his priorities. Getting a job in Aldeburgh would mean his parents could look after William during the weekends and school holidays and when he was on late shifts. The best part was that he would still get to see his son every day – which was more than could be said for his own parents during his childhood.

'What is it?' Sarah asked, catching him staring at her.

Nate shook his head. 'Nothing.' His pager went off again. 'I have to go.' He attempted to give his son a hug, but William pulled away. Nate frowned. He knew what it was about; he'd taken William from his school, his friends, his home to move here. Nate tried to explain that he'd done it for William's own benefit, so that his grandparents could look after him while Nate was at work. Although with all the hours Nate was working right now, it still felt as though he hardly saw his son.

Nate sighed and ruffled his son's hair. 'See you this evening,' he said, although he knew that William would be asleep when he got back. He didn't get a response.

'Right, I'm going to stop by my shop,' Sarah said. Nate was turning to go when he heard his mother add under her breath, 'And he'd better not have sent me more flowers.'

Nate rolled his eyes. He could guess what that comment was about. When would his father accept that she didn't want to get back together with him?

If only they'd both left the past in the past. It felt like they'd chased ghosts all their lives; and where had it got them? To the divorce courts – almost. Nate couldn't understand why they hadn't signed the paperwork. Added to that, they had a son who was just about on speaking terms with them; well, one of them, and that was only because he needed someone to look after William.

Nate hadn't spoken to his father since his return. That was the other reason he was relieved that Joseph's friend had locked the shop. It meant he didn't have to visit Cobblers Yard. Although Nate wanted his own place, and the flat was it for now, a part of him wasn't looking forward to moving in. The problem was the shopkeeper next door. Nate heaved a sigh. The flowers weren't the worst of it. He still couldn't believe the silly sod had leased the shop across the courtyard from his mother's flower shop. What was his dad thinking? That if she saw him every day, it might help to win her back. Hadn't he thought it could piss her off instead?

Like his mother, his father didn't know the first thing about business or running a shop. However, at least he'd chosen to sell things he had a modicum of experience in – art.

Nate walked downstairs, thinking about the little girl he'd met earlier that day. He wanted to take her by the shoulders and tell her to stop now; not to waste her life in the pursuit of a dream, because dreams were just that – they led nowhere.

Nate shook his head, thinking about himself as an eight-year-old boy and the parents who all but gave him up for the sake of their careers, leaving him with his grandfather. Nate knew that even if he had to give up medicine to look after his own son, he would, without question. Why couldn't one of them have done that for him?

Nate knew that nothing his parents did now could change past events. He had grudgingly asked his mother for help with William. She had eagerly accepted, no doubt wanting to right the wrongs of the past by spending the time with her grandson that she had never spent with her son. He sometimes wondered if she ever regretted putting her career before him. If she could go back, if they both could, would his parents have changed their minds and brought him home?

It pissed Nate off that he hadn't thought about his childhood for years, but that coming here had reawakened old resentments.

He knew his mother's feelings regarding the work she had done at the Art Loss Register – first in New York, then in

London – investigating the provenance of artwork and trying to reunite stolen objects and paintings with their rightful owners. He understood what her motivation was. And his father's – the famous art cop, now retired from New Scotland Yard. They looked for artefacts the Nazis had stolen from the Jews, searching for those secret depositories where art and gold had been hidden before the end of the war.

They hadn't recovered a thing belonging to Nate's great-grandfather or found any depositories. Nate shook his head. Time had passed by, and so had their careers, into early retirement; two failed artists who had spent a lifetime chasing ghosts.

Once again, he thought of Maisie. *At least my son hasn't got an artistic bone in his body. He'd get no encouragement from me if he had.* His parents had hoped their grandson, William, would inherit their son's abilities; Nate was delighted he hadn't. He knew they would have loved a little prodigy, their own grandchild, to have the talent, the gift they had not, and enjoy the artist's life vicariously through him. But it was not to be. Nate felt they got what they deserved. His grandfather had seemed old even back then, living in an old house by the windswept Suffolk coast. It might have been a dream for some children, but it wasn't for him. He missed his parents terribly. His revenge on them was giving up on his gift. He'd never painted anything since then.

The porter passed Nate in the corridor and did an about-turn, running after Nate. 'I have a message from Joseph.'

'Is he still in x-ray?'

The porter nodded.

'Well, what is it?' Nate barked at him. 'I haven't got all day.'

'Oh, er, Joseph asked me to tell you to remember his

orchids.' He hesitated. 'At least that's what I think he said.'

'Jeez, really?' Nate said, raising his eyebrows. As if he didn't have enough on his plate, now he had to water Joseph's bloody plants.

'Oh, and don't forget to feed Bella.'

Nate's eyes went wide. 'He is joking.'

The porter frowned. 'I don't think so.'

Nate shook his head. *I'm not going near Bella*, he thought.

Catching the grim look on the young doctor's face, the porter asked, 'Who is Bella?'

'You don't want to know.' Nate strode off in a foul mood. *How did he manage to fall over in his own shop, for God's sake?* Nate knew it was a stupid question to ask himself; the shop was completely full of stuff. It was a wonder he hadn't tripped over and hurt himself well before this. Nate was just pissed off with his timing. He stalked down to the minor injuries unit, thinking that at least he didn't have to call into the shop on the way home and check this so-called friend had locked up. That didn't make him feel any better, though – he suddenly realised that if he was intending to move into the flat, he would need to get hold of the bloody keys.

19

Lili was busy upstairs, cleaning the flat, when she heard the tinkle of the bell above the shop door. They had another customer. Although Maisie had insisted that she was fine minding the store, Lili put the cloth down and walked downstairs.

'Good afternoon,' Lili said, smiling. She recognised the lady with the little boy. She'd spoken to her in the café at the start of their holiday. 'It's nice to see you again.' Lili appreciated seeing a friendly face. She glanced at the lady's grandson, whose sour expression told her that the feeling wasn't mutual.

'Oh, it's you!' Sarah said in surprise. 'Small world.'

'I know! I'm Lili, by the way.' Lili wiped her hands down the leg of her jeans and held out her hand. 'We didn't get to introduce ourselves in the café.'

'No, we did not.' Sarah took her hand. 'I'm Sarah. This is my grandson, William.'

Lili caught William sticking his tongue out when he thought no one was looking. Lili put her arm around Maisie's shoulders. 'This is Maisie.'

Sarah smiled. 'Hello, Maisie.'

'Hello.'

Sarah cast her gaze around the shop. She looked at Lili, bemused. 'What are you doing here? I understood you were on holiday?'

'My friend who runs this place had a fall, so I've stepped in to help until he's back on his feet.'

'Joseph is okay with this?'

'Yes …' Lili said in a small voice. Perhaps he was, but she wasn't sure because she hadn't asked him.

'So, you're Joseph's friend?'

Lili nodded, wondering why Sarah was looking at her so strangely.

'I know about his fall,' said Sarah. 'Are you the person who rang for the ambulance?'

'I am – yes.'

'We sold a lamp this morning,' said Maisie, interrupting. 'It cost one hundred and fifty pounds.'

Sarah nodded and smiled at Maisie. 'Well done.'

'I was minding the shop on my own,' she added.

Sarah raised an eyebrow. 'Were you?'

Lili frowned at Maisie, wishing she hadn't said that. 'I was only upstairs cleaning the flat.'

'You were cleaning the flat?'

Before Lili explained, Maisie said, 'We're going to live upstairs.'

Lili stepped in. 'We're staying on for an extra week in Aldeburgh and I tried to find a holiday cottage in the town, but there isn't anything.'

'So, you thought you'd take advantage of the flat upstairs.'

Lili looked at her. She wasn't taking advantage. 'Joseph offered me the flat to rent.'

'He did?' Sarah said, surprised. 'Joseph always refused to holiday-let the place.'

'It's true.' Lili fumbled in her handbag. 'I know Joseph's not here, but look …' She handed Sarah his business card where he'd scribbled the price per week and signed his name.

Sarah stared at the card. That was her father's handwriting.

From the conversation with Sarah, Lili realised that she must know Joseph. 'Do you know Joseph well?' she asked.

Sarah looked up. 'I should think so. He's my father.'

Lili paused for a moment before going to hand over the shop keys to Sarah. 'Here, I'm sure you want to take over.' Lili felt relieved. Although the flat upstairs would have been perfect, perhaps this was for the best. She hadn't spoken to Joseph to check that he was still okay with her staying in his flat or asked him whether he wanted her to mind his shop.

'We wanted to stay on for another week, but there were no vacancies in the hotel.' Lili knew even if there were rooms, she couldn't afford it. 'If we don't find anywhere else, then I have got return tickets. We can get the next train back to London, so it isn't a problem.'

Maisie turned to Lili. 'We're going home today?'

Lili went back over and stroked her hair. 'It's quite possible, Maisie.'

'But I don't want to. I love it here. Can't we go back to see the beach and have ice cream in the ice cream parlour again?'

'I know, sweetheart, but we can come here again.' Lili walked over again to Sarah to hand her the keys.

Sarah was staring at Maisie, who had tears running down her face.

William was staring at her too. 'Cry baby,' he said.

'William!' Sarah admonished him. 'We don't call people names.'

'But she is – look!'

'Shut up!' Maisie stamped her foot, turned to the door to the flat and ran upstairs.

Lili called after her, 'Maisie, come back!'

Sarah stared at Lili. 'You know what? I haven't got time to run Joseph's shop.'

Lili turned around and looked at William. She understood. It was the school summer holidays, and Sarah had to mind her grandchild. 'Look, running the shop is no bother,' Lili assured her. 'The customers are lovely, and William might enjoy helping out. I know Maisie does.'

Lili had only seen two customers, but they were no hassle and she enjoyed meeting new people, having a friendly chat while they browsed.

Lili walked over to the cash register and picked up the payment gizmo and a ledger she'd found in which she recorded the item that had sold, copying the last entry in the book. She held up the accounts. 'Now, this is what you need to do if someone buys something—'

'Grandma knows how to run a shop,' her grandson interrupted.

'William,' Sarah scolded him again, 'please don't interrupt when someone's speaking.'

'But it's true!'

Sarah sighed. 'I own The Potting Shed across the courtyard.'

'Grandma sells flowers.'

'The flower shop?' Lili said in surprise. 'Oh, I've been in there.'

'You have?'

'Oh yes. The arrangements are amazing.' Lili didn't mention the reason she'd visited the shop – to enquire whether they had a job vacancy. It was a silly idea, formed in the heat of the moment because of that row with Alex and the possibility they might be splitting up. But Lili was now convinced that the breakup would not happen.

Once again, the last phone call with Alex came to mind. He'd wanted to know where she was staying next so that he could send her something. Lili thought of the flower shop and imagined a beautiful bouquet.

If she'd been renting the flat upstairs, it would have been lovely to arrange them in a vase and add some colour to the bland magnolia rooms.

'I just finished my horticulture degree,' Lili found herself saying. She didn't know why she'd told Sarah about it – perhaps it was their shared interest in plants.

'Really?'

'I've been volunteering at Kew Gardens. Now I have my qualification, I'm hoping to secure a permanent position. I'm waiting to see if I've been selected for an interview.'

'Congratulations. I hope you get an interview.'

'So do I,' Lili said, smiling. 'Although, I have to say, having visited your shop, it made me think …'

'About what?'

'Well, how lovely it would be to run a flower shop.'

'It is. I'm enjoying it immensely.'

Lili picked up her handbag and coat. 'Maisie – we're going now!' she called upstairs.

'You can go, but I'm staying!' came the reply.

Lili approached Sarah with the keys, apologising. 'Sorry, I'll pop upstairs and fetch her and bring our suitcases down.' Lili was just turning for the stairs when Sarah said, 'No – wait!'

Lili turned back.

'I meant what I said. I haven't got time to run Joseph's place as well, and I'm loath to shut it up when it's the summer holidays and he's still getting customers. Would you mind staying on for a bit and helping with the shop?'

'What about the flat?'

Sarah raised her eyes to the floor above and thought of Nate, wondering what his reaction would be when he found out that his grandfather, who was adamant he'd never let out the flat, had already offered it to a friend. It made her wonder what was so special about Lili.

Sarah looked at Lili. She could say no and ask her to leave. On the other hand, it was only for a week, and then Nate could move in. She didn't see a problem. It would give him time to bring William round to the idea of moving out of The Summerhouse. Besides, it sounded as though Lili was giving the place a spring clean, saving Nate a job before he moved in. God knows she imagined the flat needed a spruce up and airing.

Sarah's mind was made up. 'Stay in the flat too. It would be a huge favour to have someone around, keeping an eye on the place.' Although that was what she'd said to Nate, he worked such long shifts she couldn't see the benefit if he was here.

Lili was staring at her, trying to decide if she should accept the offer, when Maisie popped her head round the door to the stairs. Lili guessed she'd been sitting on the bottom stair listening to the conversation. She ran into Lili's arms. 'Oh, please say yes! Please, please!'

Lili sighed.

Sarah smiled at Maisie. 'Well, I think that answers that. Welcome to Cobblers Yard. We're quite the little community. I can't wait to let everyone know all about Joseph's friend.'

Lili's face dropped. This wasn't London. It hadn't occurred to her that in a small town, word would spread that a 'friend' was helping out.

Sarah noticed Lili's friendly smile fade. 'Don't worry, we're a lovely bunch of people. Now, you must tell me all about how you know Joseph.'

Lili was saved by the bell. It tinkled as the shop door opened.

They all turned around to see who had walked in.

'Not him!' Sarah muttered under her breath.

'Grandpa!' William exclaimed, running up to the man Lili recognised from the art and craft shop who she'd also seen in the flower shop, ordering a bouquet. Hadn't the young woman serving in The Potting Shed mentioned that he kept coming in to buy flowers for his soon-to-be-ex, trying to win her back? Lili's eyes darted to Sarah, who was throwing him a cold, hard stare.

'What are you doing here?' she snapped.

Lili caught Maisie staring at William in his grandfather's arms, getting a big fuss and a cuddle. Lili walked over and gave her a hug.

Ray took William's hand and approached Sarah. 'I heard about Joseph. I tried to call you on your mobile …'

Lili guessed by the look on her face that she wasn't answering on purpose.

'When I saw the shop was open, I came to investigate …'

'Did you, now?' said Sarah.

Lili got the impression that Sarah thought he'd used that as an excuse to come and see her, although there was genuine concern in his voice for Joseph.

'How is he?'

'He had a fall. Lili can tell you all about it.'

'Oh, hello again.'

Lili smiled at him.

'You two know each other?' Sarah said in surprise.

'Oh, yes, she's a regular customer.'

Sarah turned to Lili. 'You're an artist?'

Lili laughed. 'Oh, dear me, no. Maisie is the artist – aren't you, sweetheart? Why don't you run upstairs and get one of your paintings to show—'

William interrupted Lili. 'My dad says art is a pile of crap.'

'William!' Sarah and Ray said in unison. 'We will have none of that language, please,' Sarah admonished him. She looked at Maisie. 'You can show us if you like?'

Maisie became shy in front of these people she didn't know. Her eyes settled on the stupid boy holding his grandpa's hand. 'I don't want to.'

'Good,' said William. 'I don't want to see your stupid drawings, anyway.'

Ray turned to his grandson. 'Look here, that is no way to talk to the young lady.'

Maisie glared at the annoying little boy. 'My drawings are *not* stupid – *you're* stupid!' She quickly glanced at Lili and ran back up the stairs to the flat above, aware she was in trouble like William for calling him names.

'Maisie, come down this instant and say sorry to William.'

Lili could hear her stomping around on the floor above their heads. She shouted out, 'No!'

Lili turned to Ray and Sarah. 'I'm sorry. I don't know what has got into her today.' She sighed.

Sarah heaved a sigh too. 'I could say the same about William.'

Ray raised his eyes to the ceiling. 'Is she all right up there?'

Lili nodded. 'Perfectly fine. I expect she's at her easel, finishing her painting.' She caught Sarah and Ray exchange a glance before Sarah filled him in. 'Lili is Joseph's friend …'

Lili groaned. She wished people wouldn't say that, even though she knew it was her fault for telling them that.

'Lili is staying on in Aldeburgh for another week. She's offered to mind the shop.'

Ray smiled. 'That's good of you, Lili, because I wouldn't have the time.'

'Yes, me neither.'

Ray was still smiling. For once, they had agreed on something.

'Joseph has said she can use the flat upstairs.'

Ray raised his eyebrows. 'Well, that is a surprise.'

'Isn't it just?' Sarah replied.

They both turned to look at Lili.

Lili felt she was being scrutinised, but she was saved by the bell again. 'Oh, look, you'll have to excuse me – I've got a customer.'

They turned to the door. Ray shook his head. 'Nope, that isn't a customer. That's one of our neighbours in the yard.'

Lili's face fell; that meant more introductions and inevitably more questions. It made her feel like closing the shop early, but if she did, she imagined her neighbours would want to know why.

Ten minutes later, word had spread throughout the small Cobblers Yard community that their fellow shopkeeper at number five, who barely gave them the time of day, had a friend who was minding his shop. They were all intrigued to find out who she was and meet their new neighbour.

Every time the bell tinkled, another friendly face greeted Lili. She soon discovered that the person with whom everyone seemed to think she was such great friends had a reputation for being a recluse. It seemed to have made the fact that she was his friend even more intriguing.

20

As Lili mingled with the other shopkeepers in the yard, she didn't say an awful lot about her friendship with Joseph. There wasn't much to say, apart from the fact that they'd met here in this shop. At least that was true. What else could she tell them?

She left the group talking amongst themselves while she went upstairs to make tea and coffee, apologising that she didn't have any cake. She'd bought a few basic supplies in the local grocery shop on her way back from the hospital. Although she couldn't offer them much, she had a selection box of biscuits. Lili poured out two tall glasses of squash for the children and handed Maisie her juice. Sitting at her painting easel, Maisie refused to come downstairs. 'I don't want to see that horrid boy.'

When Lili returned to the shop, balancing six mugs on the tray as she walked down the stairs, she remembered the names of her guests as she handed over their drinks. Sarah and Ray were first, arguing over who had asked for what; Ray was convinced he'd asked for coffee, but Sarah told him he'd said tea. Lili sensed an argument brewing. 'It's fine – I don't mind tea.' She gave Ray the coffee she'd made for herself and offered them a biscuit.

Lili soon discovered that the little group of shopkeepers not only enjoyed a good natter with one another in the yard, they also gossiped about each other too. That was how she found out Sarah and Ray had a son, and one grandchild. They were almost-divorcees, but Ray kept dragging his heels with the paperwork. Apparently, it was common knowledge that he didn't want the divorce.

Unbeknown to them, their neighbours had started a friendly wager on whether Ray could win Sarah back. In hushed voices, they made Lili promise not to say that she knew about the bet. They invited her to join in and asked her to let them know if she found out anything that might change the odds – so far it was even-stevens. However, one of them had discovered that Sarah hadn't signed the divorce papers either. Now there was speculation over whether Ray wasn't the only one with cold feet about splitting up for good.

Lili also chatted to the two ladies who volunteered in the charity shop. Mabel and Marjorie made a bit of a pair. They were sisters who had lived in Aldeburgh all their lives and were now both widows. They were like the great aunts or great-great aunts Lili would have loved to have; the sort who gave out sage advice but then bickered like an old married couple and made you laugh with funny anecdotes. In their early eighties, they had no qualms about speaking their minds, and were very opinionated. They often said, *if you can't at our age, when can you?* Lili imagined they could easily offend someone without realising it.

Lili's smile had faltered when they'd told her they quite fancied themselves as amateur sleuths like Miss Marple or Hercule Poirot. They even argued over which detective was the best. They were avid Agatha Christie fans. Lili had left them sitting on two antique chairs by the window with tea and biscuits, still in a heated debate over which agent was the finest at detecting. Lili loved Poirot, but she thought she'd better not wade into that argument, as they might be there all day.

'Amateur sleuths,' Reggie had scoffed. He ran the music shop.

Lili got the feeling that although there was a nice camaraderie between them all, there was also a bit of rivalry too. There was bound to be, with them vying for the customers to visit their respective shops.

Lili handed Reggie a cup of black coffee.

'Those two are all mouth and no trousers.' He looked at them over the top of his half-moon glasses, 'Or should I say tweed skirts?' He grinned at Lili.

Lili was feeling better already, realising she was reading way too much into this amateur sleuthing. There had been no crime committed; she was just a young woman helping an old guy and pretending to know him so that she could stay in his flat upstairs. And hoodwink his neighbours into the bargain. Lili brushed that thought aside. She had his business card, didn't she? Besides, it was only for a week and then she would be gone.

She looked around the small gathering. What if Joseph woke up and word got back to him that his friend, Lili, was running his shop? Wouldn't he say, *what does she think she's doing – I hardly know her?* From what she'd heard about the hip operation, though, he'd be grateful for the help.

Reggie interrupted her thoughts. 'Yep, they couldn't find a needle in a proverbial haystack.'

Lili smiled at Reggie. He looked around seventy. He was tall and slim, like Ray, but that was where the similarity ended. With his mop of dyed blonde hair, long black coat and the rainbow-coloured, knitted scarf he wore, even though it was the middle of summer, he cut a bit of an eccentric figure. He reminded her of an ageing rocker.

She glanced at Reggie and decided he was more like the actor who'd played the first Doctor Who, although she couldn't for the life of her remember his name …

Reggie leaned in close. 'You know, we could do with some fresh blood in Cobblers Yard.'

Lili said, 'Pardon me?' Not sure she caught his meaning.

'Well, look around. We're all past it.'

'Who are you calling over the hill?' Marjorie said haughtily, overhearing the conversation. 'What about those two lovebirds?' she glanced at Ray and Sarah. 'They're not past it.'

'Who are you calling *lovebirds*?' Reggie shot back. 'He hasn't got a hope. They've split up.'

'It's not unheard of for couples to get back together after a split.' Marjorie retorted.

Lili thought of Alex. She must send him a text this evening to let him know where she was.

Mabel spoke her mind. 'Ah, I see our resident lothario is chatting up the ladies.' She looked pointedly at Lili.

'I bet he is,' replied Marjorie.

'What I meant is that it's nice to have another young person to breathe a bit of life into Cobblers Yard,' Reggie retorted.

Marjorie and Mabel exchanged a knowing glance. 'Of course, it doesn't hurt that the new addition is so pretty.'

That made Lili blush.

Mabel smiled at Lili. 'We all have youngsters who help in our shops. You'll meet them, I'm sure.'

Lili had already met the young girl serving in The Potting

Shed while Sarah was with her grandson. She'd seen a grungy-looking teenager opening the music shop this morning, so she presumed he helped Reggie.

Lili picked up the tea tray and collected the empty mugs. She walked over to Ray and Sarah. They had overheard Mabel discussing the youngsters who worked part time in Cobblers Yard.

'Well, it's great that Joseph has finally let someone in,' Ray said.

Lili was unsure what Ray was referring to – Joseph letting someone help in the store or having a friend.

'He could do with a hand in the shop,' Ray continued.

'Yes, he could,' Sarah chipped in.

Ray stared at Sarah. Lili could tell by the look on his face that he seemed surprised but pleased that they agreed on something.

Lili smiled at them. They were a delightful couple. She wondered why they had split up.

'So, will you be staying on as Joe's assistant in the shop when he comes back?'

Sarah butted in. 'No, Lili is a horticulturist. She's applied for a position at Kew Gardens.'

'Ah, another flower person.'

Sarah narrowed her eyes. 'What do you mean – a *flower person*?'

Lili got the sense that Ray had said the wrong thing.

'Well, what I meant was—'

Sarah held up her hand. 'You know, it is possible to have other interests, other careers besides art.'

'I know that. Look at me!'

'What do you mean – *look at me*?' she said sarcastically. 'You run an art shop.'

He grinned. 'I'm not talking about that.'

Sarah looked him up and down. 'You're not referring to your silly heir-hunting business – are you?'

Lili suppressed a smile. They were like an old married couple bickering over something trivial. *But they have been an old married couple*, she thought.

'I'll have you know that it is *not* silly. I find people.'

Lili caught Sarah rolling her eyes. 'So, how successful is that turning out to be? As successful as finding lost art?'

There was an uncomfortable silence, during which Lili got the feeling they had crossed into the old territory of past resentments which may well have had something to do with their marriage breakup.

'Grandpa, can we go now? I'm bored.'

Lili looked at William in relief. She was wondering how to withdraw from the awkward conversation.

They both turned to their grandson, who was standing between them. He slipped one hand into his grandma's and grasped his grandad's with his other. 'Come on.'

The others had overheard William and decided their break in the antiques shop was over too. It was time to return to their shops and prepare for the afternoon.

They all trooped out, thanking Lili for the refreshments and secretly looking forward to seeing a friendly face in the antique shop instead of the old curmudgeon.

Lili shut the door behind them and put the *Closed* sign in the window. It was lunchtime. She walked up the stairs, carrying the tray with the mugs to wash up. She recalled Reggie's remark about this being a novelty. He said that Joseph's shop was the one that had been there the longest, but he kept himself to himself, appearing aloof.

Lili had got the impression that Reggie didn't like Joseph. She put the mugs in the sink, thinking that perhaps it wasn't so much that Reggie or the others didn't like Joseph, but that they didn't know him. It sounded as though he had made sure of that.

What had surprised her was hearing about Joseph's supposed bad-tempered disposition. That was not what she had experienced on the two occasions she had wandered into his shop. However, now she understood why everyone had seemed a little bemused when they'd heard she was his friend. Reggie had bluntly asked Lili what was so special about *her*.

Lili had managed a joke to fob him off. 'Perhaps it's because I don't look like an ageing rocker with a bad hairstyle.' For a moment, she'd thought she had spoken out of turn; he hadn't got the joke, and would flounce out of the shop, calling out, 'How rude!' Instead, he had burst out laughing and said, 'I think you and I would have been good friends if Joseph hadn't got there first.'

'Who said you and I can't be friends too?'

'To new friends,' Reggie had said, clinking his mug with Lili's.

'Hear, hear!' Ray had replied as she joined the other shop owners, who had raised their mugs and toasted to new friends. It had rather embarrassed Lili.

Lili put the tea tray down on the kitchen worktop and called out, 'Maisie!' There was no reply. She walked into the lounge and found Maisie where she'd left her – at her painting easel.

'I'm hungry.'

'Me too. I've closed the shop for lunch. How about we buy some fish and chips?'

'Fish and chips!' Maisie couldn't get out of her seat fast enough.

'Let me just wash up the mugs. Make sure you bring a bag for collecting some more amber. We're going to have lunch on the beach.' She glanced out of the window, checking for any rain clouds gathering before they headed out. She saw William in the yard, holding his grandpa's hand while his grandparents were talking. They glanced at the shop, and then both looked up at the flat simultaneously. It made her wonder what they were talking about.

21

'I didn't know he had any friends.'

'Well, he obviously does,' Sarah replied.

'She's young. How do you think they met?'

Sarah shrugged. 'I'm not sure. She didn't say much.' Sarah looked up at the flat above Joseph's shop. She thought she spied Lili standing at the window. 'They must be *very* good friends.'

Ray followed her gaze. 'What makes you say that?'

'Well, you know my dad. No matter how much I go on at him about renting out the flat, he won't hear of it.'

'Yes, I know. Such a waste. He'd get good money for it.' Ray turned to look at Sarah. 'Is he afraid someone will steal his precious antiques downstairs?'

Sarah shook her head. 'No, I don't think it's that. It's personal. I'm surprised he agreed to let Lili stay. He doesn't allow anyone up there.'

'How come?'

'It's where he and Mum started married life together.'

'I didn't know that. Lili hasn't got the keys to his house too, has she?'

Sarah laughed. 'He wouldn't give her those, and if he did, she wouldn't want to venture up to The Summerhouse anyway – not with Bella around.'

She frowned. So did Ray. They looked at William, who was swinging on his grandpa's arm, getting impatient. They both wished Nate wasn't living in the house, even though it was only temporary. They certainly hadn't wanted him to take their grandson there.

Ray sighed. 'I've told Nate he's welcome to come and stay with me. He declined.'

Sarah laughed at that suggestion. 'Why am I not surprised?'

Ray caught the sarcasm in her voice. 'What do you mean?'

She didn't mention the obvious reason – that Nate wasn't talking to him. 'Well, for one thing,' she said, 'your home is a boat.'

'It's a houseboat.'

Sarah looked at him. 'What's the difference?'

Before Ray had a chance to dignify what he considered to be a silly remark with a response, William interrupted them. 'I want to live on Grandpa's houseboat.' William had been listening to their conversation. 'Why did Daddy say no? Doesn't he like houseboats?'

'He doesn't like me,' Ray said under his breath.

Sarah heard him. *He doesn't like me either*, she thought. She guessed the only reason they were really on speaking terms was that Nate needed childcare.

William spotted a squirrel scampering up a drainpipe outside Ray's art shop. 'Look – there's a squirrel!' He let go of his grandpa's hand and ran towards it.

Sarah heaved a sigh. 'Did we do the right thing, sending Nate to live with my father?'

It surprised Ray that she'd brought that up. 'We did what we thought best at the time.'

'But was it?' They both looked at the little boy standing by the shop watching the squirrel scaling the drainpipe.

'I can't …' She trailed off.

Ray knew what she was thinking: their grandson wasn't that much younger than Nate had been when they'd sent him to live with his grandfather. He couldn't imagine sending William away; no more than Sarah could.

'Nate gave up his promising medical career in one of the most prestigious hospitals in London to return here.'

Ray frowned. 'I know, but he didn't have to. We would have looked after William. Nate could have come and visited at the weekends.'

Sarah glared at him. 'Visited him at the weekends? I can't believe you just said that!'

Ray looked at her, contrite. 'Sorry.'

They both stared at their grandson. It took them back. It could have been Nate standing outside the shop, except that back then, Ray's art shop had been a barber shop.

'He was so young,' mused Ray.

'Yes, he was. Perhaps if we hadn't been so consumed with our careers …' she trailed off, aware that she couldn't change the past.

Ray regarded her thoughtfully. They both had regrets – of course they did. What parent wouldn't? 'Look, this was a great place to grow up, better than London. It's a nice little town, friendly people. There's even a beach. We sent Nate to an excellent school. He had everything.'

'He didn't have his parents,' remarked Sarah.

'You and I both know why we had to do it.' Ray cast a glance in William's direction and lowered his voice. 'He was safer here.'

'But if we'd told him the real reason we had to ship him out to the back of beyond …' Sarah whispered.

'And have him looking over his shoulder, everywhere he went – like us?' Ray shook his head. 'No, Sarah, we had that discussion – or have you forgotten?' Now he was being sarcastic.

She looked at him sharply.

'We had to protect our son,' Ray said. When he got no response, he heaved a sigh. 'I still think he was better off here,' he added.

'Was he really?' Sarah shot back. Sometimes she wondered.

Ray threw his hands up in the air in frustration. 'What's that supposed to mean?' he asked.

She glared at him and stormed off, in no mood to talk about what was on her mind. Their son appeared irritable and bad-tempered most of the time, and worse still, William was turning into a little version of his father.

She understood that after what had happened, losing such a reliable au pair – someone who had cared for William since he was a baby – meant Nate wasn't exactly going to be walking around with a smile slapped on his face. She remembered meeting Nate in London before he'd made the move here. He'd seemed okay, in the circumstances. However, she hadn't counted on the possibility that returning to The Summerhouse would open up old wounds and resentments. She sensed it was about his upbringing; about being sent away to grow up in that big house with a crotchety, bad-tempered recluse.

In hindsight, perhaps they should have included him in their life in London, in their world of artist friends, and told him the truth about their work with Interpol; their sideline to hunting stolen art which wasn't without its personal risks. Who knew what the repercussions of tracking down Nazi war criminals would be for them and their loved ones, if they'd ever found one?

Perhaps Nate might have understood their passion for finding lost art. It wasn't simply about reuniting stolen artworks with their rightful owners, as Nate believed. Objects looted during the Second World War didn't just reside in secret depositories. They might be in long-forgotten underground bunkers, or with unsuspecting buyers. But they were just as likely to be found in the possession of families of former Nazi officers.

Handed down through the generations. A dark legacy, if ever there was one. And that legacy would be priceless, and where there was big money, inevitably an unscrupulous criminal underworld followed in its wake. That was the real reason they sent Nate away.

Perhaps if Nate had realised back then that all they'd wanted was to protect him from the obsession that had cost them their marriage, he could forgive them. Ray's involvement with Interpol, the work they'd brought home, the conversations they'd had, the paperwork and books, the old photographs from the war – all in the name of the research that had consumed him – hadn't created an environment in which to raise a curious child.

Sarah sighed. Now Ray had swapped his obsession with hunting Nazis for an obsession with hunting heirs. Did he realise how unhealthy that was?

She didn't want to think about that, or that their son had turned his back on his gift. He could have become an artist. He might have been a great artist. But then again, he might not. The sad part was, they would never know.

'Where are you going?' Ray called after her.

'I've got things to do.' Sarah had nothing in particular to do; she just fancied a walk along the beach, on her own, to gather her thoughts. When she'd first heard that Nate needed them to look after their grandchild, and that he was coming back to live in Aldeburgh, she'd felt it would be a chance to repair their relationship. How fortuitous that she'd retired to the Suffolk coast to be closer to her father, and that her son and grandson would move here too.

One big, happy, extended family.

At least that was what she'd imagined. But who was she kidding? Nathaniel hardly spoke to her, or Ray. He just about exchanged pleasantries when she collected William in the morning and dropped him back at The Summerhouse after Nate had finished his shift.

And that wasn't the only disappointment in her life right now. Ray had followed her, irritating her enormously by not only retiring to the area too, but leasing the shop across the courtyard. There was no getting away from him.

She was convinced he wasn't that interested in running a shop; his priority was heir-hunting. Sarah wished he'd just stick to his new hobby and take his houseboat somewhere else. There must be plenty of moorings up and down the East Coast. Why did it have to be here? The trouble with small communities was that inevitably you'd bump into people you'd rather not see.

Her initial misgivings had given way to relief that she would have someone with whom to share the childcare. But that hadn't worked out in her favour either. She thought about their first week looking after their grandson. She'd assumed it was going to be shared. She'd envisaged she'd have some time to herself. No such luck. It had all fallen on her.

Every time she'd walked across the courtyard with William in tow, thinking she'd just hand him over to have a break, Ray must have seen her coming. The shop had been suddenly closed, with the door locked, and Ray had been nowhere in sight. *What is his problem?* Sarah remembered asking herself.

Then it came to her: despite Ray saying they had done the right thing, leaving Nate with his grandfather all those years ago, she guessed that William, now he was older, reminded him of his son and how he had sent him away. She knew that was why Ray had been avoiding Nate. After all, it was Ray who had taken Nate to her father's house and left him there.

She had to admit, it did make a pleasant change not to have Ray in and out of the flower shop, bothering her and bothering her assistant. But Sarah still needed time out from her grandson. He was only six. She had forgotten what hard work it was entertaining young children, not to mention how exhausting it was, being on the go all day.

It had been like that with Nate until, at four and a half, he had wandered into her studio, where she had still painted for a hobby, and had picked up a paintbrush. She'd scolded him for touching her precious paints. They'd never allowed him in the studio. It had been out of bounds. She did take him out and buy a painting set from the local toy shop, though.

Sarah would never forget the day that she and her husband, artists themselves but without the raw talent to make it professionally, had discovered they had a prodigy on their hands. They hadn't been able to drag Nate away from his painting easel unless it was for something to eat. He'd always been occupied for hours at a time.

Why didn't we nurture his gift – nurture him? Sarah sighed. She had thought when William was born that she might have a second chance, that he would inherit his father's gift, but it had soon become apparent that their grandson didn't have an artistic bone in his body. He liked to draw and colour things as much as the next little boy or girl, but she and her husband had studied fine art at university – it was where they had met – and they knew talent when they saw it. And talent like their son's was exceedingly rare.

Ray interrupted Sarah's thoughts, calling after her, 'What am I going to do with William?' as she stalked out of the courtyard, leaving her grandson behind.

And that, thought Sarah, was the crux of the matter. She glanced over her shoulder. 'Figure it out – I had to.'

Ray stared wide-eyed at his grandson. *Oh botheration*, he thought. He didn't have the first clue what to do with William. He hadn't looked after a child in so long.

'Grandpa – I'm hungry.'

'Oh, yes – right.' What did six-year-olds eat? There was nothing in the shop, only tea and biscuits and one cucumber sandwich he'd brought with him for lunch. It was the end of the week, and he hadn't been shopping, so there wasn't much back at the houseboat either.

The smell of fish and chips from the local chippy round the corner in the high street wafted up the alleyway past his nostrils. He blurted, 'Fish and chips!'

'Fish and chips!' William shouted, jumping up and down on the spot.

'Good, good.' It was such a nice, sunny day; it made a pleasant change from all that rain. The break in the weather meant they could eat their lunch outside.

As they walked to the fish-and-chip shop, Ray was thinking about the picnic bench right on the beach. It didn't look as though it should be there; the others were on the grassy bank beside the promenade. He reckoned some teenagers had probably shifted it one night for a laugh, but no one had shifted it back. So, there it was, on the shingle beach, the perfect spot.

He had the most brilliant idea. 'Why don't we have fish and chips on the beach?'

22

'No – wait! William!' It was too late. William ran off before Ray could grab his hand. He saw his grandson stop at the picnic bench and heard him shout out, 'This is our bench!'

Ray saw a young woman with a child. They'd obviously had the same idea. They were eating their meal from a polystyrene tray. There were two fish-and-chip shops in the town. They'd been to the same one; he recognised the blue emblem on the carrier bag as he drew near.

Ray grimaced. Perhaps if they hadn't had to nip back into his shop for him to use the loo, they'd have got to the seat first. He shouldn't have told William about the bench before checking it was free.

As he hurried along the promenade, intending to apologise for his grandson's rudeness, he recognised the young woman. He waved as he approached. 'Hello, there.'

Lili caught Maisie's arm, trying to stop her throwing a chip at William. 'I want him to go away!'

So do I, thought Lili. This was all she needed. She didn't want to be asked any more searching questions about how she came to know Joseph. She wondered if staying in the flat was going to turn out to be a lot more hassle than it was worth.

Lili had a thought. As soon as they finished lunch, she would have another look in the town's holiday let agents for a cottage.

She raised her hand and waved at Ray, thinking that if a rental was available somewhere up the coast like Southwold, perhaps that wouldn't be a bad idea.

Ray took the wave as an invitation to join them. 'Looks as though we had the same idea.' He held up his bag of fish and chips.

'This is our bench!' said William again.

'No it's not,' Maisie shot back. 'We got here first.'

'How about we learn to share?' suggested Lili.

'Now, I think that's a grand idea.' Ray took a seat opposite Lili.

Lili commented, 'Only child,' referring to Maisie's unwillingness to share.

'Ah, so is William.'

William sat next to Ray, opposite Maisie. A moment later, after Maisie had thrown a chip at William, and he'd thrown one back, Lili swapped seats so that she was sitting opposite William and Maisie was sitting opposite Ray.

Ray opened the bag of fish and chips, passing William a tray with the battered sausage he'd asked for and some chips. Ray took tomato ketchup sachet and emptied the contents over William's chips before handing him a disposable plastic fork. 'There you go. Is that okay?'

William nodded and stabbed his sausage with the fork. He picked the whole sausage up, balanced on the fork, and ate one end.

Ray turned and looked across the table. 'So, you bought

some more paints. I imagine you've been doing lots of artwork.'

Maisie was dipping a chip in some tomato ketchup on the side of her tray. She looked up. 'Oh, yes. I like the book of artists we got in your shop. I've been copying them.'

'Have you, now?' Ray smiled at the little girl who took such a keen interest in art. He imagined that when her holiday was over, and she returned to London, the painting set and easel would be consigned to the toy cupboard.

'We are holidaying in Constable country,' said Maisie.

'That you are.'

'I like Constable and Rembrandt but copying those can be a bit tricky.'

Ray swallowed a chip and leaned forward, elbows on the table. 'How so?' He stared at her as she talked animatedly about her art. It brought back a vivid memory of his son, aged seven, before they sent him away to live here. They'd had similar conversations about art. He'd forgotten all about that.

'If you'd like,' said Ray, 'I could give you some advice on how to improve your technique.'

'What's a teknic?'

'A *technique*? That's a good question.' For a moment, Ray had forgotten he was talking to an eight-year-old. He turned to Lili. 'Help?'

Lili tried her best to explain, in a way that Maisie would understand, just what Ray was trying to get at.

'Thanks. I'm not very good at this,' Ray said. It had been years since he'd had a small child around.

'Oh, I'm sure that's not true.'

Oh, but it is, thought Ray, feeling guilty that he had been avoiding his own grandson. He glanced at William, who was still chomping on his sausage, and was transported to another decade. His eyes wandered to a bench on the promenade where he'd sat with his son, back when Nate was Maisie's age. Perhaps this wasn't such a good idea, returning here to have fish and chips on the beach.

Try as he might, he couldn't stop the memory flooding back. Before dropping him off at his grandfather's, for a treat he'd taken Nate to get lunch and had sat with him on that bench on the promenade. They'd just arrived from London. It was the end of the summer holidays and children were enjoying their last taste of freedom, playing on the beach.

He had intended to have a talk, man-to-man, about doing his best at his new school and being a good boy for his grandfather, but neither of them had had the stomach for food or that conversation. Nate had sat there, hugging his father, begging to be taken home. Ray recalled sitting there crying into his disposable mug of tea.

Lili interrupted his thoughts.

'You'll have to come by and see her paintings – perhaps after lunch?' Lili blurted without thinking. *What happened to trying to steer clear of the locals?* she thought.

She expected Ray to say that yes, he would love to. Instead, he appeared to slide off the idea.

'Well, that would be lovely, but …' He glanced at William, wishing he didn't look so much like Nate. *Did we do the right thing?* Sarah had asked. Of course, they bloody hadn't – he just couldn't admit it.

He looked at Maisie. She had a keen interest in painting at the moment, but he was reluctant to see her paintings. He imagined Lili was after his opinion, thinking she had some sort of prodigy on her hands. Didn't all parents want to believe their children were special? Ray sighed. He knew talent when he saw it. Someone like Nathaniel came along once in a lifetime. And he and Sarah had blown it.

He smiled tightly. It made a change to talk to someone about one of his passions. He realised how much he missed those conversations with his wife, sharing details about their work and visiting art galleries together.

He'd enjoyed talking to Maisie. She was interested in art, but he didn't want to be the one to tell her mother that she didn't have the talent to become one of the eminent artists of her generation.

'I'm afraid I'm busy after lunch. Perhaps another time …'

'Yes, of course.' Lili understood. She realised what he was thinking: that as a parent, she'd think her ordinary child was gifted. She imagined he was under the misapprehension that Maisie was her daughter.

Lili knew Maisie's talent was special, though. She might not have a degree in fine arts, like Ray, or be able to tell a Rembrandt from a Constable – although the book was helping to educate her – but anyone who looked at Maisie's paintings would see what Lili saw; she was a distinguished artist in the making.

Lili had a thought. Perhaps it was for the best that word didn't get around. What if Maisie ended up in the local paper? What if people discovered Lili wasn't her mother? Not that she'd lied about that; it was just she hadn't corrected the assumption. And what if they found out how many times Maisie's mother had left her in order to go gallivanting off with a new boyfriend?

'I think you're right, about leaving it for another time.' Lili spoke her mind.

William looked at his grandpa. 'I don't want to see her stupid paintings. My dad says art is—'

'William!' Ray cut in, knowing what was coming next. 'That's enough. Eat your chips.'

William scowled at his grandpa and threw a chip at a seagull flying by, intending to bonk it on the beak. Instead, he saw it catch the chip and gobble it up. He laughed.

So did Maisie, who'd seen it too. She looked across the table at William, watching him throw another chip. She'd run out of chips, so she nicked one of his.

'Hey! That's mine.'

She threw a chip at another seagull who did the same, gobbling it up. They both giggled.

'Were you an artist, Ray?' Lili asked, picking up a piece of battered cod with her disposable fork and ignoring the two children throwing chips at the seagulls; at least they weren't fighting, which was a first. She guessed Ray felt the same.

He shook his head in response to her question. 'I wish. Although I went to art school, I'm afraid I never had the potential to be a professional artist, showing my work at galleries. It's just a hobby of mine now.'

'I'm sorry.'

'No need to be sorry,' Ray said good-humouredly. 'I had a different, but equally fulfilling career.'

'What did you do?'

William was listening in on the conversation. He said to Lili, 'My grandpa was famous.'

'Really?' said Lili in surprise. She didn't recognise him. Maybe he was in show business.

'No, I wasn't on the telly, if that's what you're thinking.

Acting was never my thing.' *Unless you count acting the fool and losing the woman you love.* Ray swept that thought aside. He turned to his grandson. 'And no, William, I wasn't famous.'

'But you were in the newspaper. Daddy said so.'

Ray frowned. Trust Nathaniel to point *that* out. It was quite the inauspicious end to an auspicious career he'd rather not think about. He glanced at Lili. 'I was an art cop.'

'What's an art cop?' asked Maisie.

'Grandpa used to hunt for Nazis.'

'That was your grandmother,' Ray quipped, deflecting that comment. He caught the expression on Lili's face. 'Oh, not directly. She worked for the ALR.'

'The ALR?' Lili raised an eyebrow. It sounded like some sort of secretive government organisation – either that or the London Underground. She stifled a smile. She was thinking of the DLR, the Docklands Light Railway.

Maisie, who had been earwigging too, stopped throwing chips, and said, 'What's a Nazi?'

Now that was a question Lili would rather not answer.

'They were the bad guys in the war,' replied William. He put two fingers together, holding his hand straight, imitating a gun. '*Pow! Pow!*'

Maisie knitted her brow, looking worried. 'What war?'

'The Second World War, of course.'

Ray rolled his eyes. On the odd occasion he'd looked after his grandson when he was a toddler, he'd let him fall asleep on his lap on the sofa in front of the old black-and-white films Ray loved watching. That was a mistake, he later realised. He hadn't counted on the fact that toddlers' minds were like sponges, soaking up every detail. To this day, William seemed to know an awful lot about the Second World War, much of it historically inaccurate. Ray knew where it all came from.

Lili replied, 'It was a long time ago. Nothing to worry about.'

'But what if the Nazis make a war again?'

Lili and Ray exchanged a smile. 'There won't be another war, sweetheart.' *Not with the Nazis, at any rate*, thought Lili.

Ray waded in. 'They would be ancient now. Too old to—' Ray stopped abruptly, staring at Lili, who was looking at him wide-eyed, shaking her head from side to side.

'Make a war?'

Ray nodded. *Or build concentration camps, or steal people's possessions*, thought Ray. He didn't say any of that. Instead, he replied, 'That's quite correct, Maisie.'

'Are they all dead?'

'Yes, most of them are.'

William was throwing cold chips at the seagulls again. Maisie, satisfied she had nothing to worry about, joined in. A chip fell on the table. A seagull swooped down and squawked at them before gobbling up the chip.

Maisie and William screamed and hurriedly got up from the picnic bench. They ran away from the seagull, along the shingle beach.

'Don't go far,' Lili called after Maisie.

'William, stay in my sight,' Ray called after William.

They watched the two children for a moment, playing tag, before Lili turned to Ray. 'What is the ALR?'

'Ah, yes, the Art Loss Register. Sarah started working for them in New York.'

'New York?'

Those were the days, thought Ray. They had been carefree

newlyweds, living in a New York apartment while Sarah was working for the Art Loss Register and progressing in her career. Ray, already a police officer, and on his way to becoming an art cop, had gone with her. He had been seconded to the New York police and had worked alongside a detective in charge of a department dedicated to retrieving stolen artwork.

Once his secondment had ended, Ray had had to return to England. Sarah had stayed in New York and, for a time, their marriage had consisted of flights back and forth across the pond; it had been a long-distance relationship.

'Ray?'

'Oh, yes, where was I?'

'You mentioned Sarah working for the Art Loss Register in New York?'

'Ah, yes. When that branch closed, she moved to the London-based ALR.'

'You said something about her hunting Nazis?'

Ray laughed. 'Oh, dear me, no. She hunted for stolen art and antiques, tracing the provenance of paintings and reuniting them with their rightful owners. She was passionate about finding those items stolen from Jews. Joseph is Jewish, so …' He trailed off.

Lili nodded in silent understanding. He didn't need to explain. She imagined something must have happened to Sarah's family during the war.

'Did she ever find any?'

Ray shook his head, no.

It was a lifelong obsession. At least, it had been until the Art Loss Register's funding was cut. They had reduced their staff and had asked for people to take voluntary redundancy or early retirement. Sarah had opted for early retirement, which had taken Ray by surprise. She had once said she'd never leave her life's work unless they carried her out in a box. But something had changed.

He knew it was to do with the birth of their grandson. She intended to right the wrongs of the past. She wanted to be there for him. To take him to Regent's Park and the museums, introduce him to art galleries and the theatre – all the cultural things they had once enjoyed as a family before they'd shipped Nate off to the back of beyond.

Except Ray didn't think this *was* the back of beyond. He stared at the sea lapping on the shore. It was a lovely little fishing community. A classic Edwardian seaside resort boasting elegant period properties, many of them along the seafront. Ray wished he'd discovered this part of the world years earlier. Before Nate had come to stay with his grandfather, they had rarely visited.

Ray's thoughts returned to Sarah. She had given up not only her position with the Art Loss Register, but her life in London. She had moved here because when her first grandchild was born, her own son wanted nothing to do with her. It was a bitter blow. She and Ray were out of the picture, as far as Nate was concerned.

Ray's reflections turned to his own circumstances. When he had taken early retirement too, he'd followed her here, hoping to build bridges and win her back. He glanced at William, who was still playing on the beach, and thought how ironic it was that when they'd moved out of London, their son's childcare arrangements, which had been in place since his wife had died three years earlier, should fall through.

With the London property market skyrocketing, there had

been no way back. Neither of them had been able to afford to return to the capital, which meant that Nate had been forced to come to them if he wanted his son to be looked after by his family. His late wife's parents weren't in good health and lived further afield up north, so they could not help out. Nate had found himself with no alternative but to follow his parents to Aldeburgh so that they could look after William while he worked.

It was just what Sarah wanted, but Ray noted how tired she'd looked this past week. He felt guilty for absconding every time he saw her approach his shop with William in tow. He'd known she was after handing him over so that he could do his share. She needed a break. Although sitting here with his takeaway coffee, fish and chips, and some delightful company – he smiled at the pretty young woman across the table – Ray wondered what Sarah was complaining about. So far, William had been no trouble – no trouble at all.

Ray didn't notice his ex-wife out for a walk along the shingle. She paused on the promenade, smiling to herself. She glanced down the beach at the waves lapping the shore. Although she enjoyed looking after her grandson, it made a pleasant change to have a bit of time to herself.

Sarah was just breathing in the sea air when she spotted two children playing. She smiled at them, then did a double-take when she realised it was William playing with another child and having fun. She could hear them laughing. What surprised her more was spotting Ray, who was sitting on a bench and enjoying the sunshine with a young woman.

Sarah started walking along the promenade towards them, wondering who the young lady was. She could see takeaway coffee cups and the remnants of fish and chips on the picnic table. They appeared to be having a leisurely lunch together. She came to an abrupt halt when she recognised Maisie playing with her grandson. Now she knew who Ray was having lunch with – Joseph's friend, Lili.

'Well, you don't waste any time, do you?' Sarah commented under her breath. She imagined Ray had used his grandson as an excuse to pop into the shop next door and ask the pretty young woman if Maisie would like to play with William and if they could all have lunch together. She felt a pang of jealousy at seeing him with another woman.

There's nothing to feel jealous about, Sarah reminded herself. *We're getting a divorce.* But the feeling persisted as she turned on her heel and walked in the other direction. Maybe it was for the best if he had found a new partner – although Lili was less than half his age. Perhaps he'd stop buying his soon-to-be-ex those blasted flowers. Sarah raised an eyebrow. Well, wouldn't that be a sure sign he was now interested in someone else?

23

Ray was watching William playing when his eyes drifted up the beach. He thought he saw Sarah walking towards them. He was about to wave when she turned around and headed back along the promenade. He turned to Lili. 'Do you mind if I ask you a question?'

I'd rather you didn't, Lili thought, *especially if it's about Joseph.*

'I'm only asking because you're a woman; maybe you could help me with what I'm doing wrong …'

Lili stared at him, wondering what on earth he was going to ask her.

'It's Sarah. Look, the truth of the matter is—'

'You're still in love with her.'

Ray looked taken aback. 'How did you know that?'

'You were in The Potting Shed last week. When I walked in, you were ordering a bouquet, but I don't think you noticed me. I commented on how pretty they were when you left. The girl who was serving mentioned that you go in each day to buy flowers for your ex. She said you were Sarah's biggest customer.'

'Ah.'

'I guessed you were trying to win her back.' Lili didn't

mention the conversation with his neighbours in the yard about the secret wager they were having.

'Yes, well, it's not working,' he said miserably. 'In fact, I believe it's doing the opposite. I'm getting on her nerves. She keeps telling me to stop buying them.'

'Then I suggest you do as she asks and don't buy her any more flowers.'

'I can't do that. She might think I've given up.'

Lili shook her head. 'No, I imagine she will be pleased if you do as she's asked.'

Ray looked at her for a long moment. 'Then what *should* I do?'

Lili was thinking about Alex. What would she like him to do to make it up to her? She would appreciate some flowers, but she'd also like him to give her a bit of space to figure things out. That was what she'd given him by agreeing to take Maisie away for the week; some time apart to put events in perspective. Perhaps having another few days' holiday wasn't turning out to be a bad idea after all.

She looked at Ray. From what his neighbours in Cobblers Yard had said, he had followed Sarah there and rented the shop just across the courtyard. For Sarah, there was no getting away from him. The flowers weren't helping either. Lili reckoned Sarah was feeling smothered. Perhaps there was a chance they might get back together. After all, she hadn't signed the divorce papers. But this wasn't the way Ray should be going about making a reconciliation happen.

Ray waited eagerly for her response.

'If I were you, I'd give her some space.' She could tell by the look on his face that it wasn't what he wished to hear. 'She knows how you feel. Give her a chance to figure things out at her end. Let her come to you.'

'But what if she doesn't?'

Lili didn't know what to say. That was what she'd done with Alex – resisted the urge to call him all week, giving him some space, hoping he would contact her. But waiting to find out if he would be in touch was excruciating.

'Look, I realise it's going to be hard, but I really think you ought to take a step back and give her some time to process things. I reckon that once you stop buying her flowers, she'll soon get the message.'

'What message?'

'That you're prepared to do as she asks, and on her terms.'

Ray smiled at Lili. 'You know what? That makes perfect sense.'

Lili thought so too, although she wasn't an expert on relationships, going by how things had worked out with Alex that week. Lili had texted him her new address at the flat. It sounded as though he was sending her something, although he wouldn't specify what it was. She couldn't wait to find out. She'd love an enormous bouquet. In her text she had cheekily mentioned The Potting Shed, which had a website; it was an unsubtle hint, but Lili didn't care.

Ray reached across the bench and placed his hand over her forearm. 'You're a good friend, Lili.'

Lili smiled at him. She was meeting such friendly people here in Aldeburgh. Living in London, although she knew folk – other volunteers in Kew and neighbours in the building that housed their flat who sometimes said hello – Lili didn't count any of them as friends.

There was no sense of community where she lived; everyone led busy lives, hurrying from one thing to the next. There was no time to stop for a natter or build relationships. No time to put a *Closed* sign in the window and go for an extended lunch hour with a friend or have your shop neighbours in for tea and biscuits.

Lili was keeping a watchful eye on Maisie, who was having fun on the beach with her new friend. It reminded Lili that she had neglected the small circle of friends she had back in London. They were under the misapprehension she was on a romantic break away with Alex. She decided she should get in touch and let them know she had extended her holiday. That reminded her she should also contact Kew and inform them she wouldn't return to her voluntary role for another week. She still hadn't heard from Kew regarding her application. She hoped her fortnight's absence wouldn't count against her.

Ray turned to look at the children too. He was pleased to see his grandson had a new playmate, even if they'd got off to a bit of a rocky start, calling each other names. It made him think about the how the end of the summer holidays would be, when William started the local primary school. He didn't make friends easily; he could be taciturn and bad-tempered. Ray looked at Maisie and thought it was a shame that she didn't live in the area. At least then William would have had one friend at school.

Ray had offered to pay for William's education out of his savings and send him to the private school up the road. It was just as well that Nate hadn't taken him up on the offer. Ray had underestimated the cost of running the shop, which had eaten into his savings. He knew the school was still open; it was the same place Nate had attended when he had moved to Aldeburgh to live with his grandfather. It had not surprised Ray when Nate had refused his help.

Ray caught Lili smiling at the children. They were collecting seashells together on the shore.

William ran up to Lili. 'Look what I've found!' He held up a gemstone.

'Hey, you've found some amber.'

Maisie, hot on his heels, overheard him talking to Lili. 'I showed him where to find them and what to look for.'

'Well done, Maisie. That was kind of you.'

'I want to make some jewellery from the pieces I've collected.'

Lili looked at Maisie. 'I know. We just need the right materials, but they don't sell them in the town.'

'Was the children's kit you bought in the shop last week not suitable?'

Lili shook her head. 'I'm afraid not, Ray.'

'Just tell me what you want, and I'll get it for you. I've got some rather good suppliers.'

'That would be fantastic – wouldn't it, Maisie?'

'Yes. I want to make a necklace for my mum.'

'That's a nice thought.' Ray's eyes drifted to Lili. 'I'm sure she will like it very much.'

Lili caught Ray looking her way. 'Perhaps we can sell some of them in the shop,' she suggested, avoiding Ray's gaze. 'As long as Joseph doesn't mind, of course.'

'I'm sure he won't.'

'Can I make a necklace too?' William asked, surprising Ray. *Since when has he been into anything creative?* Ray wondered.

'Are you going to make one for your mum?' Maisie asked.

'No – my mum is dead.'

Lili stared at William. She looked across the table at Ray.

'Cancer, I'm afraid. Three years ago.'

'Oh, I'm so sorry.'

'You could make something for your dad,' suggested Maisie.

'Men don't wear jewellery.'

'It doesn't have to be a necklace.'

William thought about it. 'My grandpa wears a ring.'

'So do I.' Ray flashed the wedding ring he still wore. 'See?'

Lili had forgotten about Joseph's ring. William had just reminded her. She made a mental note that she must visit Joseph that evening. The only thing was that she didn't want to bump into any family members while she was there – not if she was going to get a good look at his ring. She turned to William. 'Are you seeing your great-grandpa in hospital later?' she ventured.

He shrugged.

Ray said, 'Sarah and William have already been, so I very much doubt they will return this evening.'

Lili was just thinking that this was good news when Ray added, 'But I might visit.'

Lili's shoulders sagged.

'Why don't you come along too? I'm sure Joseph would love to see you. We could go together.'

Lili forced a smile. She had no intention of going with Ray or any other member of his family. She thought up an excuse. 'Maisie will be tired this evening, so I'll leave it to another day.'

'Yes, I imagine William will be too.'

'I'm going to make a ring for my dad,' William decided. He turned to Maisie. 'You could make a ring for yours.'

'I haven't got a dad.'

'How come?'

Lili's eyes went wide. She stepped in, trying to avoid what Maisie would say next. 'Crumbs, is that the time?' Lili made a show of looking at her watch. 'We must go, Maisie.'

Maisie ignored her. 'Mummy won't tell me who he is, that's how come.'

Lili's cheeks went bright red. She could feel Ray staring at her. She didn't know why she was coming over all embarrassed; it wasn't as though Maisie was talking about her – although Ray obviously didn't know that.

Now would be a good time to tell Ray that she wasn't Maisie's mother – or would it? Lili held on to that thought. He didn't need to know. Nobody did. In a week's time she'd be out of here, returning to London, and Maisie would be back with her mum.

After all these years, even though Maisie was getting older, she still couldn't shake that irrational fear that a social worker might take her away.

Lili stood up. 'I really have to go.' She gestured to Maisie to come.

'But I just wanted to collect one more piece.'

Lili sighed. 'Make it quick.'

Maisie and William scampered off, and before long came running back to the bench with a few more pieces of amber.

'We've got to go now, sweetheart – say goodbye to William and Ray.'

'But I don't want to,' Maisie replied.

'Do I have to go?' William asked his grandpa, his little face looking so crestfallen that he melted Ray's heart. Ray recalled another little boy, with a suitcase, sitting in his car on the drive outside The Summerhouse, saying, 'Do I have to go?'

Ray would much rather not relive that moment. He could have turned the car around and taken his son home. Perhaps that was what Sarah had really wanted too. They'd talked about it, going back and forward over their decision. They'd come down on the side of the sensible solution, the practical one. With their all-consuming careers, they'd decided that Nate would be better off there. That, Ray now realised, marked the breakdown in their relationship.

Ray's thoughts fleetingly turned to The Summerhouse. The name conjured up a white clapboard property with an English garden. Perhaps a pagoda covered in clematis for sitting in the shade. And family gatherings on the lawn with a blanket and picnic baskets full of cucumber sandwiches and chilled bottles of wine.

The Summerhouse was none of those things, although it had been a place of family gatherings, once upon a time. There was a photo of his father-in-law that Ray recalled seeing, taken when Joseph was a child. He had been standing on that very lawn, surrounded by a group of people – relatives, Ray imagined. He'd found the picture down the back of the old sofa where it had probably been for decades. It would have remained hidden if Ray hadn't lost some loose change out of her trouser pocket and fished down the sofa for it during one of his rare visits to the house.

When he'd returned the photo to Joseph, his reaction was not what Ray had expected – at all. Joseph had been furious and had chased him out of the house, accusing him of rifling through his things and going into rooms he had no business entering.

Ray remembered telling Sarah, when he arrived home, that her father had completely overreacted. It was almost as though he'd had something to hide. Joseph had appeared guilty, but of what, Ray had no clue.

Sarah had told Ray to stop thinking like a cop. Her father, Joseph, wasn't guilty of anything, apart from not being a good parent and husband. Sarah knew that her mother, Elspeth, blamed the breakdown of her marriage to Joseph on the move to The Summerhouse. They had been happy in the flat above the shop, but once Sarah had been born, Elspeth had wanted them to live in The Summerhouse. However, Joseph's father, George, was still alive at the time and living there too. It was his home, and Sarah imagined it had put a strain on Joseph and Elspeth's relationship.

Ray thought that it wasn't George's presence in the large house that had caused the problems. Unlike Joseph, George was the nicest gentleman you could hope to meet. Although it had been years since he'd passed away, people in the local area still remembered the kindly old man.

Sarah also believed it was the constant trips abroad that Joseph made, in search of antiques for the shop, which led to the breakup of Joseph and Elspeth's marriage. Ray could empathise; that was what had put a strain on their own relationship in the early years, when Sarah was working in New York and they hadn't seen each other from one week to the next.

But there was something Sarah had once told him that made him wonder whether there had been more to Joseph and Elspeth's breakup than they were aware of. Apparently, Sarah's mother had said that she wouldn't have minded Joseph's trips abroad if only he'd been honest about what he was doing. It had seemed an odd thing for her to say. She'd said that she didn't think the things he came back with warranted the length of time he spent away. Sarah had been too young to remember the trips abroad, but Elspeth had once told her she'd never felt she really knew Joseph; she'd felt there were secrets that he'd kept from her.

Ray sighed, thinking that the description sounded just like Joseph; always guarded, never someone you could get to know. Ray wasn't surprised that Elspeth had left him. And he imagined that it wasn't long after she'd moved to London with Sarah that Joseph had started to neglect The Summerhouse.

With peeling white paint on the shutters and a garden that hadn't seen a gardener in decades, apart from a handyman who used a motorised lawn mower and periodically sheared the grass to a crewcut, The Summerhouse was a relic of a happier past; it had not seen happiness for a long time and seemed unlikely to see it again. Even Nate, who had recently moved back in there, couldn't wait to leave. Ray didn't know whether he wanted to get away from the house or from its occupant. He suspected a little of both.

'Grandpa? Can we stay? Please say yes.'

Ray had been staring into space for far too long. He looked at his grandson, who'd been waiting patiently, hoping his grandpa would change his mind about leaving the beach.

Lili was already heading back to Cobblers Yard. He could see her in the distance. She was walking along the promenade, holding Maisie's hand. Ray imagined she didn't want to give the other shopkeepers a reason to complain. They might think she wasn't taking running Joseph's shop seriously.

Ray glanced at his watch and stood up. 'I ought to get back

to the shop.' If he was honest, he wasn't looking forward to returning to work that afternoon. He didn't know what William was going to do for the rest of the day, stuck in an art shop, of all places. Now, if it had been Nate at that age …

Ray didn't want to think about that. Instead, his thoughts turned to something else. He'd only taken on the premises to be near Sarah. He had no experience of being a shopkeeper; but he'd thought it couldn't be that hard, running a little shop in a lovely seaside town. But Ray hadn't done his homework. The lease was expensive. The monthly business rates were astronomical. Worse still, the takings barely covered the outgoings – let alone made a profit. He'd come to the realisation that unless he extended the opening hours, which wouldn't guarantee more income, it wasn't viable to keep it going.

Ray had a pension, but he couldn't continue to subsidise the business – he needed that cash to live on. However, he was loath to give up the shop if it meant not seeing Sarah. Even catching a glimpse of her in the window, or receiving a wave and *hello* at either end of the working day as they opened and closed their shops, was better than nothing. If he didn't have the shop, there was a limit to how many times he could wander into Cobblers Yard and peer at her through the shop window or buy her flowers. At least this way he had a reason to be there. That still didn't solve his money issues, so Ray had begun another venture on the side. He was an heir hunter.

It wasn't far removed from his work as a detective in the lost art and antiques division at New Scotland Yard. With the help of the Art Loss Register, he'd sometimes reunited missing artefacts with their surprised owners. This was different. This time, he reunited lost descendants with their inheritances.

In short – he found people. The sort of people who, more often than not, wanted to be found when they discovered they might be heirs to a fortune. Wasn't that everyone's dream – to discover they were the heir to a secret estate?

Ray grimaced. It would not be his dream. It might sound fantastic on paper, but from Ray's experience, discovering you had a long-lost family invariably meant secrets. Those secrets usually meant skeletons in closets and family rifts.

Ray charged a finder's fee – a small percentage of the inheritance – but sometimes the fee was not that small, depending on the size of the estate.

It gave him immense satisfaction when he found descendants. It was something he could do from the comfort of his houseboat. The painstaking tasks consisted of building family trees as well as good old-fashioned leg work in the form of phone calls and trawling the internet. Many of his resources arose from obituaries in the national newspapers. He focused on those written by friends of deceased people who, after some investigating, turned out to have no known living relatives.

In Ray's experience, everyone had someone – the trick was to find them.

24

'Now, remember what I said.' Lili paused at the door to Joseph's shop. Ray and William had caught up with them and they'd entered Cobblers Yard together. The two children skipped around the yard.

'About Sarah?'

He nodded. 'No more flowers.'

'Good.' She smiled at him.

'How's the hand, by the way?'

'Oh,' Lili held up the palm with the black support bandage and flexed her fingers. 'It was my wrist.'

'A sprain?'

Lili shook her head. 'No, I'm afraid it's a hairline fracture, but I won't need surgery. It happened when I broke Joseph's fall.'

'So, you saw someone in A&E too?'

'Yes.' Lili frowned when she thought of that doctor with the terrible bedside manner. His only redeeming quality was how he'd treated Maisie, with kindness and compassion – until he voiced his opinion on art. Lili wouldn't be sorry if she didn't see him again. At least she'd be back in London before she needed a follow-up appointment and the wrist support came off.

Ray wondered if Lili had seen Nate when she was in the hospital. He thought they would make a perfect couple. He wanted his son to be happy, but with his work and being a single parent, he said he didn't have time for a relationship. Ray believed he was shying away from dating. No one could replace his dead wife. Ray understood that. But all he needed was the right young woman to come along. Then he'd change his mind.

Ray guessed that Lili might be single too. He'd pretended he hadn't heard the comment Maisie had made about not being told who her father was. He didn't agree with that, but Lili must have her reasons. She was down here holidaying on her own. If Lili had a partner, Ray imagined she or Maisie would have said something about them.

'So, were you taken into the minor injuries unit?' Ray asked. He was about to ask if she had seen a young doctor by the name of Nathaniel Walker: tall, dark hair, brown eyes, good-looking guy – took after his mother in that department – when Lili said, 'God, that's not an experience I want to repeat.'

'Going to hospital wouldn't be my choice either.'

'Oh, I'm not talking about that. I like the little cottage hospital, and the nurses are lovely. I'm talking about him.'

Ray looked at her. 'Him – who?'

'The doctor who saw me. I wouldn't see him again if you paid me.'

Ray wondered how many doctors had been on call that day. 'What was his name?'

'Oh, I don't know. I wasn't paying attention. He was a good-looking guy, but he was rude, obnoxious and for a doctor, his bedside manner left a lot to be desired, I can tell you.' Lili shook her head. 'He could do with learning some manners.'

Ray smiled tightly. That sounded like Nate. What a shame. On second thoughts, with Maisie's keen interest in art, the last thing she needed was William's dad spouting his views about that.

'Well, I'd better get on,' said Ray, calling William over.

'Yes, me too.'

Sarah was in The Potting Shed, arranging a window display, when she saw Lili and Ray emerge from the alleyway with the children. She stopped trimming the plants and watched them chatting to one another in the courtyard. She waited to see if Ray would follow Lili inside Joseph's shop. He didn't.

Sarah sighed in relief. Then she wondered what she was feeling so relieved about. 'Why am I even interested?' she muttered. She bent down and continued with her flower arrangement.

Ray stepped into his shop and turned to William, who was standing by his side, frowning. Ray imagined this wasn't how he wanted to spend the rest of his day, hanging around a boring art shop. He eyed his grandson. 'How would you like to watch a war movie with Grandpa?'

'Like we used to?'

It always amazed Ray what a long memory his grandson had. 'Yes, like we used to.'

'Are we going to your houseboat?'

Ray decided to close the shop early. Sod it. He was going home to spend the afternoon lazing around in front of the television. 'Yes.'

'Can I have a sleepover?'

'A what?'

'Can I sleep at your place tonight?'

'Well, I don't think your father …' Ray stopped. Considering that it was a day seemed to be full of firsts – it was the first time he'd looked after his grandson since he'd retired, the first time he'd met Lili, and the first time he'd seen sense regarding Sarah and the fact that he was smothering her – he said to William, 'Why not. I shall phone him right now and ask.'

'Yippee! I'm staying on the houseboat.'

Ray frowned. 'I do have to ask your father first.' *Very nicely*, he thought to himself. Before he phoned, he put the *Closed* sign back in the window.

Sarah was still arranging flowers for her window display when she glanced across the yard and saw Ray put the *Closed* sign back. What was he doing? Even though he was looking after William, she didn't think he'd shut the shop for the rest of the day.

A few minutes later, they stepped outside. Ray locked the door while William skipped around the yard. Sarah stared at him. Where were they going? And what were they doing together that was making her grandson so happy? She frowned. All week, she had thought up activities to do with William, planning their days to perfection. She'd taken him for a picnic on a beach up the coast and to a local museum. They'd got up to all sorts of things, some of which had cost her a small fortune, but he'd never once been that excited about any of it. For future reference, she wanted to know what he was up to with his grandpa.

She was about to step outside and follow them, her curiosity getting the better of her, when Ray crossed the courtyard toward her shop. His attention was on his grandson, so he hadn't noticed her standing there. Sarah retreated from the window and scuttled past her assistant, who was at the counter. She sprinted upstairs to the area where she had a little office. Sarah walked over to the window in the eaves, which looked out over the yard. Casting her gaze down below, she saw Ray and William about to enter the shop. Her window was slightly ajar. She heard William whining, 'But why do we have to go in there first?'

She also overheard Ray's response. 'I won't be long, I promise. I just wanted to buy some flowers.'

Although she'd kept telling him to stop buying her flowers, and had at first wished he would stop, now, she quite looked forward to it. Thanks to Ray, she always had fresh blooms at home and in her office. She glanced at the last bouquet he'd bought for her, now in a vase on her desk. Sometimes he included a brief message, such as *Have a nice day* – silly things that made her smile. She just hadn't let on how much she enjoyed them. Not yet, anyway.

She waited patiently by the window for them to leave. When she heard the bell tinkle downstairs and saw Ray and William emerging from the shop empty-handed, she raced down the stairs.

'Zoe?'

'I'm in the back, preparing an order,' Zoe called out from the storeroom.

Sarah smiled. She knew who that was for. 'I'm going out – if that's all right with you?'

Her young assistant popped her head around the door. 'Of course. You weren't meant to be here, remember? I thought you were having the week off. I didn't expect to see you in the shop.'

Sarah hadn't expected to be there either. The trouble was that without her grandson to look after, she'd found herself at a complete loose end. Although she'd wanted some time to herself, after walking along the beach she was feeling bored and lonely. It didn't help that she'd caught sight of Ray relaxing and enjoying himself in Lili's company. That was why she'd walked back to Cobblers Yard; she'd decided she might as well spend the rest of the day working.

All her life she'd worked, and now she was meant to be retired, but Sarah wasn't the type to while away the days sitting at home doing nothing. *But if I had someone to while away the days with, would that be different? Perhaps painting together, or talking about the books we're reading or things that we're passionate about?* Sarah found herself thinking about Ray. 'Well, really,' she admonished herself as she hurried out of the shop, 'what a ridiculous notion. We're getting a divorce.'

Another idea, one that was not so preposterous, entered her head. Perhaps it was time she met someone else?

Sarah followed Ray and William at a discreet distance. They popped into the co-op, which meant Sarah had to mooch about, trying to be inconspicuous, waiting for them to come out. When they walked out of the shop, she noticed her grandson was carrying a huge packet of popcorn and Ray was putting a bottle of cider into a carrier bag.

Ah – they're going to the cinema for an afternoon matinee, thought Sarah as soon as she saw the popcorn. But there was only one movie on, and she'd taken William to see it already. William hadn't really enjoyed the film much; she couldn't imagine he'd want to see it again. In fact, this past week she'd discovered he didn't seem to enjoy much of anything, unless it was fish and chips on the beach and playing with Maisie. That had been a big surprise.

She recalled meeting Lili and her daughter for the first time in the café. What a shame she hadn't made more of an effort to chat to the young lady. Perhaps if she had, William would have had fun with Maisie then, instead of when he was with his grandpa. *It's not a competition*, thought Sarah, eyeing Ray's back as William skipped along beside him, chatting animatedly – although she couldn't make out what he was talking about.

Still following, Sarah noticed them pass the cinema, then turn down a small side street toward the promenade. If they were getting in his car, Sarah could think of only one place they were going – home. Even so, she wanted to be sure. As soon as she realised that he *was* returning to his car, Sarah backtracked, walking at a pace to collect her car parked outside the entrance to Cobblers Yard. Fortunately, she hadn't left her keys in the shop like she normally did.

Sarah started the engine and did a U-turn in the middle of the road. She got a honked horn from an annoyed driver for not looking in both directions before she set off. Up ahead, she could see Ray's vehicle emerging from the side street. Her timing was perfect. She spotted his car zip across the road into the street opposite. Sarah took a left turn into the same road and followed at a discreet distance as they drove through Aldeburgh, eventually leaving the town behind.

The road continued through gently rolling countryside. Sarah guessed where he was headed; the next main seaside resort on the heritage coast was Southwold. It was somewhere Sarah enjoyed spending an afternoon, visiting the bustling high street and walking along the promenade to see the colourful beach huts. She kept promising herself that one day she'd have a cream tea on the pier.

The town was much bigger than Aldeburgh, with a sandy

beach that was perfect for families and beachside attractions for children – crazy golf and a pavilion with a bowling alley and slot machines. She knew Southwold wasn't Ray's destination. Whereas she had purchased her retirement dream in Aldeburgh – a first-floor flat with a little balcony in a grand nineteenth century villa on the promenade overlooking the sea – Ray had moved somewhere quieter. It was away from the *madding crowds*, as he called the tourists who flocked to these main coastal resorts. Interestingly, Ray had chosen a place that had, apparently, always attracted artists.

She recalled that Ray had once told her that it was the birthplace of a famous film maker who had been Oscar-nominated for his World War Two documentaries. Ray loved watching war movies, so she wasn't surprised he had unearthed that titbit of information about the place.

The small village of Walberswick, which Ray now called home, lay at the mouth of the River Blyth, forming part of Southwold Harbour. Sarah knew there was a particular reason Ray had chosen this village – smaller boats could moor in the harbour on that side of the river. This was where Ray had bought his retirement dream.

Sarah rolled her eyes when she thought of his houseboat. She didn't see the point of it. It wasn't a boat that you could move around, like a yacht or a canal barge. No. Ray had to be different; he'd gone and bought a floating house. And worse still, he wasn't alone.

The little wooden framed, clapboard, single-storey floating house wouldn't have looked out of place on the Florida Keys, but Sarah thought it did in a sleepy Suffolk village. There was at least half a dozen or more moored on the riverbank. Sarah didn't see the appeal, unless you were after a permanent dizzy feeling from the floor moving beneath your feet. She didn't know if you really did feel it moving because she had never set foot on Ray's houseboat, despite numerous invitations.

Across the river was where he'd first stayed when they'd moved down here separately. Whereas she'd found a little B&B in Aldeburgh, he'd settled for a room at The Harbour Inn in Southwold while he found his bearings. He liked that it was situated on the water's edge. The old fisherman's pub was, according to Ray, full of nautical old-world charm. Sarah wouldn't know because she'd never stepped inside.

Not to be confused with the little hotel in Aldeburgh that had the same name, The Harbour Inn in Southwold wasn't really Ray's local; there were three pubs in the village. But he enjoyed the one-mile walk – or cycle ride, if he was feeling energetic – that crossed the Bailey Bridge. That was the name of the wooden footbridge over the River Blyth which separated the village of Walberswick from its larger neighbour, Southwold.

She continued to follow his car, convinced that home was where he was headed. She slowed to let a lorry come out of a side turning, which meant the lorry was then travelling between her and Ray. Further along, Sarah found herself stuck behind a slow-moving farm vehicle, and then she had to stop at a set of temporary traffic lights where the council were doing work on the road. Eventually, she lost sight of Ray's car.

Sarah was convinced he was taking William to the houseboat in Walberswick. She didn't bother putting her foot down when the light turned green. Perhaps it was for the best that she was some minutes behind.

When she arrived in the gravel car park on the harbour in

Southwold, she spotted Ray's car, but he and William were nowhere in sight. She was at least ten minutes behind them and had thought of driving the extra mile straight to Walberswick and parking on the village green, but she risked being spotted if she arrived at their houseboat before them.

Sarah left her car and took the trail beside the riverbank. A short way along, passing The Harbour Inn, she came to the Bailey Bridge. Crossing the wooden footbridge over the River Blyth, she spotted the alternative crossing from Southwold to Walberswick; a passenger ferry in the form of a rowing boat was ferrying tourists across the river.

She left the footbridge and continued along the riverbank on the opposite side. In the distance, she could see the large harbour car park on the Walberswick side and the pretty village beyond. But she wasn't heading for the village.

Still on the riverbank path, Sarah could see small fishing trawlers and the first houseboat in the row, which belonged to Ray. The houseboats each had a long wooden walkway forming a bridge from the riverbank to the boat. Sarah didn't step onto Ray's. She hoped Ray and William didn't spot her from the path. She could see them through the double patio doors in Ray's generously sized lounge. He had switched on the television and settled down on his large squishy sofa with William. She spotted the bottle of cider on the coffee table together with the popcorn.

'Well, I never.' She was feeling rather put out after all the things she'd been doing with her grandson, not to mention the money she'd spent. William appeared to be having more fun slouching in front of the television with his grandpa. Ray had his feet up on the coffee table, looking very relaxed as he settled in for an afternoon watching the TV.

Sarah stalked off in the direction of the car, wondering what she was going to do with her free afternoon. Surprisingly, the only thing that was cheering her up was the thought of returning to the shop and seeing which bouquet Ray had chosen for her this time. She had her eye on the lovely summer roses and freesias that Zoe had suggested for another customer a few days earlier.

25

'Oh, these are gorgeous. What an exquisite arrangement of summer colours.'

Zoe smiled. 'Yes, they're lovely, aren't they? There's a note too.'

'Oh, really?'

Zoe glanced over her shoulder at The Potting Shed across the yard, hoping her boss didn't return right about now, otherwise this might get awkward.

Lili stood in the doorway with the bouquet in the crook of her arm and lifted the little envelope from inside the wrapping. She smiled. She realised that Alex must have got her text, hinting she'd like him to send her some flowers. She expected there was a big apology in that note, too. Lili decided she'd take the bouquet inside and read the note there, even though Zoe already knew what it said because she'd written it.

'You're talented,' commented Lili, admiring the roses before she thanked her. 'I'll put these in some water.'

Zoe said goodbye to the nice young lady and hurried back across the cobbled yard. Sarah had been upstairs in her office when Ray had come in to order the flowers, so she hadn't seen him. Zoe glanced over her shoulder and waved as Lili closed the door. She had been surprised to discover, just as she was about to address the note to Sarah, as usual, that the bouquet was not for Sarah but for Lili. Zoe frowned as she stepped back in the shop. It was none of her business, but she thought Ray was trying to win Sarah back. Even though her boss acted as though she didn't want the flowers each time he bought her some, Zoe got the impression that Sarah wasn't being honest with herself regarding her feelings for Ray.

Zoe made up her mind that she wouldn't mention to Sarah that Ray had been into the shop that day. It would be unusual – he called in every day – but she'd rather not be the one to tell her that he had set his sights on a young woman less than half his age. Zoe stood there at the counter, recording the order in the ledger. She didn't have to write the name of the sender, just the recipient's address.

Zoe closed the book. At least if Sarah checked, she wouldn't know where the flowers for Lili had come from – unless she asked. Zoe would cross that bridge if it came to it. But she doubted it would. There would be no reason for Sarah to suspect that Ray had sent them. Besides, although Lili was in Aldeburgh on her own with Maisie, she imagined Lili had a partner. He might have ordered the bouquet. Zoe frowned. But that wasn't true.

❖

'Maisie, come and see the flowers.' Lili's day was just getting better and better. She'd had a wonderful time eating fish and chips on the beach, watching Maisie enjoying herself playing with her new friend. Lili had also enjoyed herself, chatting to Ray.

Now she had these. She'd even found a vase in a cupboard.

Maisie skipped into the kitchen. 'Wow. Those are so pretty.'

Lili smiled. She thought so too. 'Do you want to help me arrange them in the vase?'

'Yes, please.'

Lili tucked the small unopened envelope in her back pocket and got out a pair of scissors from the drawer to trim the stems.

Ten minutes later, with the flowers arranged in a large vase, Lili picked it up and walked into the lounge. 'Now, where shall I put them?' They both looked around the room.

'There!' Maisie pointed at the window ledge overlooking the yard.

'Oh yes – what a wonderful idea.' Lili thought of the note and hoped Alex might be on his way down to Aldeburgh. The first thing he'd see was his beautiful flowers as he walked into the courtyard.

Maisie moved her painting easel away from the window for Lili.

'Thank you, sweetheart.'

Maisie chose a new blank sheet of paper and sorted through her brushes.

'What are you going to paint next?' Lili asked as she turned the vase this way and that until she was satisfied.

'The flowers.'

Lili smiled. 'What a lovely idea.' She had a thought. 'May I keep the painting when you've finished?' It was such a splendid bouquet, and it would mean a lot to Lili. If Alex couldn't make it down to Aldeburgh, she would show it to him when she returned to London. She also wanted a keepsake from her holiday with Maisie.

Maisie nodded.

Lili put her arms around Maisie's shoulders. 'Wonderful, thank you, sweetie.'

Maisie set to work while Lili made herself a drink. She had left the *Open* sign in the shop window and was listening out for the tinkle of the bell above the front door downstairs in case they had a customer. She hoped no one came in. She fancied sitting in the lounge on the sofa with a cup of tea and taking her time reading the note.

She returned from the kitchen with her drink and a glass of orange juice for her resident artist. She wondered whether, along with the gemstone necklaces Maisie and William were going to make to sell in the shop, Maisie would like to advertise some of her paintings too. She'd have to find a picture-framing place to frame them, but it was worth a thought. Lili didn't broach the idea with Maisie. She had something she wanted to do first.

Before she sat down, Lili got the little envelope out of her pocket. She grinned as she opened it.

'Oh.'

Maisie looked up from her painting and caught the look of surprise on Lili's face. She said anxiously, 'What's the matter, Auntie Lili?'

❖

'Zoe, I'm back.'

Zoe was in the storeroom preparing another bouquet. She'd heard the bell tinkle above the door. She didn't expect it to be her boss. 'Ah, Sarah, I thought …?'

'Can't stay away, can I?' Sarah joked.

As she had stood on the path, staring at the houseboat and

seeing what a good time William and Ray were having, she had felt like joining them, even though she hadn't fancied what they were watching. She couldn't see the television screen from where she was standing, but she could guess what movie was on.

Despite Ray telling her he had no idea what she was talking about, she knew where William had got his knowledge of the war. Most of it was inaccurate. She had done her best to correct him, much to the chagrin of her grandson, who didn't understand that the old B-movies he'd grown up viewing were just that – movies. Until recently, he hadn't seemed to grasp that he wasn't watching the Second World War for real.

Sarah sighed. She wouldn't have intruded even if she'd wanted to. Time spent with his grandson was precious to Ray – she understood that. She felt like it could have been Nate sitting there with him, enjoying a movie like they had done together years ago, before she and Ray sent Nate away to live with his grandfather. She knew the reason Ray had been avoiding William. Regret, that was what it was.

Sarah had thought about that all the way back to the shop. Would Nate ever forgive them? Surely, he could put the past behind him. Sarah knew they should never have sent him to live with Joseph, who couldn't forget the past either – couldn't get over his wife walking out.

What was it about The Summerhouse that made everyone who lived there miserable? Sarah was thinking of her grandfather when he was alive. To the outside world, to the community at large, and to his great-grandchild, Nate, George had been the jolliest, happiest man you could wish to meet – so unlike ill-tempered Joseph. But that was his public persona, always wanting to fit in, be accepted – be liked. That was what Sarah's mother had observed. In private, it was another matter; something Sarah had found out first-hand when she visited her father and grandfather. They didn't like visitors at The Summerhouse – not even family. After his father had died, Joseph had taken some persuading to take Nate during term time. But it meant that Sarah and Ray, busy with their careers, didn't have to worry about what crowd Nate might become involved in when they weren't around.

Sarah had known that in Aldeburgh there wasn't a lot a teenage boy could do apart from help in his grandfather's shop and have beach parties with his friends. And occasionally get into trouble for hosting house parties when Joseph was away on business. She remembered that one time Joseph had had a hissy fit and had nearly thrown Nate out before he had finished his A-Levels.

Sarah winced when she recalled that episode. As it was, Nate had refused to return to London during the holidays, getting his own back on his parents. She had no doubt he'd felt they had abandoned him.

Sarah didn't want to think about that either.

Her thoughts returned to her own grandfather, George. He had settled here with his son, Joseph, after the war. The horrors he had seen and what they had been through before they arrived in England were things they rarely spoke about. For someone who was passionate about history and art, and who had studied those subjects at university, Sarah knew little of her own family's past, at least on her dad's side.

It was something she'd like to remedy, but penetrating her father's aloof, almost secretive, persona was never going to be easy. In part, that was the reason she'd retired to Aldeburgh, along with returning to a county in England she adored. She had lived there for a brief time as a child before her parents separated, and she had decided she wanted to get to know her father properly. But getting through that wall of silence that hid her father's and her grandfather's past had proved impossible. The only thing she knew for certain about their experience in the war was that they had found themselves caught up in the Nazi occupation of the Ionian Islands.

What they had been doing in Corfu, and how they had escaped, she wasn't sure. Joseph had mentioned the holidays they had spent on the island with her grandfather's artist friends, especially an English couple who had left The Summerhouse to his father. Sarah had never known her grandma on her father's side. It was obvious why Sarah's parents wouldn't talk about it; her paternal grandmother, along with their friends, had perished in the war.

Before she'd retired here, she'd imagined that when she moved, she would be in and out of The Summerhouse, visiting her father often, getting to know him. That hadn't happened. Ray wasn't the only one with a hidden agenda when it came to taking on a shop in Cobblers Yard; Sarah had taken on The Potting Shed, which she enjoyed running, primarily to have an excuse to nip across the yard to see Joseph. To this day, apart from Nate, her dad had hardly let anyone venture near the house. Perhaps his desire for solitude was the reason he had Bella.

Zoe walked out of the storeroom, interrupting Sarah's reverie. She'd been standing at the counter in her shop, thinking all this as she idly opened the ledger.

Zoe took one look at the book and said, 'I think I'll go out for lunch today.'

Sarah looked at her. That was a first. She normally sat in the storeroom with a homemade sandwich and a cup of tea, reading her latest Mills & Boon novel from the library. Although Zoe was still at school studying for her A-Levels, she seemed to have an old head on young shoulders. Zoe was already slipping on her coat.

'Okay.' Sarah noticed she hadn't mentioned the bouquet she'd been making up for Ray. 'How are the orders going?'

'I just completed one that's being sent to Southwold,' Zoe said in a hurry. She did an about-turn before she left. 'I could run it over there straightaway when I return if your car is free.'

'Er – yes, okay.'

With that, Zoe whipped around and disappeared out of the door.

Sarah stared after her. 'Someone's in a hurry,' she said, raising an eyebrow. Zoe loved her Mills & Boon novels. She could never wait to get back to them during her lunch break. Sarah didn't know whether she was single, although she imagined she was always on the lookout. 'Perhaps someone has got a hot date.'

Thinking of dates, Sarah had a date with a bouquet. It was peculiar that Zoe hadn't mentioned Ray's order. She knew that it was what he'd been in the shop for that morning, just like every other day. Perhaps Zoe was behind. Sarah opened the ledger to see how many orders they'd had that day. There were two. One for an old lady in Southwold, and one for—

Sarah slowly raised her eyes and looked towards the door. *He sent my bouquet to the antiques shop.*

Sarah walked over to the front door and peered through the glass panes to the outlet across the courtyard. The afternoon had turned out overcast, so the lights were on in her father's store.

There was also a light on in the flat upstairs. Sarah opened the door and stepped outside. There, in the first-floor window, she spied a vase with an enormous arrangement of summer blossoms.

'You fool,' she admonished herself when the penny dropped. 'He didn't send your bouquet to The Potting Shed – he sent it to *her.*' Sarah couldn't wait for Zoe to return, so she could find out what was going on. What she really wanted to know was if he had included a message with the flowers. And what it said.

Or did she?

Sarah frowned and stepped back inside, slamming the door behind her.

26

'What does it say?' Maisie asked when Lili told her the flowers had come from Ray with a little card. Although Lili was surprised that they weren't from Alex, as she'd first thought, she couldn't help but laugh when she saw the note, commenting under her breath, 'Silly old fool.'

Even though Maisie wouldn't understand the message, she read it to her, anyway. 'To a wise young owl, from a silly old fool, you're right: I shall stop sending flowers. I'm done with that. I'm sending them to you instead. It's true *you* can teach an old dog new tricks. Thank you, Lili. You're the best. Hope you like them.'

Lili put the little card on the windowsill next to the bouquet. She hadn't expected him to send her flowers, but she hoped the advice about giving Sarah some space worked. Lili looked around the room; there was a nice spot on the table for another vase. She was still anticipating a delivery from Alex.

Lili made herself another tea and sat down on the sofa, watching Maisie draw a sketch of the flowers. Although they weren't from Alex, she still wanted to keep the painting. What Maisie was creating would be a stunning design and a lovely reminder of her new friendships here in town.

Lili had been sitting there, mesmerised, watching Maisie at work, when she noticed it was growing dark outside. She looked at her watch. She was just thinking that they hadn't had a single customer all afternoon when the bell tinkled downstairs. Lili bounced off the sofa. 'We've got a customer.' Perhaps it was Ray calling in to see if she'd received her delivery, or Alex making a surprise visit.

Lili hurried down the narrow stairs. She walked into the shop and saw a stranger standing by the door. The young man wore a bright orange reflective jacket. When he spotted Lili, he said, 'Oh, you must be new. Is Joseph around?'

'Can I help?' Lili asked warily.

'Sorry, but I don't normally come to the shop. I'm not sure what's going on because he's always at home for his delivery slot.'

'Delivery slot?'

'From the local co-op. We deliver to his home.'

'Oh, I see.'

'Is he here?'

Lili shook his head. 'I'm afraid he's in hospital.'

'Oh, dear. Nothing serious, I hope?'

'He had a fall.'

The driver looked at the bags by his feet. 'What shall I do with these? I have another delivery in five minutes.'

Lili glanced at the carrier bags, which reminded her she hadn't been to buy groceries yet. There was only some milk in the fridge and a packet of biscuits in a kitchen cupboard. Eating out for another week would be expensive. The point of self-catering was that she could save money. Lili eyed the shopping bags. She didn't know what Joseph had bought, but he might just have saved her a trip to the supermarket.

'Look, I'll take them. Joseph won't need the food while he's in hospital. I'm minding the shop at the moment.'

'You're looking after the shop? Well, I'm glad to hear it. Joseph is getting on. He could do with an extra pair of hands.'

'Oh, I'm not here permanently.'

The young delivery driver eyed the good-looking young woman and mumbled, 'That's a shame.'

'I'll pay for the groceries.'

'It was an online shop. They're already paid for.'

'Ah, well in that case, I'll pay Joseph for them.'

He shrugged. 'Okay, that sounds fair. I'd better go.' He lingered in the doorway. 'Are you new in town?'

Lili nodded, wondering why he was asking.

'There's bingo at the pub and they do nice food. Would you like to—?'

Maisie chose that moment to run down the stairs shouting, 'I'm hungry! When are we going shopping?'

Lili turned and smiled at Maisie. She turned back to the young man and caught him staring at Maisie. 'Well, I'd best be off.' He backed out of the door. 'Nice to meet you.'

Lili smiled. 'Likewise.' She guessed the young man wasn't as pleased to meet Maisie. Even though they'd only just met, she had a feeling he'd been about to embarrass himself by asking her on a date. Lili was flattered but relieved that Maisie's impeccable timing had saved her from that rather awkward conversation where she said no.

'Who was that?' Maisie asked.

'That was a delivery driver, delivering—'

Maisie spotted the plastic bags from the local supermarket. 'Food!' She rushed over and looked inside. She found a sheet of paper and tossed it to one side. Lili picked it up and discovered that it was the itemised bill. 'Come on, let's take these upstairs and see what we've got,' she said. Before she did so, she checked the bill and scribbled an IOU for the amount, popping it on top of the cash register so that she would remember to withdraw the money and pay for the groceries.

Upstairs in the small galley kitchen, Lili started unpacking the shopping. She didn't know what she was expecting an elderly gentleman to buy, but she was pleasantly surprised.

'Pasta!' Maisie exclaimed. 'And chocolate buttons!'

'Chocolate buttons?'

'Joseph likes chocolate buttons, obviously,' said Maisie matter-of-factly.

On the way up the stairs, Lili told her that this was Joseph's delivery, but rather than it going to waste, they would use it and Lili would pay for it.

'Ice lollies!' Maisie's eyes went wide.

So did Lili's. *Stranger and stranger*, she thought.

'Oh wow – coco-pops!' Maisie held up the box of breakfast cereal. 'My favourite!'

The rest of the shopping was what Lili expected. Basics like bread, tea, coffee, sugar, some cheese, and porridge oats. There were quite a few ready meals – items she imagined an old man would order who couldn't cook or didn't have the inclination. The meals weren't what Lili would buy, but she wasn't complaining. There was plenty of tinned food too, from sardines to beans and soup. They'd easily get by on this for a week.

'What's this?' Maisie asked, holding up a tin she didn't recognise.

'Here, let me see.'

Maisie looked inside the bag. 'There are loads more just like it.'

Lili stared at the can. 'Oh, god, it's pet food.'

'But we haven't got a pet.'

'I know.' Lili looked inside the bag. 'But Joseph has.'

Maisie glanced about her. 'I haven't seen a pet.' She called out, 'Here kitty, kitty, kitty.'

Lili turned the can over in her hand. 'It's not a cat, Maisie, and it's not here.'

Maisie stopped what she was doing. 'Joseph has a dog?' She was getting excited. 'I've always wanted a puppy.'

Lili looked at the size of the can of dog food, then at the number of cans. She had the distinct impression it wasn't a small dog. She looked at Maisie. 'I don't think it's a puppy, sweetheart.' *Or a cute little dog*, she thought. It was a big dog, and it was a hungry dog.

'Where is it?' Maisie asked, before answering her own question. 'We have to go to Joseph's house to feed his dog. He will be hungry.'

Lili wasn't going anywhere. And she didn't have to. It wasn't her responsibility. The family could sort out the hound. She left the can of food on the kitchen worktop, walked down the stairs and out of the door, intending to call on Ray. She frowned when she noticed there were no lights on in the shop and the *Closed* sign was in the window. *Damn!* she thought.

Lili turned on her heel and crossed the courtyard. At least The Potting Shed was still open.

'I'm afraid she's gone to Thorpeness to do a delivery. I said I'd do it, but she insisted. She said she wouldn't be back for the rest of the day.'

'Oh.'

'Is there something I can help you with?'

'Is someone feeding Joseph's dog?'

'Joseph has a dog?' Zoe couldn't imagine Joseph with a pet. 'Sarah never mentioned it, but then, between you and me, the old man doesn't like visitors. She said so herself, even family, so I don't think she's been up to The Summerhouse in an age.'

'Can you phone her and ask?'

Zoe felt that she would rather not. When she'd returned to The Potting Shed after lunch, Sarah had been in a mood – she could tell. It made her wonder if her boss had looked in the ledger. But even if she had, how would she know it was Ray who had sent flowers to Lili? Unless she had been at the window upstairs and had spotted Ray entering the shop; Zoe hadn't considered that until now.

She chose not to tell Lili the other reason Sarah wasn't returning to work this afternoon. She was going to visit Joseph in hospital. It made Zoe wonder if she wanted to find out more about Joseph's so-called friend who was minding his shop.

She looked at Lili, 'Sure, I'll pass on the message,' she lied. Lili would be the last person Sarah wished to hear from right now.

'Great. When you've spoken to Sarah, can you let me know?'

Zoe nodded, although she had no intention of phoning her boss. Besides, where had Lili got the idea Joseph owned a dog? She was quite sure Lili was mistaken.

❖

Lili returned to Joseph's shop. With no customers all afternoon, Lili closed a little early to have some tea with Maisie. She cooked pasta and made a tomato sauce with one of the tins of tomatoes. She added some herbs she'd discovered in the kitchen cupboard and a dash of extra virgin olive oil. With melted cheese on top, and a sprig of basil from a packet she'd also found in the groceries as she unpacked, it was making her mouth water. It looked delicious. They sat at the old oak table by the window in the lounge to eat.

The food was delicious. The ingredients she'd used were not cheap; there was expensive extra virgin olive oil, Italian pasta, and a good quality cheese which added to the richness of the flavours.

But Lili did not enjoy her meal. *Am I a bad person for wishing Maisie would shut up?* she thought. Lili did not want Maisie to bring up the subject of the hungry dog one more time. She hadn't stopped talking about it all through their meal, which was putting Lili off her food.

'I have spoken to Zoe, and she is going to tell Sarah.'

'Yes, but what if she doesn't come back to the shop?'

Lili hadn't told her that Sarah wasn't returning that afternoon. Zoe hadn't given her Sarah's mobile phone number. If she had, Maisie would be pestering her to try again if she couldn't get through.

'What if Zoe forgets to tell her?'

Lili rolled her eyes. Maisie was still on about the hound. 'I'm sure she won't forget.'

'But what if she does?'

Lili sighed. 'I asked Zoe to let me know whether Sarah is feeding the dog.'

Maisie looked satisfied with the answer for all of two minutes until she started on about it again.

'But what if Zoe forgets?'

Lili, not one to lose her temper, was getting very irritated. 'Look, Maisie, I'm sure Zoe won't forget to speak to Sarah or let me know about the blasted dog!'

Maisie stared at Lili and fell silent.

Lili hadn't meant to get cross, but it had the desired effect.

'I'm sorry, Maisie. I never meant to snap at you.'

Maisie stared out of the window as she finished her pasta. Lili was about to ask her whether she'd completed her picture, when Maisie said, 'Zoe is locking up the flower shop.'

Lili glanced out of the window. 'So, she is.'

'Will she come over and let you know about Joseph's dog?'

'I'm sure she will.' But as soon as the words were out of her mouth, she saw Zoe turn in the other direction to head out of the yard. Before Lili could stop her, Maisie had unlatched the window and shouted out, 'Zoe!'

Lili winced as Maisie's voice echoed around the quiet courtyard. The lights were still on in the music shop. Reggie opened his shop door at the sound of someone shouting out.

Zoe turned around. Lili had no choice but to wave her over, calling out, 'Can you wait a moment?' She noticed Zoe saying something to Reggie; probably telling him it was nothing. He walked back into his shop and closed the door.

Lili reluctantly left her dinner and trudged down the stairs, Maisie hot on her heels. Lili opened the shop door. Zoe was standing outside, looking sheepish. Lili had an idea that she was intending to leave for the day without calling on her. She'd forgotten about the dog.

'I didn't forget about our conversation, Lili. Her mobile phone is switched off.' It was not a fib. In the end, she had tried to call, feeling guilty about saying she would when she had no intention of doing so.

'Did you leave her a message?'

'Not possible, I'm afraid. Her voicemail box is full.' Zoe knew who she had to thank for that. Ray kept leaving Sarah messages and clogging up her mailbox. Sarah had said she'd told him to stop many times, but it had fallen on deaf ears.

Zoe eyed Lili. *Now Sarah is going to get her wish*, she thought. She wondered what Lili saw in a man approaching sixty. *Unless she likes houseboats and pensioners*, she thought, rather uncharitably. Ray had some things going for him; he was a retired police officer with, she imagined, a good pension, and he had his heir-hunting business, which sounded as though it might be quite lucrative. The houseboat sounded good too. He often chatted about it when he was in the shop buying flowers for Sarah.

'Well, thanks for trying, Zoe. I'll try to catch her tomorrow.' Lili thought the dog would just have to go hungry for another day, although she got the impression that Zoe didn't believe Joseph had a pet.

Zoe shook her head. 'I'm afraid my boss doesn't work here at the weekends. She'll be back on Monday.'

'But what about the dog?' Maisie whined.

Yes, what about the dog? thought Lili as she closed the door. Zoe couldn't do anything about it. She'd done her best. They both had. What more could she do? Lili meant to ask if there were any other relatives nearby that she could call on, but Zoe was already across the other side of the courtyard.

'Lili,' Maisie whined, fiddling with the keys, which were hanging from the lock on the inside of the shop door. Lili glanced at them. There weren't just keys to the shop on that keyring. Maisie knew there was a latchkey too. Lili had an idea what Maisie was thinking before she even said it.

'Maisie, we are not going to Joseph's house.'

'But why not?'

There was another possibility that had only just occurred to Lili. She looked at Maisie. 'Zoe doesn't think Joseph has a dog. What if there was a mix-up and the local co-op delivered the wrong shopping bags?' It made perfect sense. Did she really see an old man in his early eighties eating cocoa pops, ice lollies and chocolate buttons, and cooking meals like pasta with sprigs of parsley? Something didn't add up. She smiled at Maisie, convinced that was it. 'I'm going to finish my pasta.'

Maisie folded her arms, a look of defiance crossing her delicate features. 'I'm taking the dog food downstairs.'

Lili shrugged. 'Suit yourself.'

Maisie smiled to herself. She had a plan.

27

Lili finished her meal in peace, listening to the patter of feet as Maisie carried the tins of dog food down the stairs, a few at a time, in carrier bags. She heard the clang of the tins being deposited on the wooden floor by the shop door.

'Good girl,' said Lili to herself. She'd think about what to do with them later.

This had worked out for the best. According to Zoe, it sounded as though Joseph didn't like visitors up at his house, anyway. Lili knew she was already taking a big liberty, staying in the flat and running Joseph's store, without intruding on his home too.

Lili put her knife and fork down and stared out of the window into the little cobbled courtyard. Lili saw Reggie at his front door, locking up his shop before going home. As he turned around, he spotted her in the window and waved. Lili smiled and waved back.

All went quiet downstairs until Lili thought she heard Maisie's voice. Who was she talking to?

Lili was sure she'd locked the door and turned the *Closed* sign around after Zoe had left. She rose from her seat, left the dirty dish in the kitchen and walked down the stairs.

'Yes, please,' Maisie was saying, 'I am at the old antiques shop in Cobblers Yard.'

Lili raised an eyebrow as she stepped off the last stair into the shop and caught Maisie on the phone. 'Maisie?'

She had her back to Lili. Maisie whirled around, still talking down the receiver. 'Cool, thank you.' She put the phone down and looked sheepishly at Lili.

'Who was that? Was it a customer?'

Maisie pursed her lips and looked at the floor.

'Maisie, who was that on the phone?'

'I called a taxi.'

'You did what?! Why did you call a taxi?' And more to the point, where had she found the number of a local taxi company? As if reading her mind, Maisie said, 'I Googled a taxi company in Aldeburgh.'

'How did you Google—?' Lili sighed and touched the back pocket of her jeans. Her mobile was missing. Lili held out her hand. 'Give it back, Maisie.'

Maisie reluctantly handed Lili her phone. The number of the taxicab was still on the screen. She asked again, 'Maisie, why did you call a taxi?'

Maisie's eyes roved over to the front door where she'd left four carrier bags, each containing cans of pet food. 'I'm going to Joseph's house to feed his dog.'

Lili threw her arms up in the air. 'How many times do I have to tell you? Joseph doesn't have a dog!'

'How do you know for sure?'

'I just do – all right?'

Lili was just reaching for the phone to cancel the taxi when she had a thought. She knew how to find out. 'I'm going to find out, once and for all, if there is a dog.' Why it hadn't occurred to her in the first place, she had no idea. Lili Googled the number for the cottage hospital. She hoped the nice nurse whom she had spoken with when she was last there was on her shift.

Lili got straight through to the ward. 'I'm afraid there's someone with him now, but I will pass on the message.'

'Oh.' Lili paused on the phone, but the nurse wouldn't divulge if he had a visitor or whether he was being seen by a member of the medical team.

'It wouldn't do any good, anyway.'

Lili frowned, losing the thread of the conversation because Maisie was pulling on her sleeve, wanting to listen in. 'I'm sorry, what do you mean?'

'There won't be any point in me asking Joseph that question.'

'Why? Is he asleep?'

'No, I'm afraid he's suffering from delirium.'

'Delirium?'

'Confusion. It came on today. It can be quite common in the elderly.'

'You mean he's got dementia?'

'No, this is different. I'm sure he will recover. That's what we've told the family member.'

So, it was Sarah visiting this afternoon. That made sense. It was probably why she wouldn't be returning to the shop and the reason she'd switched off her phone.

'A urinary tract infection could make him disorientated. It might simply be the shock of the fall or the drugs we're giving him. We're not ruling anything out. It's possible he could have had a mini stroke.'

'A stroke!'

'They're running tests.'

'Will he recover?'

'Yes, the doctor is confident he will, but it could take a few days, at least.'

Lili chewed her bottom lip. She looked around the shop. 'You mean, like a week?'

'Could be. Maybe longer than that.'

'What are they saying?' Maisie whispered.

Lili put the phone to her other ear and held up a finger to her mouth in a shushing motion.

'He is only allowed one visitor at a time, but visiting hours are between six and eight, so do pop along.'

'He can still have visitors?'

'Oh yes, it's encouraged. Even though he is confused, it's good for him to see a familiar face.'

Lili shook her head. Seeing her wouldn't do him any good, unless … she remembered he'd called her Alena. 'Can he talk?'

'When he first came to in hospital, he was quite lucid, but I got the impression he wasn't one for conversation. Now, it's the reverse. That can happen, along with hallucinations. He talks to people who are not in the room.'

'Does he?' Lili was thinking perhaps he'd talked about Alena.

Maisie grabbed her arm, miming, *What about the dog?*

Lili sighed. 'Look, if his daughter is visiting now, please can you ask her if Joseph has a—'

'Oh, sorry, I have to go.' The nurse clicked off, and the line went dead.

Lili was replacing the handset when there was a knock at the door. She looked up and saw a middle-aged woman peering through the shop window. Lili unlocked the door. 'I'm afraid we're closed.'

'Ah, I'm not after an antique. Someone ordered a taxi.'

Lili rolled her eyes at Maisie. Now she had to pay for a cab she didn't need. 'Look, I'm sorry there's been a mistake. We don't need a—'

'Yes, we do!' yelled Maisie, running to the door. 'We need to go to The Summerhouse to feed Joseph's dog.'

'For goodness' sake, Maisie.' Lili could feel her temper fraying. 'For one thing, the taxi driver will need the address of The Summerhouse, and we still don't know if Joseph has a—'

'I don't need the address,' the driver cut in. 'I know The Summerhouse. Over the years, we've often collected Joseph from the station, when he's been on his travels, and taken him home. He doesn't travel that much now though.'

'Does Joseph have a dog?' Maisie asked.

'Yes, I believe he does.'

Maisie turned around, folded her arms, cocked her head to one side and gave Lili her best *I told you so*, smug expression, looking like a proper tween.

'I haven't seen it myself, mind, but I've heard it. Proper Hound of the Baskervilles.'

Maisie frowned. She didn't have a clue what that meant. But Lili did. *Oh God – that's all I need*, she thought.

Maisie picked up two bags of pet food. 'Come on.'

Lili stood there, debating what to do. How long could a dog go without a meal? She looked at the taxi driver. 'Can you just give me a moment?' Lil got out her phone and searched for information. She sighed in relief when she read that they could survive a few days, providing they had fresh water to hand. Lili's face dropped. What if the dog had run out of water? Lili reluctantly grabbed her bag and coat. She picked up the other carrier on the way out of the door and followed Maisie and the taxi driver through Cobblers Yard to the waiting car. That was when Lili realised that she didn't have any cash.

'It's fine. We accept card payments.'

The driver put the bags of dog food in the boot before climbing in the car. She turned to her passengers in the back. 'We heard that Joseph was in hospital and that a friend was minding the store. That will be you, then.' And the inevitable question followed, 'So, how did you meet?'

Lili went bright red. Word was getting around the community.

When Lili didn't answer the question, she commented, 'Joseph doesn't have any friends.'

Lili rolled her eyes. 'I know.'

'Nice of you to feed his dog.'

Not really, thought Lili. She leaned forward in her seat. 'Out of interest, you don't happen to know what make – I mean *breed* – that dog in *The Hound of the Baskervilles* is, do you?' Lili didn't have the faintest idea about the different breeds. She'd never had a pet.

The taxi driver laughed hysterically.

Lili frowned. She got the impression the woman wasn't taking the question seriously. Lili had the impulse to Google it on her phone but resisted. She was already feeling enough trepidation at meeting the dog as it was. Minding Joseph's shop was one thing, but this was not what she had signed up for.

Lili held the keys so tightly in her hand that her knuckles turned white. She tried to relax. 'How far is it?' She glanced out of the window. They'd driven past the cinema and taken a left turn down a little side street to the promenade. After another left turn, the car passed the hotel where they'd stayed. She recognised the single-track road ahead, which ran parallel to the beach on one side and had heathland on the other.

'Hey, it's the House in the Clouds.' Maisie had ducked her head and was looking up, out of the front window. The lights were on in the house. Lili smiled. That was quite something, seeing it lit up as dusk approached.

'So, The Summerhouse is in Thorpeness,' Lili said in surprise. She had assumed it was in Aldeburgh.

The taxi driver nodded. 'Lovely place – bit run down, though, judging by the overgrown ivy around the double gates. They're coming off their hinges. I've never seen the house myself. The old man always insists on being dropped off at the entrance to his property, even though I tell him it's no trouble driving on up to the house.'

As I'm paying for the taxi, Lili thought, *I'm not walking those bags of dog food up the drive.* 'Well, this time you can take us right on up to the front door.'

She caught the cab driver grinning. 'Did you know that Joseph has lived there practically all his life?'

Before Lili asked her how she knew that, she said, 'I love local history, so I went online because I wanted to discover what the old place looked like. I assumed it had sold at some point in the past, and I could pull it up on *Rightmove,* but the property hasn't changed hands for decades. Then I remembered Joseph mentioned he'd lived in the house since he was a boy.'

Lili smiled. 'Well, today you will get to see the place. I hope The Summerhouse isn't a disappointment.'

28

It wasn't long before they turned into an unmade road just around the corner from the boating lake. As they drove up the street, Lili had an uneasy feeling. All this seemed familiar. There were older detached properties, of differing styles, along the route. Judging by their sizes, Lili guessed they ranged from two- to four-bedroomed. The road, Lili discovered, was a cul-de-sac. It ended at a pair of wrought iron double gates overgrown with ivy and set in a six-foot-high crumbling red brick wall. All this seemed familiar. She frowned. She was certain she'd been here before but could not remember when.

'Researching online, I found a photo of the place from the 1920s when it was first built. It was an Arts and Crafts house.'

Maisie looked at the taxi driver. 'What's an Arts and Crafts house?'

Lili smiled. Maisie had taken the words right out of her mouth.

'That is a good question. I had to look it up myself when I first heard the term. Apparently, in contrast to the ornate styles of the Victorian era, the Arts and Crafts homes are more individual, using traditional craftsmanship and locally sourced materials in construction. From what I've read, they share certain features. If you see a property with a gabled roof, chances are it's been built in the style of an Arts and Crafts house.'

'So, I imagine the property looks quite unusual,' commented Lili, wishing she didn't already have a good idea what the place looked like from memory.

'Oh, yes.'

There were a lot of differing styles visible, from mock Tudor to beach houses, bungalows, and terraced properties, so she imagined Joseph's house would not look out of place.

As they entered the grounds of the property, the taxi driver commented, 'I bet if you tried to close those gates, they would fall off their hinges.'

Although the drive wasn't long, it looped around so that the house didn't immediately come into view. Lili stared out of the window at the gardens. She imagined how she could transform the grounds into a beautiful country garden. There were two huge mature willow trees, their branches almost reaching the ground. It resembled a garden belonging to a house somewhere in the Deep South in the US, like Tennessee, rather than an English coastal seaside resort.

Lili sucked in a breath as The Summerhouse came into view. It was just as she remembered it.

'Isn't that something?' said the taxi driver. She brought the car to a halt on the drive, in front of the house.

'It looks creepy,' Maisie said, not making a move to get out of the car.

'It's a bit run down – that's all,' Lili commented.

The taxi driver raised an eyebrow. 'Just a bit? It's not what comes to mind when you say the word *Summerhouse* – is it?'

Lili imagined what the village must have looked like when it was formally opened in 1914. Thorpeness had been developed as a holiday village with mock Tudor homes, a beautiful boating lake, and a country club set in beautiful grounds, so it wasn't surprising that Joseph's parents had chosen to build a holiday home here.

The house had a dark red brick exterior under an unusual gabled roof; it was the signature architectural features of an Arts and Crafts house. It had a central front door and two wooden Georgian-style windows with inset panes of glass set either side of the main entrance. It was three storeys high, with dormer windows and a wraparound porch with peeling paintwork.

'I like it,' Lili said, admiring the detached residence, although she couldn't shake the feeling that she had been there before. She turned to the taxi driver, who had stopped talking. 'Are you disappointed?' she asked.

'It's smaller than I expected.'

'Smaller?' Lili said in surprise. She wasn't disappointed at all. Her attention had been captured by the long, single-storey structure attached to the side of the house. Although it too was red brick, it had four impressive floor-to-ceiling windows inset in decorative arches, and a glass roof. Now Lili knew for sure that she had been here before; it wasn't something she'd forget in a hurry.

'What is that?' Maisie asked, pointing at the unusual structure. 'It looks kind of like a greenhouse.'

Lili looked at Maisie. 'You know, I think you're right.' Even from the car, Lili could see some plants in the window. It resembled a conservatory from a bygone era. 'Why don't we go and look?' By the expression on Maisie's face, Lili guessed she'd need a bit of encouragement to get out of the taxi. For someone who had been keen to go there to feed the dog, Maisie's enthusiasm had taken flight as soon as she'd seen the house. It didn't help that storm clouds were gathering, which made everything feel more ominous and forbidding.

Lili didn't want to go in the house either, but she was there now. She got out of the car, then remembered to ask the taxi driver if she would wait. 'I'm only nipping inside to feed Joseph's dog.'

The cab driver shook her head. 'Sorry – there's another fare.'

Maisie wasn't shifting from the back seat. 'Do we have to go in there?'

Lili looked at her. *You've got to be kidding me*, she thought. 'You were the one who phoned the taxi so you could come here and feed the dog!' she said.

The taxi driver glanced over her shoulder at the little girl sitting in the back. 'I can come back in about thirty minutes.'

'Perfect,' Lili said, reaching in to take Maisie's hand. 'Come on.'

Maisie reluctantly got out of the taxi.

Lili stood on the porch with the bags of dog food and the keys. As she watched the taxi disappear down the drive, she couldn't decide whether it was a good thing or not that they hadn't heard a dog barking. Was it dead? Lili didn't want to think about that. Was it standing on the other side of the door, sniffing, waiting to pounce as soon as they walked in? Lili raised an eyebrow. Quite possibly.

Lili tried a couple of keys until she found the one for the front door. As she turned the key, she listened. There was no sound of growling or sniffing coming from inside the house. She opened the door slowly, but there was no sign of a dog appearing out of the gloom further down the hallway. Lili kept hold of the door and found the light switch. She switched it on, surprised by what she saw. Although old-fashioned, it was a generous-sized entrance with warm wooden parquet flooring, cream wood panelling on the walls and a colourful Persian rug. Under the stairs was a cosy nook with a small oak bookcase, an easy chair and a floor lamp with a large green lampshade.

'This is nice,' commented Lili.

She'd had a different expectation of the inside of the house, going by the rundown appearance of the grounds and the peeling paint on the shutters. There were white panelled doors on the left and right, and a wide, sweeping carpeted staircase at the end of the hallway that rose to the first floor. She could see there were balustrades upstairs along the landing, with doors to the rooms visible. All of which she remembered.

'It's okay, I guess,' Maisie responded. 'Let's find the dog.'

Lili didn't step into the house.

'What's the matter?' Maisie asked.

'I've been here before.'

Before Lili could stop her, Maisie had opened the door wide and run straight into the room on the right. Lili shut the front door and followed her into a cosy lounge with cream-painted walls and original wooden flooring. There were two neutral deep-cushioned loose-covered sofas offset with colourful cushions, a couple of old Regency-style chairs, and a handcrafted antique oak sideboard. Lili walked up to the framed painting over the open fireplace.

Maisie came running up to her. 'The dog isn't in here.'

Lili had gathered that. She could imagine that The Hound of

the Baskervilles, if asleep, would not still be dozing on the sofa with Maisie darting into the room. As she glanced around, something struck Lili as odd. There was not a single framed photo of Joseph or his family.

She shrugged. 'Let's try another room.' Lili stepped back into the hall and did an about-turn when she realised Maisie wasn't with her. Lili poked her head around the door. 'Maisie?'

Maisie was standing in front of the fireplace. She turned around, an odd expression on her face. Lili stepped into the room. 'What is it?'

Maisie was studying the painting. 'Look.'

'Yes, it is a fine piece of artwork. Now, let's see if the dog is in—'

'I recognise it from my book.'

'Do you,' Lili said flatly. She doubted it. That book was full of colour photos of Rembrandts and Constables, and other famous and valuable works of art. Besides, even if it *was* in the book, the picture on the wall was probably a copy. There must be dozens floating around the world.

Lili didn't have time for discussions like this. What if Sarah popped round? It might be awkward if Sarah discovered she had just let herself into the house without asking. But she did have the dog food, and Zoe had tried to contact Sarah first.

They both crossed the hallway to the other door. Maisie tried running ahead. This time, Lili grabbed her hand. 'I'll go first.'

'Why?'

'In case the dog isn't friendly.'

Maisie looked at her warily. 'You mean it might bite.'

'I don't know, maybe.'

Maisie held back as Lili opened the door a crack. Nothing

jumped out, so she walked into the room. It was a large kitchen with shaker-style cupboards that looked quite modern – Lili couldn't imagine that this was the original kitchen. She opened another door at the far end of the room and found a pantry with assorted items. She unpacked the carrier bags and placed the tins of dog food on a spare shelf, keeping one back.

She turned around and jumped with fright at the sight of a shape on the floor in the gloom. It was Maisie on her hands and knees. 'I found the dog bowls,' she said.

Lili switched on the light. 'Good.' She had an idea. She could leave the food and water in the bowls for the dog to find. Perhaps it was asleep upstairs on a bed. That was what pets got up to when their owners were out, didn't they? She'd make sure she left the kitchen door ajar before they left.

Lili held her finger to her lips. 'Shh. Perhaps the dog is asleep somewhere in the house. We wouldn't want to wake him up.'

'Her,' Maisie replied.

'Pardon?'

'It's a *she*.'

'How do you know?'

Maisie picked up a bowl. 'Look, there's a name on the side of the bowl. It says Bella.'

'Bella.' Lili relaxed. 'That's a pretty name.' She was thinking of the saying: *its bark is worse than its bite*. Some small dogs were very vocal. She decided that Bella sounded like a small dog. Cute and harmless.

The taxi driver had said that she hadn't been up to the house, which meant that even though she'd heard the dog barking, she hadn't set eyes on Bella. Even so, Lili didn't fancy being barked or growled at, so she left the kitchen door closed while she found a can opener and scooped the dog food into a bowl. Lili placed it on the floor. 'There, I think we've done our good deed for the day.'

Maisie did her bit, filling the other dish with fresh water from the sink. She put it down on the floor beside Bella's meal.

'Right, we can go now,' Lili announced. She looked at her watch. Although they'd only been there ten minutes, Lili was keen to get out of the house. She didn't mind standing outside waiting for the taxi to return. It was one thing helping in the shop, but this felt more of an intrusion into a stranger's life, even though she'd only come here to do him a favour.

'Shouldn't we check Bella is okay?'

'I don't think so, honey.' Besides, Maisie would insist on coming too, and she wouldn't want her to get upset if they discovered the dog was … well, a goner.

Lili told a little fib to placate Maisie. 'We'll come back tomorrow and check Bella has eaten her food,' she said. She was going to do no such thing. Instead, she intended to see Ray in his shop and tell him about the dog.

'Oh, okay.'

Lili was just stepping out of the door, feeling less guilty about entering Joseph's home, when she glanced to her right and noticed the conservatory. They were taking care of his dog, but what about his indoor plants? Had someone been round to water them? A voice in her head said, *do not go back in the house.*

29

'Maisie, come back here right now!' Lili said through gritted teeth from her hiding place behind a large wicker chair in the conservatory. They'd been huddling together behind the chair when Maisie had stood up. Lili had reached for her, but she was too late. 'Maisie – I mean it!' Lili's heard her own voice shaking.

'It's all right, Auntie Lili. She won't bite.'

'Then why is she growling?'

Every time Lili's head popped up from behind the rattan furniture, the dog turned in her direction and let out a long, low growl.

'Maisie!' Lili watched in horror as she made her way toward the dog.

'Good puppy – you're such a good dog.'

But she isn't a puppy, thought Lili, *and she isn't a good dog*. Not. At. All.

How could she have known the hound had been shut inside the conservatory? She hadn't been ready for the large black shape that had come hurtling towards them. Instead of turning on her heel and running out of the room, she had dived for cover with Maisie's hand in hers.

Now they were in a pickle. The animal was standing in the centre of the room. There was no way past it.

'Good girl,' Maisie said. 'You're such a clever dog.'

'What are you doing?' Lili whispered, looking at the animal. It resembled a German shepherd.

'I learnt this from television. Give them some treats every time they do as they're told.'

'What treats?'

Maisie shrugged. 'I don't know. I haven't got any.'

'So, how are we going to get out of here?'

Lili stared in horror as Maisie neared the dog, holding out her hand. 'Maisie – don't!' Lili winced, knowing what was coming next. Maisie was going to stroke it. Lili shut her eyes.

'Good doggy. Well done, Bella.' Maisie said again, her voice low and calm.

Lili didn't hear it growling. She opened her eyes and couldn't believe what she was seeing. Maisie was sitting on the floor crossed-legged in front of Bella, who had sat down and appeared to be enjoying the attention. Maisie was stroking her. 'There, you see? There's nothing to be afraid of.'

Lili wasn't sure whether the comment was directed at her or the hound.

Bella lay down, head on paws, looking relaxed. She had grey whiskers and grey fur around her snout; Lili guessed she was not a young dog. Perhaps she had been a guard dog all her life, so her behaviour was just instinct. Until a little girl called Maisie came along.

Lili glanced at Bella and smiled when she thought of what Ray had put in the note with the flowers. *You can teach an old dog new tricks.*

'Look this way,' Maisie said, moving Bella's snout.

The dog didn't seem to mind.

Lili caught her doing that and winced. 'I don't think Bella will like that,' Lili warned.

'She's okay. You need to have the dog's attention; make sure they are looking right at you before you give them a command.'

Lili sighed. By the sound of it, Maisie was enjoying herself. 'Where did you learn all this stuff?' she asked.

'TV.'

That sounded about right. She got the impression that over the years, Maisie had spent an inordinate amount of time just plonked in front of the box to keep her quiet because it was easier. Lili hadn't done that. When Maisie had stayed with her, she'd taken her out, and they'd done interesting things together. She stared at Maisie. Just then, she wasn't sorry about the amount of television Maisie had watched if it got them out of this fix.

Lili needed Bella to move so she could escape from behind the wicker chair, cross the room and get outside. The trouble was that Maisie was enjoying herself far too much, demonstrating her dog-whispering skills.

'Look, Maisie, we need to go.'

The animal sat on command.

'Well done, Bella.' Maisie gave her lots of fuss.

Lili stared at her and realised it didn't matter that Maisie had no treats to give Bella; all the dog wanted was some love and attention. *Don't we all,* thought Lili. She attempted to get up from behind the chair and make a run for it, but every time she moved, the dog growled.

'Maisie, I want you to take her in the kitchen, so I can—'

'No!'

Lili knew why Maisie was refusing; she knew it meant they would be leaving. She wasn't going anywhere right now. She was enjoying herself too much.

'Lie down!' she said to Bella.

Lili was just about to get up and run across the room, hoping the dog didn't bother giving chase, when she heard a car turn up the drive. Lili breathed a sigh of relief. 'Maisie, the taxi is here.'

'I don't care.'

'We have to go now, sweetheart.'

'I don't want to.' Maisie put her arms around Bella's neck. The dog licked her face.

Lili didn't move. She'd left the front door open. She was sure the taxi driver would poke her head in the house, more out of curiosity than concern about what had happened to her fare. Lili was ready to shout out when she did. She heard the clunk of a car door and footsteps on the gravel drive. Then Lili caught an unfamiliar voice.

'God, did I leave the front door open again? Joseph will skin me alive.' There was a pause. 'Hello, yes, I'm calling from The Summerhouse. I missed my delivery slot. My shift at work overran and I couldn't make it home in time. Can you re-deliver?'

Lili was still on her knees behind the wicker chair. She could overhear the conversation. They were right on the other side of the door, standing in the hallway. Maisie could hear them too.

'What do you mean, you've delivered it?'

Lili guessed the person on the phone had walked into the kitchen opposite; she heard shoes on the tiled floor. Their voice grew faint as they said, 'Well, I can assure you, I haven't got my shopping. Okay, I'll hold.'

Lili heard water running and someone filling up a kettle. She whispered, 'Maisie, we really have to go now.' She decided to run down the drive and meet the taxi on the road. She swallowed. It hadn't occurred to her that another person lived here. She was just whispering, 'You have to say goodbye to Bella,' when the door to the conservatory flew open. 'Maisie! What are you doing here?'

'Hello, William,' Maisie said matter-of-factly. 'We came to feed the dog.'

William spotted Bella and backed away.

'It's all right,' said Maisie. 'Come here. You can stroke her.'

Lili poked her head around the chair. 'William?' She stared at him in disbelief. 'What are you doing here?'

'I live here,' he said, shrugging his shoulders as he stepped forward. He held out his hand as he approached.

'William – no! Get away from that thing!' a voice shouted out, seconds after the conservatory door flew open again.

'It's all right, Daddy. Look …' William stroked Bella, who sat panting and wagging her tail.

'I know you,' said Nate, catching sight of Lili as she rose from her hiding place behind the wicker chair.

'What are you doing here?' Lili and Nate said in unison when they recognised each other.

William piped up, 'Daddy, this is my friend, Maisie. She came to feed Bella.'

'Your *friend*?'

Lili glanced at her broken wrist and turned to the annoying young doctor. 'You're William's dad?'

30

'Let me take a look.'

'I said I'm fine.' Lili sat in the wicker chair in the conservatory. The doctor with the crappy bedside manner had introduced himself as Nate. It surprised Lili to discover he was Joseph's grandson, and William's father.

Nate had insisted that she sat down to have a cup of tea.

When the dog had appeared out of nowhere, frightening the life out of her, Lili had dived for cover behind a large potted plant. She'd then crawled over to hide at the back of the chair with Maisie. The trouble was, she'd landed on her hand. The wrong one. It was only after Nate's arrival, when she'd got up from her hiding place, that she'd felt a searing pain in her wrist which made her feel faint.

Nate had rushed forward and helped her to a seat, then gone to make her a cup of tea and find some strong painkillers. The children had taken the dog into the kitchen out of their way.

The miserable dog growled at anything else that moved, but not the children. Nate was still wary about letting his son anywhere near the brute, but to his complete surprise, Bella seemed to be one big softie around the youngsters.

When Bella growled at Nate as he strode into the kitchen, Maisie held up her hand, and said, 'No!'

Bella stopped growling. She even licked Maisie's hand and got a lot of fuss in return.

'Can she do tricks?' Nate heard his son asking Maisie as he walked towards the door with two mugs of tea.

'Oh, yes. I can show you.'

Nate lingered at the door and watched the children. 'Remarkable,' he said under his breath. He wasn't referring to the dog's transformation, but his son's. William had been very fond of his nanny, and since she had left, and they had moved from London, William had been a miserable so-and-so.

Like father, like son, thought Nate. It wasn't William's fault. He needed some playmates around his own age. He would start his new school after the summer holidays, where he'd meet other children. Nate didn't know anybody in the local area apart from his parents and the shop owners in Cobblers Yard. He hadn't met anyone with kids, unless you counted the young woman with the broken wrist. Now he wished he hadn't been quite so abrupt with her a few days earlier at work.

'So, how do you and Maisie know my son?' Nate asked when he returned to the conservatory with the sweet tea and a box of co-codamol.

'We bumped into Sarah and William in the café in town last week, and then Ray and I met for fish and chips on the beach. Maisie and William had a great time amber-hunting.'

'You met my father?'

'Yes, I know Ray.' Lili chose not to mention the frequent trips to Ray's shop to stock up on materials. She didn't want to get into a row about Nate's attitude towards art and anyone who showed the faintest interest in it or any aptitude as an artist.

'We ran into each other at the beach, so we ended up sitting together while the children played. Your dad is interesting, isn't he? I've never heard of an art cop. I know he's retired now, but it sounds as though he's had a fascinating career.'

Nate changed the subject, which did not go unnoticed. 'So, what were you doing here in The Summerhouse?'

Lili looked at him. His manner had changed, too. *Of all the people, why did it have to be him*? Lili thought. His son's moody demeanour now made sense. William was just like his father. Lili stole a glance at Nate as he handed her a cup of tea. She recalled what William had said at the beach when Maisie had suggested he could make an amber necklace for his mum. He'd said his mum was dead. Ray had told her it was cancer, three years earlier. It was little wonder that Nate wasn't happy – that was tough, losing your wife and the mother of your child at such a young age.

Nate repeated his question.

'I was going to water the plants,' she replied.

'You came here to water the plants?' This made no sense. 'Do you know Joseph?' She seemed familiar with other members of his family. 'Did he send you?'

Lili realised they were talking at cross-purposes. She shook her head. 'I came to feed the dog.'

'You came to feed Bella?'

Lili could tell by his expression that that made no sense either. 'Look, about your missing shopping …'

'My shopping?' Nate rubbed his forehead, feeling a headache coming on. It had been a long shift. The conversation seemed to be getting nowhere. 'What has this got to do with my shopping?'

Lili downed a couple of co-codamol and picked up the sweet mug of tea. 'It has everything to do with your groceries.' Lili managed a smile. It all made sense now – the cocoa pops, the chocolate buttons, the lollipops, the pasta. She glanced at Nate. These were the items she'd expect for a young child and his dad. The soup, ready meals and pet food were for Joseph and his dog. 'You live with your grandfather, don't you?'

Nate nodded. 'It's only temporary until I get my own place. There aren't a lot of properties available around here, though.'

Tell me about it, thought Lili, although she had only been looking for a holiday let, not to rent or to buy somewhere.

'I'll probably move into the flat.'

'The flat,' blurted Lili, realising Nate didn't have a clue that it was occupied right now. 'When are you thinking of moving out of The Summerhouse?'

Before Nate responded, his son interrupted them.

'I don't want to!'

Unbeknown to them, William had walked into the room and overheard the conversation. 'I will not live in the flat.' William stamped his feet. 'I want to stay here.'

'We've talked about this, William.'

'You can't live there.' Maisie had followed William into the conservatory, wading into the argument. Lili realised what was coming next. She would much rather tell Nate herself.

'We live in the flat.'

Nate's eyes went wide. 'Wait, let me get this straight. My grandfather let his flat to *you*?'

Lili was feeling uncomfortable under his gaze. She knew what he was thinking; Joseph had never rented his flat before. What made her so special?

Maisie wasn't helping matters when she added, 'We're looking after the shop too while Joseph is in hospital.'

'Daddy, we found amber on the beach. Me and Maisie are going to make jewellery out of it and sell it in the shop.'

Nate looked from Maisie to William, open-mouthed. This was all news to him. He turned to look at Lili. 'You're running Joseph's antique shop?'

The children skipped out of the conservatory to see if Bella was still eating her dinner. Lili watched them leave the room before reluctantly turning to Nate. She didn't want the third degree from Joseph's grandson. Lili felt she had no choice but to explain how she came to be in possession of his groceries and the fact that Maisie was quite correct; she was taking care of the antique shop. She tried to gloss over how that had come to pass. Contrary to assumptions, she was not Joseph's friend. She barely knew him. 'That's why I came to the house. I found the dog food in the shopping.'

'So, you're a friend of my grandfather?'

Lili nodded. She recognised that look – one of incredulity that Joseph had a friend. It was the same reaction from the shopkeepers in Cobblers Yard who turned up to her impromptu coffee morning.

She shifted in her seat, hoping he didn't ask how she came to know his grandfather. She hated telling a fib. It was all getting a bit out of hand. Lili was back to thinking that it might not be a bad idea if the next day she looked for another holiday rental in a different town. She'd lock up the shop, return the keys, and leave before Joseph recovered. Which reminded her – she still wanted to see his ring.

She stole a glance at Nate. Her wrist was throbbing. All she wanted to do was go back to the flat. She glanced at her watch; the taxi would be here any minute.

She was about to get out of her seat when Nate said, 'So, you're the friend who is looking after the shop. I didn't know it was you, but my mum, Sarah, mentioned it. She was pleased. You're doing us all a huge favour.'

'Am I?'

'None of us have got the time. We could have closed the shop, but with the outgoings, even selling the odd item helps the bottom line for Joseph.'

Lili thought of the expensive lamp she'd sold a few days earlier. She was having second thoughts about just walking out and leaving them in the lurch, especially as Maisie had made a friend and was having such a good time here.

The only blot on the horizon was when Joseph recovered from the delirium and found out that a stranger was minding his shop and living in his flat. She wondered if he would even remember giving her his card and inviting her to stay.

31

Nate cut across Lili's thoughts with a comment she wasn't expecting. 'That's fine, you keeping an eye on the shop and selling the odd item, unless your idea is to make some money on the side.'

Lili stared at him. 'Just what are you implying?'

Nate said, 'I think you know.'

Lili shot back. 'I certainly do not.' Although she had indeed guessed what he was suggesting. 'For your information, I sold a lamp for one hundred and fifty pounds. I haven't taken a penny from the sale. Maisie and I have kept the shop open, and I am well within my rights to take a wage for working in the shop, but I haven't, out of respect for Joseph. He allowed us to rent the flat at a knock-down price, so I thought minding his place was the least I could do.'

Lili finished her diatribe, wishing she hadn't blurted the bit about the peppercorn rent.

Nate didn't comment on that. 'Sorry, I shouldn't have said that. It was out of line. There's a lot on my mind.'

Lili stared at him for a long moment. He was a single dad, a widower, and by the sound of things, he'd only just relocated.

She imagined he wasn't having an easy time of it. She'd heard William; he didn't want to leave The Summerhouse and move again. Lili was beginning to understand why the new locum doctor was so irritable and tetchy.

'You don't have to apologise,' she said, and changed the subject. 'So, how is Joseph? I haven't seen him since the ambulance brought us both in. I heard he is a bit confused?'

'Delirium, I'm afraid.' Nate frowned while he repeated just what the nurse had told Lili on the phone. 'By the looks of things, it might take him some time to recover. It doesn't help that he needs hip replacement surgery.'

'Did he break it in the fall?'

'No, it turns out he needed one well before that.' Nate had seen the x-ray. 'He's been suffering in silence, not wanting to make a fuss, I imagine. I think the fall did the old fool a favour.'

'You do?'

'Yes, now he's got no choice but to have it done; I'll see to it that we don't discharge him until he does.' Nate offered Lili a rare smile.

Lili suddenly felt a little shy. She'd thought he was good-looking before, but that smile took her breath away.

Nate glanced over Lili's shoulder. 'To be honest, I keep forgetting to come in here and water his plants.' He had an idea. 'My mother mentioned that you're a horticulturist?'

'Yes, I am.'

'You said you were going to water the plants, while you were here.'

'I saw the conservatory and thought, why not?' Lili frowned. 'I didn't realise the dog was in here.'

'Will you take care of them? Look, I haven't got the first

clue. What if I swamp them? If I kill them off, I'll be in real trouble. I don't know if you're aware of Joseph's prized orchids …'

Lili looked at him blankly.

'I didn't expect you would. He has told no one, apart from me. He's waiting for one to flower. Will you take a look before you leave?'

Lili followed Nate to the end of the room where there were two rows of work benches.

'Oh, my goodness.' Lili spotted the orchids. She rushed over and stared at the plants. 'Where did he get these?'

Nate shrugged. 'Joseph travelled a lot, collecting antiques, but I think his real passion had always been flowers. He'd often bring them back from his trips abroad.'

'So, how come he runs an antique shop?'

Nate shrugged. 'The family business – I guess. It was my great-grandfather who opened the shop. They used to run it together. Joseph took it over when he died.'

Lili stared at the orchids. 'Do you know how rare these are?'

'Nope.'

The look on Nate's cute face said he wasn't all that bothered to know either. Lili gave him a sideways glance, wishing he wasn't so good-looking. He looked like he'd just stepped out of a Hollywood movie or the drama series *Grey's Anatomy*. Not that Lili found the fact that he was a doctor all that appealing, especially when she'd been on the receiving end of his none-too-charming bedside manner.

Lili's wrist still hurt, but that didn't stop her from reaching out and touching the delicate plants.

'By rare, I mean, *rare*,' she emphasised. 'This plant,

Dendrophylax lindenii, is also called a ghost orchid because it grows away from sunlight, preferring places that are not well-lit. And it doesn't bloom every year.'

There was more. Lili couldn't believe what she was seeing. 'Oh, my goodness,' she said again, spotting something else. 'Do you know what this is?' It was a rhetorical question – of course he didn't. Lili was so excited. She pointed at a plant that, to Nate, was nothing special. 'This is a night-flowering orchid! Do you know how—'

'—rare they are,' Nate finished her sentence, his eyes glazing over. 'Yes, yes,' he added dismissively, even though he didn't have a clue. 'What I want to know is whether you'll water them for me?'

Lili looked about her. 'Have you got a watering can? I'll do it before my taxi comes back to pick me up.'

'That's not what I meant … well, it is.' Nate was aware he was sounding flustered. Lili was so damned attractive, with her large brown eyes, her naturally blonde hair, those little freckles over her cute button nose, and her full lips. He wanted to lean in and …

'Nate – are you okay?'

Leaning toward her, he stopped just in time. He had nearly made a right prat of himself. 'God, I don't know what came over me!' he said. He hadn't meant to say it out loud.

'Long shift at work?'

Nate nodded. Lili was putting his weird behaviour down to tiredness. Nate wiped his brow. He was sweating. It was always quite a few degrees hotter in this part of the house. Either that, or he was getting hot under the collar.

Lili noticed that every time she glanced at him, he was

staring at her. What was that about? Maybe, like her, he had the distinct feeling they'd met before. She hadn't felt it when she'd first seen him in the hospital and he'd been wearing scrubs, but dressed down in jeans and a sweatshirt, he just seemed so familiar.

'What I meant to say …' continued Nate, stepping back and thinking that perhaps it would help him to think straight if he wasn't standing so close to her, '… is that I'm asking if you could come and water the plants every day.'

'Every day?'

'Yes. I'd pay you, of course,' he added.

I can't be bought, Lili thought, nearly blurting it out but stopping herself. She suspected she felt that way because she was already working in Joseph's shop and she was feeling like the family's hired help. 'I'll think about it.'

Lili looked at the plants and couldn't bear the thought that something might happen to such rare orchids. She wouldn't be surprised if they had taken years to nurture. 'I'm only on holiday here, so I won't be staying beyond next week.' She noticed the look of disappointment cross his face.

'Is that a yes, then?'

'Yes, all right. But you don't have to pay me.'

'Okay.' Nate found the watering can. 'There's an outside tap. You can step out here.' Nate showed her to one of the floor-to-ceiling windows that was cleverly disguised as a door.

Lili reached for the watering can, but Nate didn't hand it over. 'Wait a moment – I think there's a smaller can around here somewhere.'

'Oh, yes – right.' She'd forgotten she had a broken wrist.

Nate looked about him and found it. 'What about this? I

know it's tiny, so it will mean more trips back and forward to refill.'

'That's perfect. Thank you.'

There was an awkward moment when Nate handed it over and they stood staring at one another.

Nate broke the trance. 'Right, let's get some water.'

'Yes, good idea.'

They both stepped into the hall and halted. Lili and Nate looked at each other, and said, 'The dog.' They exchanged a knowing smile.

'I'll show you the outside tap, instead.'

Lili eyed the kitchen door. 'Good plan.'

Lili followed him outside and watched Nate filling up the watering can. They'd just stepped back into the conservatory when Lili heard a car pull into the driveway. 'Oh, that must be my taxi.'

Nate frowned.

'Maisie, sweetheart, it's time to leave,' Lili called out.

Maisie looked in on Lili watering the plants. She said in a petulant voice, 'I don't want to go.'

William was hot on her heels. He ran straight up to Nate. 'Daddy, please can they stay?'

Nate looked at his son. He didn't want them to go either. 'Will you stay for dinner?'

'Dinner?' Lili turned around, surprised by the invitation.

Nate knew that it sounded like he was asking for a date. He didn't want to put her off, so he quickly added, 'It's the least I can do.'

She realised it was a thank you for looking after Joseph's plants. Even so, she felt uncomfortable at the thought of accepting his offer. It wasn't the house, or the dog – it was the company. Nate was too attractive by half.

Lili dropped her gaze from those searching brown eyes. 'I'm afraid we've already eaten. Besides, what were you intending to cook?' She looked at him askance. 'I have your shopping – remember?'

'Oh, yes. Perhaps *you* should invite *me* for dinner,' Nate joked.

They exchanged a smile again, both looking away this time and feeling shy, like teenagers.

Teenagers. Lili stared at him. Now she remembered. He hadn't been a boarder; he'd been a day pupil at the private school she'd attended. He'd been skinnier back then, and not as broad-shouldered; he had filled out. His hairstyle had been longer back then, too. Now his dark hair was cut close and his face was more angular, but she was sure he was the boy she'd seen in this house.

Lili remembered the time she and Hannah had gate-crashed a party in Thorpeness. It had been Hannah's idea. She'd heard about the party from the kids who hung around Aldeburgh town centre on a Saturday night. Lili hadn't wanted to go. She'd found out they hadn't been invited and would have to catch a lift in a car with some local lads.

She recalled Hannah telling her to lighten up, stop being a prude, and get in the damn car. That wasn't all she'd said, either. Hannah had told her she'd be ruining her evening if she didn't go too. Against her better judgement, Lili had caved and got into the car. She hadn't taken much notice of where they were going; she remembered her heart thumping in her chest, anxiety levels rising when she caught sight of the speedometer she could see over the shoulder of the teenage driver. Would they get pulled over by the police? Did he even have a driving licence? That was what had been going through her mind. She had only noted her surroundings when they'd arrived at a large, rundown house at the end of an unmade road full of expensive properties. She hadn't felt so bad about the trip when she saw the neighbourhood; it was the two boys they'd come with that she hadn't been so keen on. Lili recalled feeling uncomfortable, hoping that it was just a lift and that Hannah hadn't set her up on a blind date.

Lili remembered the house, packed with teenagers. When they'd arrived, she had wondered whose party it was until Hannah sent her to a makeshift bar to get some drinks where she had overheard a conversation. Two girls had been talking to Nate. She'd recognised him from school. He'd been a popular kid. Bright, loud and opinionated, he'd fitted right in with the popular crowd of school girls with wealthy parents – just like his, she'd assumed.

She recalled overhearing one of them asking Nate, 'What are *they* doing here? Did you invite them?' Their voices had been incredulous; they'd spoken about her and Hannah as though the pair of them were dirt on the bottom of the popular crowd's shoes.

Lili had wanted the ground to swallow her up. Then Hannah had disappeared. She'd spent the rest of the evening trying to find her and the louts they'd arrived with, worrying about how they'd get home. The house had been so packed with kids from the school, spilling out into the grounds, that Lili hadn't been able to find her anywhere. Then there she was, one arm around Lili's shoulders, an empty wine bottle in the other hand, whispering in Lili's ear, 'You'll never guess what? I did it!'

In hindsight, Lili felt silly for saying, 'Did what?'

Lili glanced at Maisie as they sat down together in the back of the taxi. She looked up at the house. It was little wonder that Hannah wouldn't divulge who Maisie's father was – or couldn't; she had been drunk, and she'd done the deed right here in this house with one of those local lads who'd brought them to the party – or perhaps with both.

William ran up to the car and banged on the window. Bella was barking in the background.

'See you tomorrow!' he shouted out.

Maisie turned to Lili. 'Are we coming again?'

Lili nodded and smiled. 'I'll pop round every day to water the plants.' Lili was thinking she might do this at lunchtime, just to avoid bumping into Nate. Although she'd insisted that she didn't want to be paid, she knew she couldn't keep forking out for taxis; they were expensive. So, they came to an arrangement. Nate told her he'd leave some money for the taxi on the kitchen table.

'Will I see William and Bella?'

That was the other thing. Nate had been feeding the dog, but he'd much rather not have anything to do with Bella. 'Nate has asked if you wouldn't mind giving Bella her dinner while I'm watering the plants,' Lili told Maisie. 'You're going to get some extra pocket money.' He had insisted and Lili had accepted. It was nice for Maisie to top up her holiday fund, even though Lili knew Maisie would have done her bit for free.

'What about William? Will I see him too?'

'Maybe. It depends on what he's doing with his grandparents over the coming days.' Lili imagined that when Nate was working at the hospital, William would spend time with Sarah or Ray.

'Can we go to his house one day when he's there?'

'We'll see,' Lili replied, aware that it was what all parents said to avoid committing to something when they would rather not. She didn't tell Maisie that Nate had invited them both to dinner the next evening. It was a thank you gesture for agreeing to take care of his grandfather's plants and feed the dog. She'd declined, telling him she had other plans.

On the way back to the shop, the taxi driver talked to Maisie about Bella. She'd seen the dog sitting on the driveway. Her first impression was that Bella was quite old. The taxi driver thought she was lovely, with the spattering of grey around her muzzle and her shaggy, black and tan German shepherd coat.

The taxi driver got the impression that, given the way the little girl was talking about Bella, she had already formed quite an attachment. Not the best idea with a dog that age. What she needed was a puppy. That was what she and her husband had bought their youngsters; a little Labrador puppy – the perfect playmate for children.

She glanced in her rear-view mirror, about to mention it to the young woman sitting in the back, when she caught her far-off expression. She seemed preoccupied.

Lili stared out of the window as they made their way to Cobblers Yard. They passed the hotel where she and Maisie had stayed the previous week. It brought Alex to mind. Apart from the phone call from Alex, they hadn't contacted each other since. She was still waiting for the delivery he'd said was on its way. At this rate, she'd be home before he'd even sent it – whatever *it* was.

Lili had the impulse to get out her mobile and ring him, but every time she thought about it, someone else came to mind. Nate. She wished she wasn't now regretting her decision to refuse that dinner invitation.

32

'I must admit, I'm surprised you accepted my invitation to dinner after all. I thought, you know, something had come up.'

Over the past five days, he'd kept asking, and she'd kept declining, always coming up with an excuse. This time something had come up all right, which was the reason she had accepted.

Maisie picked up her knife and fork. She saw William copying her. She smiled at her friend and glanced at Lili, her smile waning.

Lili caught Maisie looking at her, no doubt checking she was okay. She offered her a disarming smile to dispel any anxieties. Poor Maisie. Lili had felt awful breaking down like that in front of her, but it was the shock more than anything; Lili had received something in the post from Alex.

The previous evening, after tending to the plants, feeding Bella and chatting to Nate, who had been home with his son because he was on an early shift, she had returned to the shop to find something on the doorstep. And it was not at all what she had been expecting. She hadn't got flowers, chocolates, or Alex turning up at her door with either of those things and an apology. What Lili had got, delivered by FedEx, was a large cardboard box. Nothing could have prepared her for what she had found inside. Lili thought how callous Alex was, emptying all her possessions into a crate and just getting rid of them in the post. He hadn't even told her that was what he was doing or given her the opportunity to return to the flat they shared to pack her own things. That one single, albeit large, box was the sum of her life. Her only consolation was that if this was it – it was over between them – then at least she didn't have to see him in order to collect her stuff.

Lili bit her bottom lip, thinking back to the phone call she'd made just the day before. She'd texted him her new address days earlier. He'd said he was sending her something. She had been wondering if he had forgotten.

Lili had phoned their flat to speak to Alex and had got a shock when a woman answered. She now guessed that the ensuing conversation must have precipitated what she'd received the next day. She couldn't help but think back to that call …

'Oh, hi Lili.'

Lili had recognised her voice. It was Penny, the secretary she'd seen when she'd popped into the solicitors' office where Alex worked.

'Oh, you're wondering what I'm doing here. It's a work thing … hold on.' Another voice came on the line. It was one of his male colleagues. 'Hi Lili, how's your holiday?'

So, he'd told his team she was away on holiday, but nothing about splitting up or anything like that.

His colleague had said, 'The office is being refitted, and we needed to work late, so we had to bring our laptops over to yours. Hope you don't mind?'

'Why would I mind?' Lili had replied, trying not to think

about the buxom young woman called Penny. They had all been there, the team he worked with, although Penny had said she might stay on, catch up with some stuff later with Alex.

'I need to speak to Alex.'

'He's on a conference call now.'

'This can't wait,' Lili had said through gritted teeth.

The first thing she'd said to him when he'd got on the phone, was, 'I spoke to Penny.'

'Yes, and you spoke to Sean too.' There was a pause. 'Oh, right, you think I'd just jump into bed with someone else the minute you're gone. What do you take me for?'

Lili had not liked his tone. 'You're right,' she blurted, 'we need a break.'

'Fine!'

'Fine!' Lili had slammed the phone down, and thought, *what have I done?* Not only did she need a job, but now she had to find somewhere to live too.

'What are we doing today?' Maisie had asked the next day.

Job hunting, she had wanted to say. *Flat hunting. Life hunting.* She had sat on the shingle beach with a takeaway mug of hot chocolate at lunchtime while Maisie searched for more amber. She was not inclined to return to London. Rents were cheaper here – if there were any rentals available. She thought over her options, yet again. She had some savings in her account, but she'd still need a job. That was when she'd decided *to hell with it*, had taken the entire afternoon off, and had gone to The Summerhouse. Maisie had wanted to play with Bella, and Lili had been bored hanging around the antiques shop, waiting for customers who didn't appear. In fact, she'd felt anxious about why she wasn't selling anything, and hated the thought that she was letting Joseph down. She'd looked at his ledger and discovered she'd been doing much better than him. He sold next to nothing.

Ray had come up trumps with the jewellery-making kit. Between the four of them, they'd sat shaping amber necklaces, bracelets, and rings, which sold surprisingly well. A percentage of the profits went back to the shop. Even Sarah had joined in, making them with William in her spare time and telling Lili that she found it quite therapeutic.

At first, Sarah had been standoffish. Lili knew she was sliding off certain of Sarah's questions to do with how she had come to know Joseph. Sarah's distant manner had soon dissipated, though. She'd told Lili how much she appreciated the way they included William. She was seeing the happy, carefree William again, and had told Lili, 'That's down to you and Maisie.'

'And Bella,' Maisie had said, overhearing the conversation.

Sarah had even confided in Lili that she had joined a dating agency and met someone. Well, she hadn't met them yet. It was all in the early stages; they were communicating online. Lili got the impression she was almost thanking her. She didn't know what for. Surely, Ray hadn't told Sarah about the advice Lili had given him about the flowers? Lili realised that the plan had backfired. Poor Ray. When was she going to pluck up the courage and tell him that the plan wasn't working – and that it was all her fault? Deluded Ray was assuming that the time they were all spending making bracelets in Joseph's shop would bring Sarah and him back together. When would he find out he was mistaken?

Deciding it wasn't necessary to open the shop all day, Lili had been spending more time at The Summerhouse in the afternoons, tending to Joseph's prized orchids. She wondered what Nate's reaction would be if she told him just how valuable those plants were – five or six figures. One of them alone, if it flowered, could be worth a hundred thousand pounds. It was little wonder that Joseph had a guard dog.

With not much to do, Lili had tended the gardens outside, getting a ticking-off from Nate when he'd arrived home early and caught her carrying a heavy garden sack of branches and leaves to the bin. He hadn't complained about her taking on the extra work, though; he'd just doubled the taxi fare money, and Lili had pocketed the extra.

She knew what she was doing there. She'd been going to The Summerhouse to avoid facing up to the end of the week. It had been a stupid thing to do. The days were flying past and Lili still hadn't figured out what she was going to do when Saturday arrived and she took Maisie home. She hadn't even searched for a rental or a job. She was avoiding dealing with those issues.

'Earth to Lili …'

Lili looked up. 'I'm sorry – what?'

'You were staring at your plate? Is the meal okay?'

Lili glanced across the table at Nate, but not before she caught Maisie frowning at her. 'Is everything okay?' she asked.

'Yes, sweetheart. I was just thinking about the end of the holiday – that's all.'

'Do we have to go home? I like it here.'

So do I, Lili thought. She had it on the tip of her tongue to say to Maisie, *but what about your mum?*

Lili looked across the table at Nate, who was still under the misapprehension that Maisie was her child. She didn't see the point of putting him in the picture; they'd be leaving soon.

'The meal is wonderful.' So were the candles and the bottle of wine. If it wasn't for the two children talking incessantly, dominating the conversation, or the dog prowling for scraps from the table, it would have been a lovely romantic dinner. Not that Lili was after romance.

Or was she? The thought of Alex dumping her possessions into a box had led to this: accepting an invitation on the spur of the moment for dinner with a very handsome doctor.

She smiled at him across the table. It felt strange being here at The Summerhouse. Lili was thinking about that house party again. Her best friend had been gorgeous and slim. Lili had not been. Now, she hoped to goodness he didn't recognise her. She convinced herself he wouldn't because she'd been quite podgy back then. Her hair had been different too – very long and dead straight – and she'd still had braces.

Lili finished her meal and put her knife and fork down. She glanced at Bella, doing as she was told for the two children, but giving her and Nate a wide berth – which was a vast improvement from having her growling at them. At least now they could all be in the same room together.

She turned to Nate. 'I found something at the bottom of the garden …'

33

Speaking to Nate up the dinner table, Lili told him that she had made a discovery in the garden earlier in the day, although she couldn't take the credit; it had been Bella and Maisie who had found it.

Lili had been busy clearing some borders for planting. When she'd looked up, Maisie had been nowhere in sight. Lili knew she had been playing with Bella only a moment earlier, throwing her a ball and giving her treats; Maisie had been spending some of the money she was earning on the dog. Lili had called out. Her heart had skipped a beat when there was no answer. Lili recalled hearing Bella barking. She had been about to investigate when Maisie had reappeared, running up the lawn, shouting, 'We found something at the bottom of the garden!'

Lili hadn't yet ventured that far down the garden. What Bella and Maisie had discovered was a wooden house that looked like a log cabin. It stood at the bottom of the garden, which sloped down to the water's edge at the far end of the boating lake. There was a small beach where ducks and geese gathered away from the crowds.

The building had a wraparound veranda, an old wooden

swing on the porch and plenty of cobwebs around the window, suggesting that it hadn't been used in years – decades, even. Lili had tried the door handle. It had been locked. Despite there being several keys on Joseph's keyring, none of them had fitted the lock.

She'd wiped some dirt off one of the windows and peered inside. The curtains at the window had obscured her view. Standing on the small shore, Lili had been able to see the boathouse – now converted into a tearoom – in the distance, and the little canoes in rows bobbing on the water.

'That old thing,' Nate said, after Lili told him what she'd found. He'd forgotten about it, because it was hidden from view by creeping ivy. 'It's probably full of a load of old junk. I don't know where the keys are, and I suspect Joseph doesn't either. I dread to imagine what the state of it must be inside. It needs tearing down.'

'Oh, that would be a shame,' commented Lili. 'Is that the reason this house is called The Summerhouse, because it has one in the garden?'

Nate looked at her. 'You know, I've never really thought about it. What I can tell you is that you found the *original* summerhouse. When my great-grandfather moved to Thorpeness, that old place was all that was here. He had the house built on the land after the war when they both came to England. Maybe he kept the original one for sentimental reasons – who knows.' Nate recalled that his great-grandfather had often sat in the swing seat on the veranda, smoking his pipe and gazing out over the lake for hours at a time.

However, the building brought to mind the only function he'd ever thrown here. And his biggest mistake. How could he have foreseen that Joseph and his great-grandfather would arrive home early from a trip on the one occasion he'd had a house party? He stared at Lili across the table. 'God, now I know where I've seen you before. It's been bugging the hell out of me …' His eyes darted to the children. 'Excuse my French.'

Lili froze. *Did he remember …*

'Did you come to a party here when we were teenagers?'

Lili saw no point denying it. She held up her hands, 'Guilty as charged, I'm afraid.'

'Why didn't you say something?'

Lili confessed, 'I gate-crashed your party. Sorry about that. I realise the apology is belated.'

He laughed and shook his head. 'Who would have thought?'

'I know.' It surprised Lili that he remembered her. 'Small world.'

'Isn't it just?'

Lili and Nate stared at each other, the silence broken by the clatter of spoons on dishes as Maisie and William finished their dessert of jelly and ice cream. They asked to get down from the table and retreated into the lounge to play board games. Bella followed them.

For the first time since Lili had come to the house and Nate had discovered her hiding from the dog, they were alone together.

Lili confessed, 'My friend got drunk, so we left early.' Lili left out the part about what Hannah had got up to in one of the bedrooms. 'Let's just say it wasn't an episode I wanted to revisit.'

'Me neither.' Nate grimaced.

'Really?'

'Yeah – my grandfather came back early.'

'Oh dear. I'm guessing he didn't know about it?'

Nate shook his head. 'He went ballistic.'

'Because of the mess?'

'No, because someone tried to force an entry into the summerhouse.'

'You mean the old wooden house at the end of the garden?'

'Yes. It was just some wasted teenagers. They didn't get far, but even so …' Nate trailed off. He decided not to dwell on the memory. He looked across the table at Lili. 'So, did you grow up here in Aldeburgh?'

'I suppose you could say that. I went to the same school you did.'

'I thought you were one of the local kids that crashed the party.'

Lili shook her head. 'We came with some local boys, but no, I don't have family here, if that's what you mean.'

'I don't remember you at school …'

Lili hadn't thought he would. She'd noticed him, but they'd moved in different circles. 'I was a boarder. Since I was eight.'

'That's tough. I thought I had it bad having to go and live with my grandfather. I came here about the same time, though.'

Maisie skipped into the dining room at that moment to ask if they could watch television and overheard the conversation. 'Lili is an orphan. Are you an orphan too, Nate?'

'Might as well have been,' Lili heard him say under his breath. He smiled at Maisie. 'No, my parents were too busy with their careers. You've met my mum and dad, Sarah and Ray.'

'Oh, yes. Can we watch TV?'

'Of course.'

When Maisie left the room, Nate turned to Lili. 'I'm sorry.'

'What about?'

'Your parents.'

Lili shrugged. 'It was a long time ago.' She didn't go into the details; not because she didn't want to talk about it, it was just that she didn't know what had happened to them – although she did say, 'I grew up in care.' She'd only shared this with a few people before Nate – Hannah, Alex and the two couples in London whom she counted as her closest friends. It was as though she felt there was a stigma attached. 'I was found wandering on a beach in Corfu, alone.'

'Corfu?'

Lili nodded. 'I was three when they found me. I knew my first name, Lili, but that was it. You hear of children going missing all the time, but parents going missing?'

'That's …'

'Bizarre – yes.'

'Do you think something happened to them? Maybe they had an accident?'

Lili hoped so, because she didn't like to think about the alternative – that they'd just abandoned their toddler.

As if reading her thoughts, Nate commented, 'Nobody just abandons their child.'

Unless they didn't want me. It was the reason she hadn't tried to trace them. What if was true, and they hadn't wanted her, so they'd *ditched* her? Would she be able to forgive them if they were alive, and they came forward now, all these years later? Her best friend came to mind. She was beginning to understand why Hannah wanted nothing to do with her parents, and why Nate was still hurt by Sarah and Ray's decision to send him to live with his grandfather.

There was nothing worse than the feeling of rejection. Lili frowned. She tried to push thoughts of Alex to the back of her mind. She knew she was putting on a brave face during the day, but at night, when she was alone in bed, that was when it tended to hit her. The way he had dumped her after all those years together. She still couldn't get over how callous he had been. Her one consolation, which was why she was having dinner with Nate, was the knowledge that if Alex could act like that towards her, as much as it hurt splitting up, she was better off without him.

Lost in thought, Lili jumped when her phone rang. 'I'd better get this,' she said, heading into the conservatory to take the call.

It wasn't Alex, thank God. After he'd sent her that box in the post, full of her possessions, she'd decided that if he rang or sent a text, she was going to ignore him.

She answered the phone. It was Hannah. Lili expected she was calling to arrange to collect Maisie when she got home.

'Hi Hannah, how's things?'

'I'm at the airport, catching a flight …'

'Great.' For a moment Lili wondered if there was another reason she was calling; had she extended her stay abroad even further? Lili would not put it past her.

While she was on the phone, Lili meant to ask if she could take Maisie home and crash at Hannah's house for a few days while she sorted out finding a place of her own. 'Hannah, I was wondering …'

'Oh, blast, the gate has opened already. Look, gotta dash. Is Maisie okay?'

'Yes. Would you like to speak to her?'

'I haven't got time. She can tell me all about the holiday and her trip to London with you when I get back.'

'Ah.' Lili hadn't had a chance to mention that they hadn't gone to London. 'The thing is …'

'I've got to go. I just called so you know I'm not on my way home.'

Lili frowned. 'Wait, did you say you're *not* on your way home?'

'You wouldn't believe it, but this fantastic deal came up in Bali. It's too good to pass up. My fiancé was like, why wait until we're married to have our honeymoon? Let's do it now. Then we could have a second honeymoon – it's all the rage, you know.'

No, Lili didn't know. 'But what about Maisie?'

'Maisie?' Hannah said it almost as though her daughter was an afterthought. 'Yes, well she wouldn't want to come to Bali. It seemed a pointless waste of money just to fly to England, only to travel back out at some later date.'

Lili was still frowning. Hannah hadn't answered her question. Then again, she didn't have to. Hannah had never had to ask if Lili would look after Maisie. It had always been a given; why should this time be any different?

Lili hadn't put her in the picture about her split with Alex.

'See you soon. Well, in about two weeks.'

'Another two weeks!' Why was she acting surprised? That took her nicely to the end of the long school summer holidays.

'I knew you wouldn't mind, Lili.'

Mind? Of course, she wouldn't mind – under different circumstances. But not like this. Lili had enough of her own issues going on right now, without the worry of keeping a roof over Maisie's head. 'Look, there's something I need to tell—'

'God, the gate is closing. Gotta go. Luv ya.' Hannah rang off.

Lili stared at her phone. She couldn't fail to see the irony of her situation. All these years, she'd been the dependable one. She'd provided a place for Hannah and her daughter to crash during their frequent bouts of homelessness brought on by Hannah's many failed relationships, along with her inability to settle down and get a job. Now the tables had turned. Lili was the one in a failed relationship, reaching out, homeless and jobless.

34

Nate popped his head around the door of the conservatory. 'Everything all right?' He walked into the room when he saw her face.

Maisie appeared at the door. She'd heard Lili's phone. 'Was that Alex?'

Lili shook her head. 'No.'

'Good, because he is not nice.'

Nate raised an eyebrow.

Maisie turned to Nate and said, 'Alex dumped her,' and ran out of the room.

'Why do children do that?'

Nate smiled. 'What? Speak their minds and tell everyone your business?' He sighed. 'Because they were born to vex us.'

'Sorry, about that, Nate. Alex is … *was* my partner. We've split up.'

Nate didn't say he was sorry to hear that because he wasn't. In fact, it was the best news he'd had in some time; the woman he was falling for was single. He didn't know Alex, but he was an idiot, a fool, a complete dick to split up with Lili. Nate stifled a grin.

Lili sat down in a wicker chair, tears rolling down her face. 'I don't know what I'm going to do. He sent all my stuff in a box by FedEx.' Lili didn't mention her other problem – what would she do with Maisie?

'He did *what*?'

Lili sighed. 'It's a long story.' Now she wished she had corrected the misconception from the start that Maisie wasn't her daughter. But how could she have known she'd get more involved with Nate and his family as time went on?

'You could stay here,' he ventured.

'Here?' Lili looked around her, shaking her head.

'I meant, in Suffolk.' Nate would love her to stop here as a guest. There were plenty of bedrooms. The problem was Joseph; Nate had had to twist his arm to let him live there with William for a bit. He stared at Lili. 'Why go back to London?'

'I need a job, and somewhere to live.'

Nate smiled. 'You've got all that here. Don't worry about Joseph. I'll talk him round to letting you stay on at the shop. He needs help.'

Lili could think of all sorts of reasons why that wouldn't work. The shop didn't earn much money. Besides, she didn't want to work in an antiques shop.

'I know it's not your thing – antiques,' Nate said as if reading her mind. 'But it could tide you over until you found something else.'

That was true, but that something else was a situation in Kew which would mean a move back to London. She thought about the job application she'd submitted almost a fortnight ago; it was bothering her that she still hadn't heard whether she'd got an interview. She knew she'd have to phone them and find out, but like everything else, she'd been putting it off, afraid of bad news.

Nate came and sat down in the wicker chair beside her. 'You could landscape people's gardens. Look how you're transforming the garden out there.' He pointed. 'You could be a freelance gardener – have you thought about that?'

Lili had not. Working in the shop, she'd discovered she enjoyed running a business; it was something she had never considered before.

It all sounded perfect, apart from one problem: what would happen when they all found out she had told an enormous whopper of a fib and Joseph didn't have a clue who she was? And what about Maisie? How would Lili explain it when Maisie went home to her mum – especially to Nate, a single parent himself?

Lili got out a tissue to wipe her eyes. Although Nate was trying to come up with ideas, he wasn't helping. Lili felt guilty that she'd spoiled a lovely meal. 'I'm so sorry. I know this isn't what you invited me here for, to hear all about my problems.'

Nate sat there shaking his head. 'Don't apologise.' He reached for her hand.

They both looked round when the door Nate had left ajar opened. Lili was expecting Maisie to walk in again and say something else to embarrass her. Instead, Bella appeared.

'Oh God,' they said in unison as the hound made her way towards them.

'Maisie!' Lili called out, letting go of Nate's hand as Bella walked right up to her.

Lili didn't have time to jump out of her seat. Instead, she sat still. Out of the corner of her eye, she saw Nate about to reach for the dog's collar. 'No, leave her. Listen, do you hear it?'

'What?'

'She's not growling at us.'

Nate relaxed a bit.

Bella sat down at Lili's feet and put her head on Lili's lap, nuzzling her hand.

'Oh,' Lili exclaimed in surprise. She finished wiping her eyes dry and stroked her head. 'Good dog.'

'Bella! There you are!' Maisie exclaimed, running into the room. 'Come here!'

'Well, you really can teach an old dog new tricks,' commented Nate, staring at Bella's head on Lili's lap.

Bella stood up at the sound of Maisie's voice. She growled at Nate as she passed him on the way out of the door.

'Well, sometimes,' Nate added.

That made Lili laugh.

Nate smiled, watching Maisie walk out with the dog. He spotted William waiting for his playmates on the other side of the door. 'Let's play,' Maisie said.

He heard two sets of footsteps and the patter of paws running up the hallway.

'Don't run in the house, Maisie!' Lili called out.

'It's fine, really it is. It's great to see him smiling again, having fun.' He turned to Lili. 'So, how about it?'

Lili looked at him. 'How about what?'

'About staying?' He felt they were just getting to know one another. He glanced at Lili, hoping she would change her mind about returning to London. If she was going to start over, then why not make that new beginning here? Nate wished he could persuade her to stay.

35

'So, it's agreed. We're all set then.'

Lili stared at Nate. 'I feel like you've railroaded me into a decision, to be honest.'

'It wasn't all me,' Nate replied, smiling as he glanced at the two children in the rear-view mirror.

Lili turned around in her seat and frowned at them. She looked at Maisie. 'Are you sure you're okay having a sleepover with William at The Summerhouse?'

Bella woofed.

Lili rolled her eyes. 'I didn't ask you.' She couldn't help but smile at the dog sitting on the back seat in between the two children.

They'd been on their way out when Nate had said, 'I'll get the car.' He'd parked it around the side of the house. The mention of the word *car* had had Bella jumping up and down as though someone had just said *walkies*. She had seemed to know that everyone was going out, and she'd wanted to go too. *Who can blame her?* thought Lili. After years stuck in The Summerhouse being a guard dog, Lili felt it was time Bella retired and had a chance to smell the roses – or in this case go on a little trip in the car down the road to Aldeburgh.

'We'll stop at the flat so you can pack some things in an overnight bag.'

'You've got it all planned.'

Nate looked at her sheepishly, trying to stifle a grin. It was all part of the plan. He just hoped it worked. But that wasn't up to him. It had to be her decision.

Lili glanced over her shoulder at Maisie. 'So, you're okay with this?'

Maisie was busy playing a card game with William. She didn't look up. 'Yes, I'm fine.'

'Okay, well, if you're sure.'

'Hey!' William exclaimed. 'Give that back!'

Lili smiled at the dog again. Bella was sitting there, her head bobbing left and right, watching the children slapping cards down between her feet as they played *snap*. She'd decided to join in, putting her paw down on William's card. She'd then leant over and picked it up in her jaws, refusing to give it back.

'Bella,' William warned.

'What's going on?' Nate asked, glancing in his rear-view mirror.

'They're playing snap. Bella decided to join in,' Lili said.

Ten minutes later, Nate parked on the high street in Aldeburgh, as close as he could get to the little lane leading to Cobblers Yard.

Lili opened the car door, then turned to Nate. 'You know I could just spend the night here. Then it wouldn't cost you any money.'

'Yes, I realise that, but it's not the same as being pampered at the hotel. You do like The Harbour Inn, don't you?'

Lili liked it very much, although she wondered what this was all about. 'Yes, it's where I stayed with Maisie when we arrived. We spent our first week there.'

He was after her staying around – she knew that. Perhaps he thought a night in a lovely hotel in the town, on her own, with no distractions, would give her time to reflect on just what she would be missing if she returned to London.

If that was what it was about, she didn't want to burst his bubble. He had gone to the trouble of booking the room. She'd thought he might book an evening meal in the restaurant for the two of them and ask Ray or Sarah to babysit. He hadn't mentioned it, but perhaps it was going to be a surprise. She'd seen the sheepish look on his face when she'd said, *you've got it all planned.* It was as though he was hiding something. She'd wondered what else he was up to.

It had all started when Maisie had begged for a sleepover. Lili had understood why Nate hadn't asked her to stay too. That might be awkward. But his reasoning for treating her to a night at the hotel still eluded her.

Lili was thinking all this as she walked into the flat. When she returned to the car, the expression on Nate's face said that he wasn't happy.

He frowned at her. 'What's all this?'

Lili had packed her suitcase, and Maisie's Trunki. She sighed. 'Look, it seems pointless packing an overnight bag.'

'But I thought—'

Lili knew what he thought. This was why she didn't want him to pay for a night at The Harbour Inn, if his expectation was that she would stay around. Nate would bring Maisie along to pick Lili up in the morning. She didn't say it, but if their bags were packed and ready, then he could run them straight to the train station. Staying overnight at the hotel had its benefits, she realised, which was why she hadn't point-blank refused the offer. She would have time on her own to figure out what she was going to do next. She intended to phone her two friends in London to see if one of them could put her and Maisie up.

Lili was aware that she could have done all that from the flat while Maisie had her sleepover, but if Nate insisted that she spend a night in the lovely Harbour Inn, then Lili thought she might as well; it would be nice to end her stay at the hotel.

She had another reason for accepting; Lili had become attached to Cobblers Yard and the little flat above Joseph's antique shop. This was for the best. It would make it easier to leave when the time came – at least, she hoped it would.

They arrived outside The Harbour Inn. Lili sat in the car for a moment, staring at the hotel. It seemed peculiar being back. So much had happened in the fortnight since she'd been there.

'Is everything alright?'

Despite her intention to phone her friends and organise staying with one of them in London, she was having second thoughts about leaving.

'What's the matter?' asked Nate. 'Have you changed your mind?'

'What?' She turned to Nate, realising he was talking about stopping here, or her plans for catching the train in the morning. 'Er no, everything's … great. I'd better get going.'

'Maisie, now are you absolutely sure you want to have—'

'I'm fine!' Maisie insisted. 'I do want a sleepover!'

'Okay.'

'I will give you a hand with your suitcase?'

Lili opened the car door.

Nate got out too and walked to the back of the car. Lili joined him as he lifted her case out of the boot. 'What about Maisie's case?'

'You can leave it in the car.'

'Oh, alright.'

'You are picking me up in the morning?'

'Of course.' Nate stood there staring at the Trunki. He shut the boot and turned to Lili. 'Are you thinking of going straight to the train station tomorrow and returning to London?'

Lili breathed a sigh. He had to tell him. 'Yes.'

There was an uncomfortable silence.

'Nate, look I—'

'You're going back to him aren't you, that … idiot who dumped you.'

'No, no I'm not. I have some friends who will put us up.'

Nate stared at her. *Thank god*, he thought. All was not lost. What if her friends couldn't put them up? She still had a night in the hotel to think things through. Perhaps she'd reflect on what she'd be missing.

Nate had one more thing planned that might convince Lili to stay. He smiled, but then he caught sight of Lili picking up her suitcase. He realised she didn't need to return to Cobblers Yard. That might be a problem. But it would not deter him. He had all night to find a way around that conundrum.

Lili picked up her case. 'Right, well I'm off then.'

'Are you sure you don't want a hand with that?'

Lili heard Bella barking and the children laughing in the back of the car. It wouldn't be long before they got bored – and then they'd argue. 'No, I'm fine. Why don't you head off?'

They lingered a moment, both unsure of the etiquette for people who weren't together but wanted to be. *Is it too forward to kiss her goodbye?* thought Nate.

Is it too forward to expect him to kiss me? thought Lili. In the end, they both settled for an awkward hug. Lili drew away. It was just as well Nate had the kids, otherwise she might be tempted to ask him up to her hotel room. And that wouldn't do at all. She was meant to be leaving the next day.

'Oh, I almost forgot. I booked an evening meal in the restaurant.'

Lili tried to act surprised, even though this was just what she'd expected. 'You did?'

'Yes, I thought that as you're staying overnight, then you might as well have dinner. Round off your day. You don't mind dining alone – do you?'

'Oh, er … no. Of course not.' Lili was taken aback. She'd assumed that he'd find a babysitter, like his mum and dad, and return to have an evening meal with her. Mind you, with her suitcase packed, it was obvious she was leaving. Why would he want to have dinner with her if she was leaving for London in the morning?

'How would you feel if we all had breakfast together tomorrow?'

'In the hotel?'

'Um, no.'

Nate shook his head. She recalled her and Maisie's first morning there, when they'd had breakfast on the beach. Lili smiled. 'Okay.'

She walked to the front of the car and poked her head inside. 'You will be good for William's dad, won't you?'

'Cross my heart,' Maisie replied, drawing a heart shape on her chest with her finger.

'Good.'

Lili didn't notice the two children snickering into their hands as soon as her back was turned. Nate had already told them the plan, but they were sworn to secrecy. It was a risk because William found it difficult to keep a secret.

Nate followed Lili around the vehicle and stood leaning against the driver's side door as he watched her carry her case up the path to the hotel. She turned around and waved.

Nate waved back. So did Maisie, staring after her from the car window. She'd seen Lili carrying her Trunki from the flat and handing it to Nate to store in the boot. She knew what that meant; they were going home in the morning. She didn't want to go home to her mum and that boyfriend of hers. She wanted to remain here with Lili, Nate, and William. And William's grandparents, Ray and Sarah. That was why when Nate had made her and William promise to keep a secret, it wasn't the only one she was keeping. She wouldn't breathe a word that Lili wasn't her mum, otherwise that might mean she couldn't stay – and she didn't want that to happen.

As Lili walked inside the hotel, she still thought it all very strange. Surely, dinner together would be better than breakfast? But once again, she was thinking that perhaps it was for the best; a lovely meal and a few glasses of wine might be just the sort of thing to release her inhibitions, and she might find herself inviting him back to her room for a nightcap. And who knew where that would lead?

36

'Just the one case?' asked the friendly concierge.

Lili smiled at him for being so diplomatic. What he meant was; *You must be alone, on your own, single, with no boyfriend, husband or partner.* Lili glanced back through the open doorway. The car had gone. She'd had half a mind to invite them all in to dine at the hotel instead. She'd have footed the bill. She was missing them already.

'We'll run this up to your room,' said the young man behind the counter. He glanced at the computer screen in front of him. 'I see there's a reservation in the restaurant for dinner.'

'Yes, about that …' Lili had changed her mind about dining alone. 'May I have dinner in my room?'

'Of course. That is not a problem.' He handed over her key. 'The honeymoon suite.'

Lili frowned. That was the very room Alex had booked for the two of them, when she'd thought he might propose.

The young man looked at the keys. 'Is it not to your liking? According to this, you have stayed with us in that room before.'

Nate had chosen one of the most expensive rooms, not realising the significance.

'The thing is,' the young man continued, 'I'm afraid there are no other bedrooms. We are fully booked.'

Lili sighed. Of course they were. It was the summer holidays. Who wouldn't want to come here on holiday? And stay forever?

She raised an eyebrow at the thought, which had come out of nowhere. Lili reached out and took the keys. Her other choice was to return to the flat for the night, but it seemed rude after Nate and gone to all this trouble – and expense.

'When would you like your meal brought up?'

Lili wasn't one to have a late supper, but on this occasion, she was going to make an exception. 'Eight – if you don't mind.'

She knew what she wanted to do; have dinner in her room, on her bed, in her PJs. The sort of indulgent things she imagined most people with children would love to do but never got around to. *But Maisie isn't my child*, she thought. At least she wouldn't have to tell her new friends that Maisie wasn't hers. She was leaving in the morning.

Lili followed the concierge with her case up the rickety stairs, across the landing, up and down more small flights of stairs and along narrow corridors that seem to double back on themselves. She arrived at the familiar door. She almost cried when she saw Maisie's chair – the one the hotel had found for her to sit at and paint. It was still positioned in the window.

A few minutes later, Lili headed out, leaving the hotel and making her way along Crag Path. For the first time, she could follow the trail alongside the beach without keeping an eye on Maisie collecting amber from the beach. Lili could just enjoy the peaceful surroundings, the colourful cottages and townhouses fronting the path, and her thoughts.

But her thoughts were not peaceful. She was consumed with

thinking about the next day. She knew she had to call her friends. She should have phoned the moment she'd got to the hotel. She knew she was putting it off.

She found a gap in the low wall alongside the path with five small stone steps that led up to the beach. She stepped through and took large strides down the beach until she neared the water's edge. She paused and sat down on the shingle. She looked out to sea, listening to the lapping of the water and watching the gentle ripple of the waves as the tide came in. She recalled her conversation with Nate in the conservatory in The Summerhouse, and Nate trying to persuade her to stay. Closing her eyes, she took a deep breath. Could it work? But what about Maisie? When was she going to tell him Maisie wasn't her daughter?

She heard children laughing and a dog barking, and felt a wet doggy nose sniffing her hand.

Lili smiled. 'Bella?' She opened her eyes to find a woman approaching along the beach with her youngsters. The dog wasn't Bella. She was calling to her dog and apologising to Lili.

Lili shook her head. 'Don't worry, I love dogs,' she said. She was surprised to realise what a change of heart Bella had caused her to have. *And children*, she thought, missing them already. *And Nate.*

And Nate? She barely knew him. *So why not give it a chance to get to know him? You've got nothing to go back to London for.* Was she considering Nate's offer and thinking of staying?

37

'Miss, Miss!'

Lili had returned to the hotel and was starting up the stairs when the young man on reception came running after her. 'There's a letter for you.'

'A letter? For me?'

'Yes. I am so sorry, but it arrived just after you checked out last time you stayed with us, and we … we didn't have a forwarding address.'

Lili took the letter and looked at the envelope. For a moment, she thought Alex had sent it, but why would he send it to the hotel when she'd given him the address of the flat above Joseph's antique shop? It looked official, but she recognised his handwriting where he'd crossed out their address in London and scrawled The Harbour Inn to redirect it here to Aldeburgh.

Lili glanced at the young man standing at the stairs. His expression suggested he thought the hotel might be to blame, but it wasn't his fault. Lili frowned. Alex must have forwarded this letter before she and Maisie left the hotel for the flat above Joseph's antique shop; he hadn't even had the decency to tell her he'd sent it.

'I hope it's not important,'

Lili sighed. 'Look, don't worry about it.'

He smiled in relief. 'Can we get you anything?'

Lili looked at him. 'Now you come to mention it …'

Lili fancied a soak in the gorgeous en suite bathroom with the sunken bath. It was something she hadn't had time to do when she'd stayed here with Maisie. Then she intended to have a TV dinner and watch an on-demand movie. In fact, Lili was looking forward to an indulgent evening alone. The only thing missing was some scented candles to help her relax. That was what she requested when the concierge asked if there was anything he could get her.

Not long after she stepped into her room, there was a knock on the door. She'd expected a couple of candles. What she got was a large gift basket from one of the upmarket shops in the town. The basket not only contained candles, but sweet-smelling soaps, some bath bombs in strawberry, apple and vanilla which melted in the water, giving a lovely aroma, and bubbles. There were bottles of shower gels, and crème body rubs too.

Lili ran the bath, threw in the small, round bombs, and lit the candles, placing them in strategic positions around the tiled bathroom to make for a soothing atmosphere.

She got undressed, folded her clothes and placed them on the stool beside the bath. Stepping into the sunken bathtub, she gradually lowered herself into the water, the bubbles tickling her skin as she did so. She glanced to her left and caught sight of the letter she'd stuffed in the back pocket of her jeans. She reached for the small hand towel that was draped over the side of the bath, dried her hands, and leaned over to pull the envelope from the pocket.

She knew it was a daft thing to do, in case she dropped it in the water, but she couldn't imagine it was that important. She opened the envelope. Inside was a folded single sheet of notepaper. She unfolded it and read the contents, then sat up with such a start that she almost dropped it.

'Oh, my God! I've been offered an interview at Kew Gardens.' The thought that she'd missed it tempered Lili's excitement. After all, the letter had been sitting on reception for over a week. She skimmed the contents and breathed a tremendous sigh when she saw the interview date. 'It's the day after tomorrow,' she said to herself. 'I must make a phone call.'

Lili's long soak in her luxurious bathtub was forgotten in an instant. She climbed out of the bath and slipped on a robe hanging on a peg behind the bathroom door.

She found her phone in the bedroom and called one of her two good friends in London. 'Abigail, it's Lili. I have some fantastic news!' Abigail would be shocked when she learned that Lili and Alex had split up. *First things first*, thought Lili. She would tell Abigail about the job interview at Kew and slip in her request for the huge favour of crashing at her house until she figured out what to do about finding a place of her own.

But I have the flat above Joseph's shop, and Nate, Sarah, and Ray, she told herself. There were friends here who would look out for her. *Everyone in Cobblers Yard would want me to stay.* Lili dismissed that thought. She couldn't commute from here if she got her dream job.

Lili realised that Abigail was quiet at the end of the phone. She could hear her breathing, so she knew she was still there. 'Abigail, I have some fantastic news,' Lili said again, a little surprised that her friend hadn't asked what it was.

'Toby's dead.'

'I'm sorry – what?' Lili was on her mobile. She couldn't have heard her right. Abigail had been the first of the three of them to marry. Toby was a lovely bloke. And it was as though it was meant to be; they shared a birthday. 'What are you talking about?'

'He died, Lili, at work.'

Lili knew that Toby worked as a paramedic. Something must have happened on the job. As far as she was aware, Toby, in his early thirties, was in good health. 'Can I visit?' Lili asked. She wasn't after staying at Abigail's place; that wouldn't be possible in the circumstances – but she would like to see her.

'Not right now. My family is down, so is his. I … I just wanted you to know. Alex said he would get in touch and fill you in.'

Lili recalled the calls from Alex that she hadn't answered – and the text messages she'd deleted. She'd had no idea that he might be trying to get in touch about Toby.

'God, I don't know what to say.' Lili wanted to ask how it had happened, but she guessed it was quite recent. Understandably, Abigail wouldn't want to talk about it.

'You don't have to say anything.' Abigail paused. 'What was it you had to tell me?'

Lili looked at the piece of paper in her hand. 'It doesn't matter.'

'It does. I am so happy for you, Lili. It's what you wanted, isn't it?'

Lili frowned when she realised that Abigail had assumed she was phoning with news of getting engaged to Alex or setting a date for their wedding – not a job interview.

'Hold him, Lili, for me. You've only got one life – live it, Lili.

Don't let opportunities pass through your fingers. They might be here today but gone tomorrow.' Abigail fell silent.

So did Lili. 'I am so sorry,' she said again.

'I must go, Lili.'

'I will come and see you.'

Abigail rang off.

Lili stood there, staring at her letter. She jumped at the sound of someone knocking on her door, then ran back into the bathroom and wrapped a towel around her wet hair before answering the door.

'Oh, my.' Lili stared at the concierge as he stepped inside, carrying an enormous bouquet of flowers. He placed it on the windowsill where Maisie had sat and painted during her stay. When he'd gone, Lili walked over and found a little card amongst the flowers. She stood there for a moment, staring out of the window, wishing Maisie was there with her. After that phone call, she didn't want to be alone, and no longer felt like celebrating. She put the letter down on the bedside cabinet and opened the card. She thought the flowers were from Nate. They were from Ray. The card has a simple message: *You'll be missed*. Word had got around already that she was leaving.

Lili was intending to phone her other friend about staying over in London, but after speaking to Abigail, she didn't fancy making that call right now.

She blow-dried her hair and got dressed. The next knock at the door was her dinner. Lili wasn't feeling hungry or in the mood for that romcom she'd promised herself. In fact, all she now felt was lonely. She wished she hadn't agreed to Maisie's sleepover.

Lili sat down in the chair by the window and rang Nate. She

needed to hear his voice and check on Maisie. When he answered the phone, she could tell he was surprised to get her call.

'I'm just checking Maisie is okay.'

The sound of his voice when he replied gave him away. He sounded disappointed that Maisie was the only reason for her call. Lili didn't admit that it wasn't.

'So, you're sure she's fine?' Lili could hear a film in the background. It was the theme tune to that old movie, *Ghostbusters*. She wasn't the only one who had designed an evening around the television.

'They've got popcorn too.'

Lili heard Bella bark.

'Ah, that's the dog. I think she's more excited about the sleepover than—'

Lili burst into tears.

'Crumbs – what did I say?'

'It's not you, I just spoke to a friend, and her husband has died. It made me realise …' Lili was still sobbing.

Nate said, 'I'm coming to get you.'

'No, seriously – don't. You are all having such fun …'

'So, we can have fun together – you included. Besides, you sound as though you need some company.'

Lili didn't argue. Nate was still on his mobile to her, but she could hear him turning off the television and asking the children to get their coats on. 'I'll be with you in a few minutes,' he said.

'Will you come straight up to the room?' Lili asked. 'I don't feel like waiting in the lobby.'

'Sure.'

Lili ended the call and sat down on the end of the bed. She felt bad for dragging the children away from their movie. Lili tried phoning again to tell him not to come, but she imagined they were already on the road. His phone went straight to voicemail. She knew they'd be there in a matter of minutes.

Lili was staring at her phone when she heard children's voices and footsteps running down the corridor. Then there was a loud knock on the door.

Lili stood up and opened it. Maisie was in first, throwing her arms around Lili and giving her a hug. 'Nate said you were feeling sad, so we came to cheer you up. Look, we brought our popcorn.' Maisie ran over and sat down on the bed as though she had been here, in this suite, all along and they hadn't just spent the last week at the flat.

William came racing in next. He threw his arms around Lili's waist. 'Don't be sad,' he said, before running over and jumping on the bed next to Maisie. 'Where are the TV controls? I want to watch the movie.'

Nate appeared at the bedroom door, casting a furtive glance over his shoulder. Lili wondered what the matter was until she saw he had something in his hand. It was a dog lead. 'You brought Bella?' Lili said in surprise.

He put a finger to his lips in a shushing motion and was pulled into the room by an excitable Bella. She'd spotted Lili.

Lili knelt as she bounded over. 'Oh, you sweet dog.'

Bella furiously wagged her tail and lay down, legs in the air, to have her tummy tickled.

Nate took one last look down the hallway before closing the door. He let out a huge sigh. 'I don't know how I passed the concierge and the front desk without somebody noticing, to be honest. I shouldn't have brought her.'

'They allow dogs in the hotel,' Lili replied. There's no way

Nate would have passed anybody unnoticed with a dog Bella's size. Even so, Lili looked up and said, 'You could have left her at home.'

'Bella insisted on coming.'

'What do you mean?'

'She knew we were going out. I made the mistake of not shutting her in the conservatory. I opened the car door, and there she was. She'd snuck out of the house. I tried getting her out of the car, but she wouldn't budge.'

'She wanted to come too,' Maisie added. 'Oh, look here it is.'

Lili heard the theme tune to *Ghostbusters* again. The two children lay down on the bed together, heads propped on pillows, a large tub of popcorn between them.

Bella sniffed the air and jumped up on the bed. Flat on her stomach, Bella inched her way up the bed.

Nate spotted her. 'Oh, and Bella likes popcorn.'

Lili laughed. She got up and sat down on the sofa. Nate joined her. 'So, are you okay?'

'I am now you're all here.'

Nate put a tentative arm around her shoulder. 'Do you want to talk about it – your friend, that phone call?'

Lili shook her head, no. 'Can we watch the movie first?'

Nate smiled. 'Of course.'

She felt his arm tightening around her shoulders, pulling her closer.

'Hey, Bella!'

Lili turned around and caught Bella poking her nose into their popcorn bucket. She looked at them and Bella before turning back to the movie. She glanced at Nate. She was thinking of what her friend had said. *Hold him, Lili, for me. You've only got one life*

– live it, Lili. Don't let opportunities pass through your fingers. They might be here today but gone tomorrow. Lili's eyes roved to the letter on the bedside table. She had a decision to make.

38

Lili awoke. The two children were still fast asleep either side of her in the large queen-sized bed. They'd all watched another long movie, staying up way past their bedtimes. Lili had told them a bedtime story, snuggled down with them, and ended up nodding off too. When she woke, she was under the duvet. She smiled. Nate must have placed it over the three of them while they slept. She slowly sat up so as not to rouse them, but she did wake Bella, who was sprawled out at the end of the bed. Her head popped up.

Lili carefully got out from between the children and pulled the duvet over them. Maisie turned over but didn't wake up. Lili glanced at Nate, who was asleep on the sofa, his legs hanging off the end. A blanket was on the floor. She crept over, picked the blanket up and draped it over him. He stirred. It was early, but now Lili was awake, she had a lot on her mind.

She walked over to the window and sat down in Maisie's chair. It reminded her of the beginning of their holiday and the discovery she'd made about Maisie's artistic talent; she knew that Maisie could be a famous artist when she grew up. Bella joined her, sitting by her side, looking out of the window too. Lili put her hand on the dog's head and gently stroked her nose. She let out a soft whine.

Lili looked at her and whispered. 'You want to know whether I'm staying.'

As if she understood, the dog put her muzzle on Lili's lap, giving her the sad puppy dog eyes treatment.

Lili smiled down at her. 'Well, that might work, you know.' Her eyes shifted to the simple message written on the card from Ray, and the beautiful bouquet from The Potting Shed. It made her think of the others she'd met in Cobblers Yard. And Joseph and his antique shop. She fingered the ring on the chain around her neck. She still wanted to speak to him and find out why they had the same ring. Was it just a coincidence – or was it something more? She glanced over her shoulder at Nate. There were more reasons to stay than not.

She turned to the window, feeling the warmth of the rising sun on her face. The shingle beach was deserted; the fishermen had yet to arrive with their catch of the day. She stared at the calm sea in the distance, the sun's first rays casting a soft shimmering glow on the rippling surface. This wasn't called The Sunrise Coast for nothing. She knew this stretch of coastline had the most beautiful sunrises. This was the first time she'd had been awake to see it. She smiled. It was the dawn of a new day, and a new chapter in her life – one way or another.

Lili didn't realise she'd fallen asleep in the chair until she felt a gentle hand on her shoulder. 'Lili?'

She stretched and yawned. When she glanced out of the window, there were people walking along the promenade, fishing trawlers out at sea, and the black wooden huts on the beach, their doors open ready for business.

'What's the time?' She spotted Maisie and William sitting in bed, playing on her Nintendo.

'It's seven. We didn't want to wake you.' Lili noticed a blanket draped around her knees.

'You must have woken early. Did you catch the sunrise before you fell asleep again?'

'Oh, yes. It was beautiful.'

'They don't call this The Sunrise Coast for nothing,' commented Natė, echoing her sentiments. He paused. Lili could tell there was something on his mind. 'What is it?'

'I wondered if we could all have breakfast together downstairs?' he ventured. 'In fact, I was a bit presumptuous and booked a table this morning while you were sleeping.' He glanced at her suitcase by the door. 'I didn't know whether you'd have time …'

Lili had all the time in the world. 'Yes, I'd like that very much.'

Nate lingered, a question on his lips. *Did this mean she was staying?* He was plucking up the courage to ask, his heart pounding in his chest at the thought she might say no, when Maisie jumped off the bed and ran over to Lili. 'Look, I'm on to the third level on the game!'

Lili put an arm around her and smiled. 'Well, that's amazing, sweetheart.' Her smile faded when she remembered that Nate still didn't know Maisie wasn't her daughter. 'Nate, there's something I need to tell you.'

Nate, his heart pounding in his chest, thought this was it. She was leaving. 'Don't tell me now – let's go downstairs and enjoy breakfast.' He hoped their remaining time together at The Harbour Inn would persuade her to change her mind.

Nate had originally wanted to surprise her by treating her to breakfast in the flat above the antique shop. He had even ordered several bouquets of fresh flowers. With the help of the two children, he'd placed them in vases around the flat and had decorated the outside of Joseph's shop with bunting. They had all mucked in to create a big homemade banner which read *Welcome home, Lili.* She would have seen it after her sojourn in the hotel. It had all been part of a bid to persuade her to stay.

The fact that she'd taken her suitcase had thwarted that plan, although Nate had still gone ahead with it all, hoping he could find an excuse to bring her back to Cobblers Yard first thing in the morning. In hindsight, it had been a stupid idea. If she was leaving, would she appreciate the surprise? He now realised it might have just upset her or made her cross. Probably a bit of both.

Nate sent William into the bathroom to wash his face. Maisie went in next. Nate had to go to the car to get her Trunki so that she could change into a clean set of clothes, but the mention of it sent her into a grump; it reminded her they were leaving that day. She cheered up when she realised that they were going down to breakfast first.

Lili had a wash too, applied a bit of makeup, and put on a pair of jeans and a floral blouse – although they really could have done with an iron after being in her case overnight.

Nate took her suitcase. As they left, he spotted a letter on the bedside cabinet. He picked it up. 'Is this yours?'

Lili glanced at the invitation for an interview from Kew Gardens. She shook her head and smiled to herself. 'No, actually, it isn't.'

Nate left it where he'd found it, raising his eyebrows as he walked out of the door. He could have sworn he'd seen her name on the envelope.

Maisie, William and Lili took their seats in the small dining room overlooking the promenade. Bella was well-behaved. She lay under the table and didn't make a sound, even when she spotted Nate outside through the floor-to-ceiling window.

Bella wasn't the only one watching Nate. Lili was watching him too. He walked to the car parked outside and put her suitcase in the boot. Maisie saw him too. 'Am I going home today?'

Lili smiled. 'No, sweetheart.' She glanced at William, who was busy playing on Maisie's Nintendo, looking too absorbed to be listening to their conversation. 'Mummy phoned yesterday. She's visiting an island called Bali for a month. It means you'll be staying with me. Is that okay?' Lili knew she didn't have to ask that question. Maisie nodded. 'Can we stay here for the rest of the summer?'

For the rest of our lives, Lili thought, *if it were my choice*. But Maisie would have to go back to London at the end of the holiday.

'I wish I could stay here forever.'

'I know, sweetheart.' Lili wished Maisie could stay too.

Maisie turned to look out of the window. Lili followed her gaze. She spotted Nate walking back to the hotel from the car. Lili smiled. 'Nate doesn't know we're staying yet. It's going to be a surprise.'

William looked up from the Nintendo. 'What's going to be a surprise?'

Maisie said, 'We're not going back to London. We're staying here.'

William, a sensitive boy, didn't react in the way Lili was expecting. His bottom lip quivered before he burst into tears.

Nate walked into the dining room and saw Lili with her arms around his son. William's face was streaked with tears. He stopped dead. *Oh God – she's told him they're leaving.*

Lili hugged William, thinking of the letter. She'd imagined the job at Kew would be the start of her new life. She'd thought that it was what she wanted but coming here had changed everything. However, it had taken that phone call to Abigail for her to realise what was important. She wasn't just looking for a new job; she was searching for a place to call her own. A place where she felt she belonged.

She recalled the start of their holiday, staying at this wonderful little hotel, and thought how fitting it was that she should come to that realisation right there at The Harbour Inn.

Nate looked at her and then glanced at his son. William wiped his nose with the sleeve of his jumper and smiled up at Lili. Nate saw his son's smile. Had he got it wrong? Were those tears of joy because William had just found out they weren't leaving?

Lili raised her glass of orange juice. 'To new beginnings.'

Nate took a seat at the table. 'Does this mean …?'

'I'm staying, Nate.'

He raised his glass too, staring at her across the table. He couldn't quite believe what he was hearing. 'To new beginnings.'

'At The Harbour Inn,' Maisie added.

Lili turned to her. Growing up an orphan had meant that something had been missing all her life – the family she'd never had. But a family could be lots of things, Lili realised – not just a home with parents. It could be a community of people who cared for one another – she was thinking of Cobblers Yard – and a single dad she was falling for.

Now it was Lili's turn to shed a tear of joy. She smiled at Maisie. What better place to toast new beginnings than at The Harbour Inn, where her journey home had begun.

The Sunrise Coast Series continues in

The Secret of the Summerhouse

Paperback and Kindle eBook available
from Amazon

If you enjoyed *New Beginnings at the Harbour Inn* I would be grateful if you'd leave a review on Amazon.

For further details about the author and her novels visit the author's website.

www.elisedarcy.com

Printed in Great Britain
by Amazon

22856018R10182